The Romanov Episode

Clive Radford

CONTENTS

Chapter One: Last Roundup Part One

As the hit-men closed in, Gavin Anderson's pulse rate took an upwards surge. For the last time, he imagined, images of his wife and children splashed across his mind.

From behind his enforcers, the sinister figure of Julius Fyodor Austerberg emerged out from the shadows of the Mövenpick's car park.

"Mister Anderson," he griped, "I warned Mister Richmond, Mister Fraser and yourself not to interfere in my dealings. Yet here are the three of you, continuing to be caught in the act. You are not going to enjoy the oxygen of further publicity."

Anderson exchanged spooked gawps with Richmond and Fraser.

Stepping nearer and peering at them, Austerberg lectured, "Smart operators would have quit the Romanov caper by now. You've left me with no choice but to eliminate you from future proceedings." Turning to his henchmen, he snapped, "Viktor, Stanislav, you know what to do."

Edging in, they aimed their shooters at the victims...

Chapter Two: The Stars Align

Gavin Anderson never had a positive word to say about I.T solution consultants, and even less about financiers. Habitually forecasting an astronomical return on investment over an incredibly short timescale, the former's track record on delivering on promises remained woeful. Fairing no better, though the latter had no hesitation in bankrolling investments, the risk versus reward model always favoured the lender, their contracts forever ensuring capital return plus interest, way before his company made a penny on the deal.

As Oxalite global futures director at their Welwyn Garden City plant and company headquarters, it fell to Anderson to cobble together a requirements specification when one of the pharmaceutical's business units needed I.T to mechanise a research programme, solve a production business driver, or manage the administration of the company's huge international operation.

Based on worldwide market research, the board had decided to authorise Project Unicorn, a 'hit to lead' drug discovery scheme aimed at finding a cure for motor neurone disease, a life-threatening ailment affecting significant numbers of people. Often, drug discovery life cycles fell into the plus ten-years time frame, necessitating the use of powerful software applications to aid in the modelling, design, development and certification phases before the end product became licensed for production. Correspondingly, inward investment in tandem with company capital funding the venture could run into the hundreds of millions of pounds bracket.

Anderson had called in Brunswick Scorpio, Oxalite's contracted I.T consultancy services supplier to discuss the I.T necessities for Project Unicorn, their account manager, Dave Sedgewick, agreeing to meet him at Welwyn Garden City.

"Damn it!" Anderson blurted, as Sedgewick entered his office.

"Something wrong, Mister Anderson?"

Issuing him a peeved visage, he bawled, "Why is it, even the most tried and trusted software applications have a habit of crashing, just when the user is at a critical point in the work?" His irritation increasing, he wailed, "Here, take a look at this."

"What are you running?" Sedgewick enquired, as he joined Anderson behind his desk.

"*MS Excel* spreadsheet on *Windows 8.1*."

"I'm no expert, but I'll check what's happening."

Making a few keystrokes, Sedgewick pulled up the resource utilisation application on Anderson's laptop. "Ahh, it appears you're suffering from network contention. *Excel* is running fine. It's your data server that is slow in responding to your calls to populate the spreadsheet, giving the impression the application is crashing. Could be you've just hit a client end user usage peak, and the server farm is maxed out."

"But we invested in load balancing software some time ago."

"True. However, since that investment Oxalite has added further users and applications to your network."

"So, I suppose the solution to that is to beef up the server farm?"

"In principle, yes."

"Huh, more expense."

"Well, under the terms of your support agreement," Sedgewick voiced, "we could examine the problem."

"Never mind that," he jabbered, waving the offer aside. "I want to talk to you about I.T provisioning for Project Unicorn. Take a gander at this."

Thrusting a mission statement towards Sedgewick, he awaited a succinct response.

"Hhmmm, this is more complex than previous Oxalite requisites," he assessed, after reading the summary page. "Might need some special configuring."

"Quite."

Thumbing through the paper in depth, Sedgewick tabled some qualifying questions. Satisfied the Brunswick Scorpio man had a solid grasp on the stipulation, Anderson then enquired as to the next stage.

"I'll ask Colby Richmond to scrutinise the document," Sedgewick declared. "He recently joined Brunswick Scorpio from IBM in the role of global sales director for industrial solutions. He has extensive background experience in enterprise resource planning applications including for pharmaceutical programmes. Project Unicorn fits neatly into his worldliness portfolio."

"Did you say…" Taken aback at the name, he furrowed his brow. "…Colby Richmond?"

"Yes."

"Huh." Anderson's mood lightened. "I used to have a junior school friend named Colby Richmond." Rubbing his chin, he dwelt for a moment. "Do you know where he originates from?"

"Somewhere in Cheshire I believe."

"*Good god*, I come from Cheshire. It couldn't be the *same* person…could it?"

"If you think it would help progress the business, I could arrange for Mister Richmond to meet with you."

"Mmmm, okay. No doubt we will have to get together at some stage in the enterprise, anyway, so let's bring it forward."

~ * ~

A week later, Richmond made the trip to Welwyn Garden City, Anderson taking the trouble to pick him up from the Oxalite reception.

Approaching the Brunswick Scorpio global sales director, he uttered, "Colby Richmond?"

"Yes."

"Originally from Christleton?"

"Indeed."

"Hot damn, it is you."

"Yes, when Dave Sedgewick told me your name, I to made the possible connection."

Shaking hands and beaming at each other like long-lost brothers, neither could quite believe the stars had aligned in the heavens to bring them together.

"It must be forty-six years since I last saw you, Colby."

"Indeed, at Christleton Junior School. Lot of water under the bridge since then."

"For sure. Come on, let's do some business and catch up on past times."

Retiring to Anderson's office, the Cheshire men discussed Project Unicorn followed by a protracted chinwag about their lives subsequent to Christleton Junior School.

"After we moved from Christleton to Neston," Richmond informed, "eventually I took my GCE O and A-levels at Chester College, then studied computer science with business studies at the University of Surrey, whilst sponsored by Marconi Avionics. Post-graduation, I spent a further three years with Marconi before being headhunted by Dowty Defence and Air Systems. Then after five years, I left for mainstream I.T and industrial strength commercial software, first with the ACT Group, then IBM. Before I joined Brunswick Scorpio, my career moved into director level international sales and marketing management during my eighteen years with IBM."

"Are you married?"

"Yes. I met my wife, Carolyn, whilst on business for Marconi in 'the colonies'. We have two daughters, Amanda and Suzi. How about you, Gavin?"

"Oh, I went to King's School Chester followed by the University of Edinburgh to major in chemical engineering with business management. After graduating, I joined petrochemicals giant, Scale UK. Twelve years later I moved to Oxalite as operations director before becoming global futures director. I met my wife, Francine, when I worked at Scale's Nexus House on the Embankment. We have two children, Michelle and Wyatt."

"Some degree of commonality and cross-over in our lives since university graduation."

"Absolutely. And I've met others with a similar background to ours."

"Country boys made good hey?"

"*Cheshire* country boys," Anderson emphasised.

"Hah, in my teens and early twenties, I often referred to the county as 'Royal' Cheshire."

"Yes, on the infrequent times I visit Chester and the Wirral, I always come away with a feeling of being immersed in the majestic and the imperial. Thankfully, it hasn't changed much since we were junior schoolboys." Tarrying, he appended, "Now that we've become reacquainted, Colby, we mustn't let our friendship lapse again."

"Definitely. By the way, where do you live?"

"Potters Bar, and you?"

"Hempstead in Kent."

"We'll have to get Roger Fraser in on the act. He's another *Royal* Cheshire boy, hailing from Middlewich. He also lives in Kent at Hazelwood. Roger represents the acceptable face of financial services and is director of analysis and international trouble-shooter for The Firm, one of four investment houses used by Oxalite."

"Oh yes, in my formative IBM years, we provided an ebusiness technology refresh for The Firm, an investment house steeped in mystery, and some say possible infamy."

"So I have heard. Howbeit, no wholesale bank is squeaky clean. Intrigue and chicanery seem to go hand in glove with that industry. Aside from that, Francine and I have been to many socials held by The Firm at Roger's invitation. You'd really like him."

"Well, what do you suggest as a forum for a threesome?"

"Oh, some R n R at a top-rate West End restaurant."

"How about the Belvedere in Holland Park?"

"Splendid nomination. I'll make the booking."

~ * ~

Completing the trio's life C.V attainment over dinner at the Belvedere two weeks later, Richmond enquired of Fraser, "What's your story to date, Roger?"

"Well, in summary, my family moved from Middlewich to Kent when I was very young. After Chelsfield Grammar I attended Kings

College Cambridge, graduating with a degree in economics, then joined JP Morgan Chase as an analyst and achieved chartered financial analyst status, before moving on to Merrill Lynch, and finally The Firm. I met my wife, Charlotte, while at Cambridge. We have three children, Wendy, James and Heather."

"Hah, another success chronicle."

"Well, it's not all been plain sailing," Fraser assured. "There have been some domestic issues mainly caused by my predilection for rugby. I'm a member of the Kappa Corinthians Rugby Football Club based at Farnborough Kent and still play for the veterans."

"Back in the day, I used to be an avid rugby and cricket player," Richmond recalled. "But it lapsed soon after graduation due to work pressures at Marconi and domestic responsibilities."

"I was never a great sportsman," Anderson admitted. "Certainly I played rugby at King's School, but I can't claim any noteworthy exploits in the sporting arena. Though I still play tennis in the summer, outside of the work environment, I'm much more the observer of sports and cultural events. And I have a penchant for rock music, particularly the Rolling Stones, cultivated from a very early age."

"I seem to remember you engaged me in rock music discussions at Christleton Junior School," Richmond acknowledged. "The Rolling Stones became one of my favourite bands. Still are."

"Huh, that's another thing we have in common," Fraser attributed. "The Rolling Stones have been high on my music agenda since I was on the rusks."

"And here we are decades later," Anderson reviewed, "involved in three of the biggest worldwide industries."

"Quite," Fraser accredited. "What would you say have been the most significant milestones in pharmacology?"

"Oh, that is best answered by referring to the rate of rise of discoveries, beginning with the smallpox vaccine by Edward Jenner in 1796. That really marked the advent of modern pharmacology. Surprisingly, though it had been known for over 300 years, nobody had adopted ether as an anaesthetic until Dr. Crawford Williamson Long in 1842. But arguably, the most momentous, cure-all, discovery was

Alexander Fleming's penicillin in 1928. Naturally, others have also made weighty contributions, such as Frederick Banting's insulin in 1921, and Jonas Salk's polio vaccination in 1953.

"Moving forward, the twenty-first century has seen the first complete sequences of individual human genomes encoded as DNA within the twenty-three chromosome pairs in cell nuclei by the Human Genome Project on 12th February 2001. This allowed a switch in drug development and research from traditional drug discovery by isolating molecules from plants or animals, or creating new molecules in the treatment of illness in humans, to pharmacogenomics. That is the study and knowledge of how genes respond to drugs. These advances are improving personalised medicine and allowing precision medicine.

"And all this transcendence in just over two centuries since Jenner's breakthrough."

"Impressive," Richmond voiced. "Though you may think I'm astonished by the rate of computer advancement from Alan Turing's Bombe at Bletchley Park in 1940 to the advent of practical quantum computing by IBM in the late 1990s, it's really aerospace that astounds me from working at Marconi and Dowty. A timeslot of just sixty-six years saw the first powered flight by the Wright Brothers in 1903 to the Apollo 11 moon landing in 1969. To use an art simile, it's as monumental as when nineteenth century romanticism gave way to twentieth century expressionism. In comparison to aerospace, road, rail, and sea travel has persisted relatively pre-historic."

"What about banking, Roger?" Anderson fished.

"Ohh—" Chuckling and shaking his napper defensively, Fraser confessed, "Compared to your illustrious submissions, the world of finance cannot claim such groundbreaking epiphanies benefitting mankind.

"All I can point to is that without the institution of banking, first brought about in the fourth millennium BC, commerce could not have prospered bringing about man's desire to conquer illnesses and fly to the moon. Without financial investment, very little or nothing can be achieved, because invention relies on the purchase of plant and materials for research, as per Gavin's Project Unicorn."

"Mmmm, quite right," Anderson affirmed. "I suppose all this business; domestic and cultural commonality is down to the times we grew up in. We willingly joined the rat race, and its attendant mind games."

"For sure," Richmond upheld. "We climbed aboard the ambition carousel. But on reflection, like most people, whether they know it or not, what we were engaged in amounted to pleasing others. Our parents, our teachers, our church ministers, our employers, and our loved ones. We constantly seek their approval."

"You mean, we've become approval junkies?"

"Indeed, I do. Makes us feel good when someone who we love or respect or both, pats us on the back. It's like a drug. We must have it."

"Categorically true." Stopping, a vexed demeanour came over Anderson. "I don't know if this is just rose-tinted thinking, but back then, I had a distinct feeling of unrestricted freedom of thought and expression. Whereas today, we seem to have to be careful about everything we say, just in case it offends the PC brigade."

"Well, after the monochromatic haze of austerity following World War Two," Fraser illuminated, "we were born into the colourful second English renaissance. A time for limitless horizons, exploration and excellence in the arts, the sciences, and societal improvements. Today, the sciences continue to amaze, but the new arts amount to minimalist charlatanism, and English society has become a cauldron for every damned Johnny foreigner under the sun to tell the English what we must think and say, and how we must behave."

"Entirely right, Roger," Richmond endorsed. "The old political maxim is, you run for government in poetry, but you govern in prose, meaning manifestos promise what the people want, but once elected, politicians kowtow to prevailing forces. Effectively, we've been in the reformation since that twat Blair came to power and started the destruction of England. Mind you, the writing has been on the wall from the late nineteen-seventies onwards, so-called progressive politics eating away at English culture and traditions with every in-coming administration.

"Without doubt, the drive for meritocracy and excellence in all spheres has been trumped by the advent of the globalist's reformation, with its ever lowering of standards ideology producing worldwide banality via multiculturalism and pandering to the lowest common denominator."

"Oh, for sure. An industry exemplifying that reformation is Hollywood," Fraser forwarded. "Back in the day, the first gen movie moguls produced outstanding films. When they died, the bean counters took over the big five studios, and film excellence became degraded. Now the globalist conglomerates with liberal elitists at the helm own Hollywood, and film epics have been replaced with their socially engineered political dogma output designed to indoctrinate and enforce their repressive worldview."

"Yes, you're both correct," Anderson backed. "Plus, our own institutions have been infiltrated by the invaders to gain power over the indigenous population. Long gone are the days when the English ruled England. Now we are dominated by interlopers imposing their agenda on us. Worse still—" He frowned. "It can be said, there are no great people anymore in all walks of life, just shades of mediocrity which filters downwards into the ranks. Those at the top of the pyramids have neither the gravitas nor the presence to impress and inspire.

"And depressingly, none of the main political parties are opposing this wholesale takeover of our country." Faltering as if saddened by his own words, he then supplemented, "We all seek the clarity of permanence, but that sacred asset has been dissipated, even stamped on, by the new masters of the universe — the politically correct flock. I dread to think what our beloved England will look like to our children when they are our age."

"A salutary picture, Gavin," Fraser categorised. "And one that has plagued me for a long time."

"It seems that the only time we can get away from the witchfinder general, virtue-signalling, lefties dominated society consuming us, is when we are holidaying abroad with our families."

"Let's not spoil the evening with our grievances against the *nouveau* status quo," Richmond encouraged. "There's a host of other topics we can consider, primarily what we have been doing since we left

Royal Cheshire."

"You're right, Colby," Anderson reinforced. "To hell with the PC zealots, death to the traitorous bastards."

"Slow death," Fraser interjected.

"Yes, slow and painful death." Resting, he then said, "Speaking of fanatics, Roger—" He winced. "Have you come across one, Griffin Allard, on your travels within the investment banking sector?"

"Indeed, I have. Odious creature, a toady of the first order. 'Didn't you play the lead in your school's production of A. A. Milne's *Toad of Toad Hall*?' I once asked him. He replied, 'It was *Wind in the Willows*.' 'As Mister Toad, known as Toady?' I countered. 'Yes,' he conceded…. case proven. What about him?"

"He's with BNP Paribas, another investment house used by Oxalite."

"Yes, often I have to go mono-e-mono with Allard. I take it you've been subject to his somewhat forthright *modus operandi* for positioning investment opportunities?"

"*Hah*, to say his rottweiler-like, bludgeoning technique becomes overwhelming is an understatement. The man comes onto me like a Panzer tank, firing from every angle. It's not what he says, it's how he says it, coupled with that masterful, no arguments please comportment. I'm not usually disconcerted in business, principally with service providers, but his bombast is so strong that I feel obliged to take his word as gospel."

"Oh, I admit he is invariably right. It's just as you've found, his attitude is vociferous."

"Why is he a toady, Roger?" Richmond interjected.

"Ahh, that's because as well as being pushy, he is an accomplished arse-licker, ingratiating himself with the upper echelons at BNP Paribas."

"Hah." Grinning, he prescribed, "All industries contain their fair share of rectal fanciers. My father calls them jackals, lackeys, and flunkies — most combing the ranks for patsies and dupes to compensate for their own shortcomings. This toady fellow may have a history of being right, but he may also still fit into this *user* pattern."

"Unfortunately," Anderson asserted, "we cannot pick and choose who we do business with. We have to accept there will be good ol' boys, who know how to behave, and those falling beneath the passable level."

"Changing the theme to something lighter," Richmond commenced, "can I tell you a funny story?"

"Go on."

"The Brunswick Scorpio London office in Cannon Street is next door to Marlowe and Associates, a firm of quantity surveyors who use the same drinking establishment as us. That is the Candlemaker in the basement of the Wallbrook Building. I've got to know their projects manager, Ted Ruggles. A very personable chap with a capacity for seeing the humorous side of life, he told me one of their staff, who lingered unnamed, had matured a difficulty raising a stalk. To alleviate the embarrassing encumbrance, he'd taken some anti-impotence pills, Viagra possibly, or coated his hampton in stallion cream."

"Did it work?"

"Apparently, it worked too well. After achieving a massive erection, and doing the business with his girlfriend, his member still abided rock-hard. It just wouldn't go down! Pushed for time, he got dressed, his stiffy poking out in his loose-fitting trousers, left his highly-satisfied sweetheart, and jumped onto a Piccadilly Line train at Hammersmith en route for Finsbury Park. Unbeknown to him, a woman saw his arousal, got off the train at Gloucester Road, called the police, and told them, there's a pervert on the Piccadilly Line traveling east. The cops intercepted him at Covent Garden and escorted him to the local nick, still with a massive hard-on poking out his trousers. The desk-sergeant said to him, 'It's not funny you know.' He retorted, 'I *know* it's bloody well not. I can't get the damn thing to go down!' Even worse, if he couldn't cough up the bail money, the police will keep him in custody overnight, pending a magistrate's appearance to answer charges of sexual harassment and lewd and lascivious behaviour. So, he calls Ted Ruggles to supply the wonga. Apparently, he still had the stiffy when he appeared before the magistrate and the woman complainant the next morning."

"Good god, talk about the unexpected," Anderson trumpeted. "He must have had a severe allergic reaction to whatever potion he took."

"Quite. That's what he claimed to the magistrate."

"Was he sent down?" Fraser inquired.

"No, but he was fined, bound over, and instructed not to enter the public domain in an aroused state ever again."

Tickled by the corollary, Anderson and Fraser burst into laughter.

"And there's me thinking," Fraser declared, between chortles, "things like that only happened in the investment banking sector."

For the next few hours, the Cheshire boys tabled more life maturation stories. Anderson freely recalled many episodes from his private and professional palette effecting his thinking, and thereby his strategy to settling issues, whilst Richmond divulged his lack of self-belief to address academic studies demarcated appreciably with his workplace natural constituency. Completing the testimonies, Fraser owned-up that after some hesitation, he had embraced his trouble-shooter role at The Firm, and given the choice, he'd ditch his analyst duties in favour of fulltime troubleshooting.

Becoming evident to the three campaneros that they had both much in common and a shared outlook on life, the interconnections between them expanded exponentially. Though Anderson had acquired a raft of pals at Scale and Oxalite, none possessed the level of charisma and zest pouring out of Fraser and Richmond under playtime conditions. Notably, he also fielded an extra piquancy whilst in the company of his fellow Cheshire men, something never surfacing when he chatted to other friends. Almost as if they had been hatched from the same batch, he also dctcctcd that Fraser and Richmond were coming to the same conclusion.

Buoyed up by the assumption, towards the end of the dinner, Anderson proposed, "We really must have a longer get-together. In fact, we need to get totally away from the daily dose of PC indoctrination issued by our cursed oppressors and the fiendish traitors — at least for a while."

"How do you mean?" Richmond canvassed.

"Well, in addition to inter-family shindigs, how about the three of us take a vacation abroad?"

"That would involve selling the idea to wives and getting extended pass-outs," Fraser put forward.

"Undoubtedly," Richmond bolstered. "But it shouldn't deter us. What were you thinking of, Gavin, in particular?"

"How about a trip to Lausanne via Geneva-Cointrin Airport? During the day we can explore the city and sail on Lake Geneva, and at night take in the Casino Barriére at Montreux."

"I take it you've got a sailing qualification?"

"I started out on *Topper* dinghies on Aldenham reservoir with the Aldenham Sailing Club. After attaining Royal Yachting Association levels one through five ratings, I then got my day skipper license after completing a course at the Royal Harwich Yacht Club. We've had a family usable, multi-masted schooner moored at Harwich for the past twenty years."

"You've become a very proficient sailor then?"

"Well, I wouldn't go as far as that, Colby, but I've clocked up over 2,500 hours on the North Sea and in the English Channel."

"So," Fraser began, "we'd use your sailing credentials to hire a craft at Lausanne?"

"Got it in one, Roger." Dwelling, he then subjoined, "You two done any sailing?"

"Acting as a host to clients," Fraser explained, "I did a couple of trips around the Solent when I was with Merrill Lynch on a dual-masted schooner. Got to take the wheel for a while and provided crewing services."

"How about you, Colby?"

"Oohh, apart from rowing on the River Dee in my late teens, the extent of my water endeavours has been taking the overnight ferry from Harwich to the Hook of Holland, and Southampton to Guernsey." Halting, he then certified, "I don't mind sharing with you that I've never been able to kick my low threshold of boredom. I've had it since my schooldays. So, what Gavin is promoting floats my boat, if you'll forgive the pun. Bring it on."

"Right, I'll make some enquiries regarding flights, accommodation, car and boat hire."

"*When shall we three meet again? In thunder, lightning, or in rain?*" Fraser quizzed.

"I see you know your Shakespeare," Richmond complimented. *"When the hurly-burly's done. When the battle's lost and won."*

"You mean," Anderson prompted, "when we have pass-outs from our trouble and strife's?"

"Exactly," Fraser confirmed.

"One rule of engagement I'd like to advocate," Anderson vented. "No talking about wives, children, and unequivocally, business."

"Positively," Richmond buttressed with vim. "And no taking mobile phones or laptops with us."

"Well, if we are going to make the most of this sojourn," Fraser submitted, "domesticity and professional matters will also need to be parked on the back burner."

"Hhmm, let's just hope we can sell our vacation intent to our families," Richmond caveated.

"No doubt it will take a lot in terms of monetary, presents, favours and promises compensation!" Anderson predicted.

Over the course of the succeeding few months, the Anderson, Richmond and Fraser households got to know one another — visits carried out to each other's homes, collective trips made to see London shows, and in general, the families intertwining and generating cordial relationships. Ideal for the men to gently weave their vacation plan into proceedings without causing ripples.

Chapter Three: Three Cheshire Boys

To say Gavin Anderson's Lausanne proposal amounted to a near juxtaposition of his weekly *modus vivendi* could be classified as an understatement. Cautious by nature, Anderson had achieved his professional and personal successes by means of careful planning, seldom, if ever, straying into rash and impulsive territories. Though capable of being exceedingly personable, customarily suspicion crept into his machinations when assessing newcomers.

Born under a full harvest hunter moon looming large above a cloudless night sky, as time passed Anderson deduced growing up to be a cast of mind, evident from minute-to-minute circumstances as they arose, the maxim gaining more credence with the relentless passage of time. That observation had fostered a prudent and defensive mindset ensuring he rarely got stung, his apprehension of the unknown safeguarding him until he had made friend or foe qualification. Of course, in the bosom of his family, his protective shield came down. They only saw his light-hearted, jocular side saturated in smiles and laughter, plus his still ripe appetite for the Rolling Stones fostered in his nascent years.

By his late teens he had evolved into a handsome young man. His slender, slightly shy of six-feet tall frame, radiant, russet-brown merging into fawn eyes, raven-black hair, and an engaging demeanour, his primary merits. Over the ensuing decades he'd broadened out, his eyes becoming strained due to many hours spent glued to a computer monitor necessitating the take up of reading spectacles, and his barnet came to be sprinkled with slivers of grey due to the aging process.

Mixed-doubles tennis partnering Francine lasted as his single recreation for shedding excess calories. The only other pastimes he prolonged from bygone years were theatre and rock concerts — his other extramural passions. A trait inherited from his father; workaholic

Anderson could never visualise retirement. Even out of the work environment, his Oxalite business challenges were never far from his immediate attention. He thrived on them. They topped up his goodies well like the elixir of life. Without them he knew he'd feel hollow, useless, redundant. They were his drug of choice, the rush of adrenalin released both during the solving treatment and at their successful termination, producing his professional high. Thankfully for Anderson, uniformly his roster comprised a multitude of trials, all overlapping ensuring no recitatives, to use a musical term. Just the medicine to ensure his interest by no means flagged, he never lapsed into timepiece-watching or hankering for the working-day to finish.

Adversity had nearly befallen Anderson during a Christleton Junior School trip to Snowdonia. Nearing the upper reaches of Mount Snowdon, the pathway gave way under a torrent of rainwater rushing over the slopes, Anderson and two other juniors losing their footing and slipping off the passageway for about ten feet, before stopping precariously just short of a 200 feet high precipice. Scrambling to the rescue, the accompanying teachers hauled the threesome up, and the party continued to the summit. Typical of the times, the potential gravity of the instance never became recounted to parents by either pupils or the school. Albeit, when either Michelle or Wyatt participated in school treks, the Snowdon plight re-emerged into his consciousness, and he fretted for their wellbeing. The same safety reservations happened with Francine. Although she was an excellent driver and had never been involved in a road traffic accident, if she drove alone, often he imagined the worst. The fear all came down to love for his family and the knowledge that fate could fall on any unsuspecting soul. Conversely, he had no qualms about protracting his life under the risky conditions he often encountered in his profession.

Taller than Anderson with broad shoulders, sapphire blending into midnight blue eyes, wavy blond hair and a mouth designed for kissing, Richmond cut quite a striking figure in his teens. A girl magnet, fillies had flocked to him, though heartache dogged him after one breakup, the desolation sustained until Carolyn entered his life. As he grew older and his face perfected more character, his attractiveness to women blossomed further. Drawn to him like iron filings to a magnet, they craved to be in his company, though they accepted he only had eyes for his ravishing wife.

Never ceasing to amaze him, the contrasts between Richmond's pre-graduation and post-graduation lives were stark. The former, a cauldron of educational trials and tainted girlfriend relationships. The latter, a crucible of stability and equilibrium since meeting Carolyn.

Wavering and diffident about his intellectual standing, he had agonised over his aptitudes from the start of his university education, vowing on graduation never to return to academia. Contrastingly, with the workplace his natural comfort zone, he excelled in his chosen sales and marketing profession, quickly establishing a reputation for getting things done on-cost and on-time at his first employer, Marconi Avionics. An attribute serving him well throughout his career all the way to Brunswick Scorpio, he never underestimated its value. Often what set him apart as far as customers were concerned centred on his innate communication capabilities, Richmond able to read subtle nuances and react accordingly, the trait resulting in contract awards and correspondingly high earnings for him.

Shrewdly, he also played the Carolyn card at both company events and client socials. As well as providing stunning features and a vibrant personality, she also brought charisma to the party. Corporate level executives were charmed by her divine abilities. Together they formed a golden couple, able to take on the world and often prevail against the odds. As far as Colby Richmond could see, it didn't get any better. Even if oodles of tempting sirens came on to him all at once, hell would freeze over before he betrayed Carolyn. Not alone, she had her own fan club, men mesmerised in her wake, but like her husband, she never strayed. They were the perfect combination, just about everybody they knew assessing their marriage to be unconditionally solid with zero contradictions.

Growing up in the arcadian atmosphere of Neston and Chester, as a young person Richmond assumed it represented a microcosm of the world as a whole. A rude awakening hit him as he soon discovered at university and in the workplace that little of the outside world lived up to the carefree environment of his home territory. His sensitive nose became acutely tuned to detect skunks in all their nefarious and charlatan forms, the baptism imbuing him with the necessary wit to survive and prosper. Though he never pre-judged people and steadfastly gave them the benefit of the doubt, nonetheless when his weasel spotter did twitch, he went out of his way not to become embroiled with its owner. Carolyn also possessed the asset, but on occasion he sensed a miscreant that had breached her scallywag barrier, and he had to intervene to prevent her being taken to the cleaners. Hoping their children had inherited the self-preservation trait, both parents impressed upon Amanda and Suzi the need to be vigilant when faced with the unknown.

Though Charlotte restricted his rugby crowd joy-time, the third Cheshire boy, Roger Fraser, never lacked for confidence at any stage in his life. More than competent at Cambridge, a barnstorming success with The Firm, and embossed with a keen sense of humour, Fraser rose up to meet paradoxes and conundrums toe-to-toe. As tall as Richmond and built like a sleek god in his early twenties, he had put on a few pounds over the subsequent decades, his original dark floppy mop starting to grey, and his once clear violet-blue eyes becoming slightly bloodshot.

Altogether appealing to the opposite sex, like Anderson, Fraser's excursions into girl territory had been sparse until Charlotte bagged him. Incontrovertibly, he'd put it about in his teens, but whereas Richmond's conquest total had quickly hit double numbers, his remained a single value. Teenage girls were largely a mystery to him. Their often-erratic behaviour and partiality to change their minds several times, all in the space of a few minutes, had him flummoxed. Whereas his male playmates were consistent - that is consistently good or bad - and exhibited a uniformity of views and decisions, girls were flighty and fickle. In many ways, Charlotte was no different, but she had an X-factor, an indefinable talent for making him see clearly. Waving her metaphorical magic wand, she quelled all his anxieties. That plus the fabulous things she did to his tallywhacker, had her by a long shot above her contemporaries - Fraser smitten.

Where he got his supreme investment banking analytical talents from, he could never fathom. He traversed the same mechanisms as his work colleagues, but unendingly he could find the sliver of an emerging market trend, the pearl in the dross, or a money-bearing opportunity cloaked in many deceptive layers, that they failed to recognise. Often providing the kernel for market-leading stock trading campaigns, Fraser had become a crutch for lamebrain, stockbrokers, the go-to guru for steers when a bear market threatened to engulf the industry, the fount of reliable analysis in the face of convoluted market conditions. Always goodhearted, if not prone to having fun at the delinquent trader's expense with a tirade of witty putdowns unfailingly going over their upper storeys, nevertheless he eternally delivered.

When Toby 'Top Cat' Chalcroft, equities director for The Firm's London SBU, sounded him out about a troubleshooter role additional to his analyst function, at first Fraser rebuffed the notion, pigeonholing it as way beyond his talents. Countering, TC insisted he possessed the necessary gravitas and interpersonal skills, and The Firm had a lot of faith in him. Abashed by the compliments, he acceded, taking on the supplementary role. Once he'd got a handle on the function after a few hair-raising escapades, he relished battling to resolve more out-on-the-rim business problems.

Amounting to his weak point, often after a little squirming, Wendy, James and Heather were able to twist him around their little fingers. Also adept at getting her way with him using sex or threats, Charlotte tended to rule the domestic roost. The latter distilled into secession of conjugal rights and doghouse blues penance, if he'd come home three-sheets to the wind after a Kappa Corinthians Rugby Football Club celebration, or if he'd failed to carry out his household duties to her satisfaction. Not grounds to invoke divorce proceedings, he took his punishment with good humour.

~ * ~

Though they had entered their early middle years, collectively the Cheshire boys were alluring fellows, receiving admiring glances from women of all ages, and the esteem of their contemporaries. Personality wise, they were open, gregarious in trusted company, could always see the funny side of thorny situations, and took whatever life threw at them with a good heart and a determination to overcome difficulties.

They had all travelled extensively abroad and been involved in risky hijinks or witnessed tragic happenings. Anderson had been catapulted off a North Sea oil rig when blowout preventers failed, causing a gas and oil explosion. He had also narrowly avoided major injury when granite pieces and pane shards fell groundward from a skyscraper in Sumatra after an igniting gas leak resulted in a huge blast. During a trouble-shooter mission in Grand Cayman to snare a money-laundering operative, the bag-carrier had been cornered in a bank and pulled a gun on Fraser, The Firm's man seeing his life flash before him until secret service officers persuaded the scoundrel to surrender. Conversely, Richmond had never been touched by any near-to-death brushes. Though while at Marconi, he was a passenger in the company Britten-Norman Islander aircraft taking off from the Royal Aircraft Establishment Farnborough, when it became caught in the downdraft from a twin-rotor *Chinook* helicopter about to leave the ground. The Islander's portside wing dropped abruptly causing the aircraft to stall, the pilot recovering steady-state flight a matter of feet from a treeline.

With their jobs demanding sweeping international jet-setting, they had all amassed between one to two million air miles. Though statistically the safest form of travel, notwithstanding, with increasing frequency of flights, the probability of becoming involved in an air incident also increased. During a jaunt from Damman to the remote Scale oil-drilling site at Rayda, the light aircraft carrying Anderson and Saudi Scale employees hit a sandstorm necessitating a forced, bumpy landing, short of the Rayda airstrip. Often a pulse-raising journey for Richmond in winter, hostile weather conditions at Tampere Pirkkala Airport, close to the Arctic Circle in Finland, often obliged incoming flights to divert to Helsinki Airport. One time, the SAS *Boeing 737* ferrying him tried three times to land at Tampere in a snow blizzard. Now short on fuel, navigating to Helsinki was not an option, the *737* finally making a very turbulent landing at Tampere at the fourth attempt, before stopping at the runway extremity, yards from the airport boundary fence. Daunting for Fraser, landing at Kai Tek Airport between Hong Kong's skyscrapers during his early career with JP Morgan Chase often proved to be a fine line between a successful touchdown and crashing into the downtown buildings. Similarly, taking off from the short Quito Airport runway, high up in the Andes, involved aircraft dipping down into the valley below to pick up speed before resuming the balance of the take-off path, Fraser often thinking his end would come in an Amazon jungle air crash.

Taking the incidents philosophically, the Cheshire boys placed them as part and parcel of their occupations. Little did they know their Lausanne sojourn would call upon their nerve and calmness to a much greater extent.

Chapter Four: The Sisters Grimm

Congregating at London Gatwick Airport, after checking in at the Geneva desk, the three Cheshire boys retired to the BA Executive Club Lounge to await their flight.

"My god," Fraser blurted, as they sat sipping gourmet coffee and scoffing hors d'oeuvres, "this will be the first time I've been on a men-only holiday since I went to Malta with school pals after our A-level examinations."

"Hah, my men-only excursions have also been far and few between," Anderson allotted. "What about you, Colby?"

"Oh." Nostalgically he divulged, "My late teenage years were filled with romances, so if memory serves, all of my vacations were with girls. Needless to say, the counterpoint to that became a memorable duration of playing rugby and cricket and thereby entering into the brotherhood of men."

"I still have that fellowship furnished and gilded by Kappa Corinthians," Fraser identified. "Some of my closest male friends were at school with me and are also members of the rugby club. Furthermore, the same clique are the founders of the Hazelwood & District Gentlemen's Club."

"What's that, Roger?" Anderson enquired.

"Oh, you'd both like it. It's a forum for engaging in lewd and boisterous pastimes, whilst consuming vast amounts of alcohol and gorging ourselves silly on haute cuisine. It goes without saying, to participate in these raucous, bacchanalian junctures requires an extended pass out from Charlotte. She's always suspicious about what we get up to. Conversely, her mother, Davina — Lady MacBeth as I call her — positively encourages all-male activities. She's somewhere to the right of Atilla the Hun when it comes to political philosophy but sincerely believes we men need our space away from the female of the species."

"Huh, mother-in-law's can be either dragons or empathetic when it comes to male independence," Richmond portrayed. "One of my IBM account managers had a torrid time with his monster-in-law, as he called her. Every time he went to a men-only event, she jumped all over him like a virulent rash. In response, when he and his wife visited his in-laws, he'd give his mother-in-law packets of *Paxo*, but she didn't seem to take the hint *vis-à-vis* getting stuffed. He even sent her a Christmas card made from a *Paxo* packet, and on one Yuletide occasion when the mother-in-law came for Christmas lunch, he asked her in a demonstrative tone, 'Do you want *stuffing*?' Did she catch on, did she hell as like."

"Indifference," Anderson delineated, "or worse still, a badly, tuned-in, personal antenna can make the most cantankerous foe oblivious to the subtlest of tag lines. It often occurs in life's cruel laboratory."

"Frequently I cogitate," Fraser outlined, "that we need protection from the glare of civilisation."

"How do you mean?"

"Well, good manners and social etiquette can be abused, as in the mother-in-law case Colby recounted. A *quid pro quo* does not necessarily result from person-B when person-A adopts a civil stance. So-called civilisation produces both politeness and impertinence, courtesy of freedom of expression. The former equates with a sense of propriety, whereas the latter is manifested from a contemptuous attitude. Thereby we can be subject to the shimmer of both the genteel and the boorish.

"You might consider, we three going on holiday is a reaction to the maelstrom of uncertainty we find ourselves in on a daily basis. And thereby, we crave the consistency of predictability that only commonality of background, personality and purpose can provide."

"So subconsciously," Richmond postulated, "because we all suffer fools in one form or another, the prospect of getting away from it for a while melded a convergence of acceptance to the Lausanne sojourn?"

"Yes, if you will. Think of it as a profound communion."

"Interesting that you base the theory on commonality factors, Roger," Anderson observed. "Indisputably you're quite right. I wouldn't have suggested the break if there were no binding agents between us."

"One of the most irritating things is lack of tact and finesse," Fraser tabled. "Never ceases to amaze me how the terminally stupid come out with the most appalling foot-in-mouth blunders. For example, someone asks, 'Who's the fat, ugly, specky bastard?' only to be told, 'That's your new boss.'"

"Hah, that reminds me of a senior field engineer I knew at Marconi," Richmond recalled. "He was great company but no diplomat, especially when it came to three-baggers. He'd wander up to a girl not blessed with good looks and blab, 'Have you got a license to be out with a face like that? You'd be done for sheep-scaring in Wales.' Being insensitive, unsurprisingly he was immune to comebacks."

"I suppose none of us enter into unkind putdowns," Anderson verified. "Though we may think it."

"Oh undoubtedly," Fraser corroborated. "I must have lost at least half my tongue, biting it when on the brink of a riposte to the most outlandish outpourings from the bumptious and the arrogant. Often, they are like the Facebook originators - high on intellect but low on personality."

"Just let's hope we don't come across such brass and impudent rascals in Lausanne."

"Here, here," Fraser and Richmond underpinned in unison.

Moving on the conversation, Fraser enquired, "Are you still an ardent Liverpool FC devotee, Colby?"

"*Huh*, that's become a sore point. It's now impossible to get hold of away fixture tickets when the mighty Reds play London clubs. And most Anfield Road matches are sold out in advance to season ticket holders. Long gone are the days when I could roll up to home games and pay at the turnstiles or fax the club requesting tickets be reserved."

"A massive change came about with the creation of the Premier League, and the sport became flooded with TV coverage rights money, principally by Sky Sports," Fraser insisted. "The sports business model became replaced by the commodity business model engendering the rise of infernal player's agents to haggle over player transfer, sign-on and other package fees. With that came a broad assault of targeted marketing of the product by Sky, and an accompanying huge increase in ticket prices.

"Whereas pre-1992, when the PL was created, football clubs were largely supported by local working class aficionados, who could afford to attend matches week-in, week-out, post that watershed, football became egocentric merchandise attracting a much more affluent stratum, capable of shelling out for eye-watering season ticket prices. Correspondingly, this pseudo-supporter group has a propensity to brag about their club support to their plastic partizans, singularly when it comes to a legendary club like LFC. Consequently, local low- paid Liverpudlians have been priced out of the entertainment."

"Yes, this new narcissistic set has no hesitation in buying every blessed ticket for every competition, be it national or European, leaving no scope for the genuine life-long supporter. I converted Carolyn into LFC allegiance when she landed in Blighty. We used to watch the Reds home and away. When Amanda and Suzy were old enough, we'd also take them along as well. Be that as it may, the last time I was able to procure tickets for Anfield Road was April 2009, when we attended the fixture against Blackburn Rovers, a milestone marking the twentieth anniversary of the Hillsborough disaster."

"Not being a football fan," Anderson revealed, "much of what you both say has passed me by, but I do get the impression from the media that today's players are preened and pampered."

"Undeniably," Fraser upheld. "They play on snooker-table-like surfaces throughout the season with a light ball designed to fly. Whereas in the early 1990s and going back to the dawn of football in the nineteenth century, as soon as winter arrived, football pitches were turned into quagmires. Nowadays players lack the skill to skate over the *ploughed* fields and snow-bound surfaces that the likes of George Best, Stanley Matthews, Tom Finney, Kevin Keegan and Kenny Dalglish had to negotiate. Put those same players on today's incessantly manicured pitches, and they'd take modern defenders to the cleaners."

"Hah, you mentioning quagmire pitches," Richmond began, "reminds me of a Stoke City versus Nottingham Forest match my father took me to when I was at Noddy's Junk Shop, er…Neston Junior School.

The Victoria Ground pitch was coated in so much sand to compensate for the cut-up surface that my father quipped, 'I'm surprised they weren't handing out deckchairs, and buckets and spades, when we came through the turnstiles.'"

"That bad," Anderson queried, grinning at the satirical comment.

"Unreservedly, Gavin."

When BA announced the Geneva flight, the Cheshire boys made their way to the departure gate, two elderly women dressed in the style of governesses sauntering up behind them, clearly unsure they were in the right queue.

"I tell you; this is the line for Geneva."

"No, it's not, Evelyn. That airport attendant said it's at the end of the concourse."

"He was wrong."

"No, you are."

"Excuse me, young man," Evelyn said to Anderson, pulling at his jacket sleeve.

"Hah, it's a long time since I've been called young man," he cheerfully replied.

"Don't quibble," she insisted. "Is this the right line for Geneva?"

"Indeed, it is," he validated, maintaining his helpful mug.

Lured by the burgeoning contretemps, Richmond and Fraser about turned to observe proceedings.

"*See*, I told you it was, Gertrude. Why don't you ever believe me?"

"Because, Evelyn, you rarely get things right."

"Now don't start arguing in front of these gentlemen. They'll think we are harridans from hell."

"Really, Evelyn." She scowled. "You'd show me up in Woolworths. Have some decorum."

"Woolworths stopped trading in 2008."

"Very well, Poundland. I think they're still in operation. Now, control yourself."

"Don't tell me how to behave, particularly when I'm right."

Grimacing at the slight, Gertrude then dialed the Cheshire boys. "I apologise for my sister's outburst, gentlemen. Anyone would think her finishing school got bombed."

"Don't make excuses for me, sister darling. Roedean was never bombed, as you know full well."

"Once she starts, I can never get her to stop," Gertrude moaned, her phiz inviting sympathy from the threesome.

"Well, you are definitely in the right queue," Anderson reconfirmed.

"Are you going to Geneva, Mister…?"

"Anderson, Gavin Anderson, and these are my companions, Colby Richmond and Roger Fraser."

"They all look like very eligible young men," Evelyn observed. "Handsome devils. I bet they're gigolos in pursuit of rich continental heiresses."

"You must excuse my sister," Gertrude begged. "She has the habit of opening her mouth before engaging her brain."

Radiating at the amusing vilification, Anderson guaranteed, "We are nothing more than vacationers, ladies, out to sail on Lake Geneva and gamble at the Casino Barriére at Montreux. We're staying at the Mövenpick Hotel Lausanne."

"Oh, I see," Gertrude acknowledged. "We're at the Carlton Lausanne Boutique Hotel." Facing her sister, she blasted, "*Really*, Evelyn, what must these young men think of you."

"No harm done," Richmond assured. "We've got thick skins."

"Ohh, that's very considerate of you, Mister Richmond." She turned to her sister again. "See, I told you, not all young men are philanderers and Philistines." Unfolding charitable features, she polled, "Tell me, Mister Anderson, does your diet include Panax ginseng?"

"Erm…er, I don't think so."

"You really should have a helping of Panax ginseng every day." She petted his arm reassuringly. "It's *very good* for the penis."

"Do come along, Gertrude," her sister pressed, "or we'll miss our flight."

Fiddling to find departure tickets in their handbags, they left the Englishmen open-mouthed, still shocked by Gertrude's gastronomic advice.

*

Wandering up the aisle of the *Airbus A320* to his designated aisle seat, Anderson found it already occupied by a gorgeous young lady dressed in business attire.

"Excuse me, I think you're in my seat."

"I'm so sorry," she replied. "I get air sickness, so I need the aisle seat for quick access to the toilets."

"Oh, I see. No matter, I'll use the centre seat."

"That's very kind of you. I'm Suzannah Arliss."

"Gavin Anderson."

She got up to allow him access to the inner seat row.

"I discovered I had an aversion to flying during my first flight in my late teens," she disclosed, hoping to elicit more understanding from Anderson. "Presuming it'd go away, alas, it didn't, and I've had to live with it ever since."

"Do you fly very often?"

"My job demands some European air travel."

"What do you do for a crust?"

"I'm a model for Revlon."

"*Really.*" His complexion lit up at the exposure. "I've never met a cosmetics model before."

"It's my face and hands that really got me the job."

"I can see why. You're a very pretty girl, and your facial makeup is immaculate."

"Hah, we have to sustain the Revlon image constantly," she shared, lifting her eyebrows to emphasise the requirement. "We're never allowed out in public without makeup, just in case a press photographer is lurking."

"I take it you're travelling to Geneva for a shoot?"

"Yes. Inside the sixteenth century in origin Hôtel de Ville at the heart of the old town. It's actually a family-owned brasserie with some spectacular rooms, ideal for affiliating Revlon products with the high society, jet-set lifestyle."

"Oh, I see. A marketing ploy."

"Precisely. I'll be joining three other models coming from other parts of Europe. This will be my third time at the Hôtel de Ville for a Revlon shoot. On one previous occasion, a group of suspicious-looking characters came out of its restaurant and watched proceedings. The apparent group leader, a tall aristocratic grandee, had such a domineering presence, that our photographer refrained from asking them to leave."

"Must have been intimidating."

"Certainly for the photographer. Anyway, thankfully, most of my assignments are at British locations where I don't have to fly."

"How did you become a model, Suzannah?"

"I was spotted in an art gallery in my nineteenth year by a Garnier rep. He persuaded me to attend an audition. Garnier liked what they saw and sent me to the London Finishing Academy to learn deportment and for elocution."

"So that soft seductive voice comes from your training?"

"It does. You see, sometimes I have a short speaking role in TV adverts. As well as looking good, we have to sound sophisticated." She stopped abruptly as she felt the forward momentum of the aircraft. "Oh, we're rolling for departure. During the flight if I suddenly disappear, don't be offended. It means I may be on the edge of vomiting."

"I quite understand. Do you take anything for air sickness?"

"I'm already dosed up to the gills on tablets, and I keep hydrated throughout the flight. Albeit, the antidote is not totally successful. I suffer a range of symptoms from dizziness to actually being sick."

"Hah." He chuckled. "The things we subject ourselves to for our professions."

"Have you undergone any health difficulties through your profession?"

"More the case, I've been in some hostile environments where I could have been injured or even killed."

"I suppose most occupations come with some risk, or by enacting them you open yourself up to hidden phobias, in my case, air sickness."

"True. We must be masochistic because it doesn't prevent us from doing them."

She smiled at him. "Talk to me about your pleasant occurrences, Gavin. Sometimes, if my mind is engaged on someone else, it stops me becoming nauseous."

"Be my pleasure."

Whilst Anderson entertained the luscious Revlon model, Fraser and Richmond discussed life issues in seats across the aisle from him.

"Tell me, Colby, why did you give up playing rugby and cricket after university?"

"Oh, after graduation I did play for about a year for Marconi in the local inter-company rugby and cricket leagues. But I had little time to train because of work commitments abroad, plus I was unavailable on some match days for the same reason. Ergo, my form waned. Howbeit, I was mainly selected because of my track record for Surrey."

"That aside, I wanted to be with Carolyn as much as possible." He became quixotic. "You see, she took me past the outer limits of my fancies when we became an item. Virtually an avalanche effect, the before and after we met were markedly different. I'd finally found Miss Right, my life-long soulmate, and felt the need to be with her as much as possible. Something had to give, and it became rugby and cricket. I played racket sports occasionally, still do, but the team games went for a burton. I also had to give up my private pilot's licence within a year of attaining it, because of domestic calls on the fiscal purse, mainly the house mortgage."

"Is private flying expensive?"

"Very, but it depends on what real estate you hold on the *Monopoly* board. It's a rich man's plaything. Marconi covered the cost of attaining my PPL, but after that I had to pay for everything. Ironically, I could afford it now, but because my license lapsed, I'd have to repeat flying training. However, I did a bit of gliding at Challock with a Marconi buddy qualified as a pilot, but that happened way back when." Grimacing, he enquired, "How do you find the time for rugby at Kappa Corinthians?"

"Ohh, put that down to tradition. I started as a colt at the club when I attended Chelsfield Grammar. Then after Cambridge, I really got my teeth into it. Played for the first team until aged thirty-five. Now I play for the vets. You see, it's not just participating in matches—" He sparkled as if he'd been chosen by a super-deity. "The club became an epicentre for social activities, a home away from home, if you will. Sure, I get heat from Charlotte for crossing the domicile threshold plastered after a rugby club jamboree, but she has never asked me to give it up.

"Quite frankly, Colby, I love my home life, and emphatically, my jobs at The Firm, but I'd be lost without Kappa Corinthians to act as a counterpoint."

"Yes, I can see that. I suppose in my micro-universe, Carolyn and the girls are my counterpoint to work. It's funny, in my teens I always assumed I'd be playing rugby and cricket well into my thirties, independent of what else came along. But I was wrong. With the marriage came a sacred union. Thereby, I set myself to taking on all the associated responsibilities. Apart from work calling for so much international travel, and domesticity drives, everything else became sidelined."

"Just goes to illustrate, everyone is different." Pulling a repugnant kisser, he enquired, "How do you get on with home duties, such as gardening and shopping?"

"I'm no gardener, Roger, and in all frankness, I loathe both."

"My own pet hate is supermarket shopping at Sainsburys, mainly because the staff stand about like tits in a trance with their thumbs up their arses meditating, instead of opening up more check-outs to service huge queues."

"Yes, I have the same dread. Huh, it's become just as bad at Marks and Spencer and Waitrose." Pausing, he then augmented, "Just returning to rugby, I still go to the Stoop occasionally with my buddies from IBM to watch the mighty Harlequins, and if there's televised rugby on the box, I tune into it if there are no other demands."

"Ahh, you must have seen Sierra Franklin introducing the BT Sports fixtures."

"Indeed. A very attractive girl."

"Ohhh, she's pure angel delight incarnate, a honey. Although she's in her early forties, she's in *lovely* condition."

Snickering at the portrayal, Richmond adjudged, "You make her sound like a vintage BMW."

"Ahh, you've connected with my other love."

"What's that?"

32

"My Ferrari red *BMW M3*. Next to Charlotte, she is my divinity, my godhead. We've got a *Mercedes Viano* MPV for family ferrying, but the beamer is mine, and mine alone. Naturally, she's a fair-weather car. She's never seen rain, let alone snow. Once I get behind the wheel of my *M3*, a surge of electricity energises me marking the advent of uncontained joy and freedom." As if blessed, he confided, "She is my go-to redeemer when I need solace away from everything else. When I went to pick her up from the BMW concessionaires in Aylesford, all shiny and new, emblematically speaking, I got a massive hard on and ejaculated all over her bonnet. She was that beautiful. Sometimes I go out to the garage and just stare at her from every angle, and the same thing happens."

"Do you kiss her goodnight?"

"Absolutely. I'm zealous about protecting her. Last year we visited Vanessa Lafontaine, an old university classmate of Charlotte's, living in Gosport. We were standing next to the *M3*, when suddenly Vanessa's latest boyfriend leaned against it. My eyes bulged and I let out a low frequency growl in response. Sensing he had transgressed, he recoiled. I had to tell him, touching another man's motor is as bad as touching his dick! It's an instant hanging offence."

"*Hah, hah.*" Richmond scintillated. "I can see you are serious about your beloved *M3*."

"Too right. The blaggard also queried her nought to sixty time, saying the official time was four-point-three seconds. I told him red ones go faster due to reduced drag, and my *M3* did the time in four-point-one seconds."

"And he believed you?"

"I'm very convincing when it comes to all *M3* matters."

"I used to have a *BMW 850 Ci* coupé in the late-1990s."

"Oohh, very sleek. A resplendent car."

"Yes, she drew some beat. Since then, I've owned an *Audi A8 4.2 quattro*, and currently I drive a *Maserati Quattroporte V*. Carolyn has a *Porsche 911-997*."

"*Nice* cars," Fraser complimented. "Is Carolyn a good driver?"

"Very much so. She knows how to drive in ways that are best for the car."

"Huh, I wish Charlotte could do that. I cringe when she drives the *Viano*, and I *won't* let her anywhere near the *M3's* driving seat."

"Not a sympathetic car driver then?"

"She is superb at everything apart from driving."

With their sparky conversations eating away at time, the flight passed very quickly. Before the Cheshire boys knew it, the *A320* touched down at Geneva-Cointrin. After clearing passport control and collecting their baggage, they strolled through the arrival's concourse.

"Mister Anderson," they heard a female voice call.

Stopping in their tracks, the sisters Grimm drew up beside them pushing a trolly containing their luggage.

"I do hope you and your friends have a wonderful holiday," Gertrude urged.

"Many thanks. We trust that you and your sister will similarly be enthralled."

"What a lovely sentiment. Don't you think so, Evelyn?"

"Do come along, Gertrude. I want to get to the Carlton before they stop serving lunch."

"You're being self-centred again," she criticised, beetle-browed. "You promised me you'd be more courteous with people while we were on holiday."

"Stop carping, Gertrude. Come on, I'm hungry." She started to push the trolly.

"You had something to eat on the plane. *Really*, Evelyn, what am I going to do with you?"

As Gertrude trundled off after her sister, the squabble continued. Magnetised by the amusing tiff, the Cheshire boys watched them as they disappeared into the crowd and exited the airport, still fencing with each other.

"Right, gentlemen," Anderson said, gleaming. "Let's collect that *BMW M5* hire car from Avis, and drive to Lausanne. Our sailing and gambling sorties await."

Chapter Five: On Lake Geneva

On a baking hot July day in the Swiss Alps, the three campaneros took the sixty-odd kilometre scenic drive around Lake Geneva to the Mövenpick Hotel Lausanne, just a hop, a skip and a jump from Port Lausanne-Ouchy, mooring dock for their rented schooner, the Argonaut.

"My God, this is breathtaking," Richmond praised, as they stood on the quayside taking in a panoramic vista of Lake Geneva and the coastline. "I've been on business in Switzerland, but this is the first time I've actually taken the country in. It's as beautiful as the scenery around Lake Como and the other Italian lakes."

"Smell that air as well," Fraser invited. "After London's diesel fumes, it's as fresh and pure as a woodland fragrance."

"I predicted you'd both be impressed," Anderson hailed. "Wait until we're out on the lake. It will be even better."

*

That evening they got togged up in their penguin suits and drove to the Casino Barriére at Montreux. After the old Montreux Casino, immortalised in the Deep Purple classic, *Smoke on the Water*, burnt down in 1971, the Casino Barriére was built on the same site to replace it. Not as palatial as its predecessor, nevertheless the successor comprised multiple large gambling rooms, a spectacular cabaret circus, and a plenitude of bars and restaurants. Oozing sophistication and elegance with its mock regency décor, mirrored passageways, soaring ceilings with crystal chandeliers, and thick-pile carpet everywhere, the new building had become the go-to epicentre of choice for both locals and tourists. Though the Cheshire boys were not serious gamblers, they had put aside sufficient disposable funds to play the roulette and blackjack tables for the duration of their stay.

Whilst on business in Monte Carlo and Singapore, Anderson had dabbled with casino gambling, Richmond the same in Las Vegas, and Fraser in Hong Kong and at the London Playboy Club. Nothing more than fun to all of them, at best they won a small amount of money, or at worst, lost their conservative stakes completely.

What amazed Anderson during his first visit to the Marina Bay Sands Casino Singapore amounted to how international the high stakes gambling circuit appeared to be. Punters from every continent cloistered around every roulette and card table. The recognition had passed him by at the Casino de Monte-Carlo because of focusing on a high-powered client giving him concerns about a licensing contract with Oxalite. Conversely, he'd already finalised a licensing deal with the Yamanouchi Pharmaceutical Company when their CEO took him to the Marina Bay Sands Casino. He began to appreciate that for the super-rich, casino gambling represented the equivalent pastime of him taking Francine to a Rolling Stones concert or a West End playhouse.

Largely immune to the temptations of wholesale gambling, at the most Richmond had participated in sweepstakes and been to the Aintree Grand National and Royal Ascot with Carolyn and their intimates. His meagre betting at the horse racing meetings had indeed produced some winnings. But over the course of the cards, unremittingly he lost his entire hundred-pound initial stake. Though he visited at least ten hotel-gambling resorts and stayed at the Dunes Hotel and Country Club in Las Vegas whilst representing Dowty at an aerospace symposium, he prolonged his indifference to gambling, only placing hundred-dollars on bets and losing all of it. Instead, and much more memorable, he chose to take in the cabaret and indoor circus shows.

When Fraser entertained a private investor at the bunny venue, it drummed home to him how much punters were prepared to bet. His guest, liquid to the extent of owning his own Learjet, lost 40,000 pounds in a matter of twenty-minutes, and didn't even flinch. Not alone, the stock analyst come trouble-shooter witnessed other gamblers losing or winning up to hundreds of thousands of pounds, their heartbeats apparently never rising above normal. Pro-rata, he compared it to going over to the Kappa

Corinthians Clubhouse in Farnborough Kent and buying a round of *Shepherd and Neame Master Brew* for the entire first-fifteen, and that didn't happen very often.

Having made a bundle from their professions, the Cheshire boys lived like kings, but kings of ridiculously small countries. Whereas the heavy-duty gamblers they had witnessed splashing the cash in huge bundles, lived like kings of large countries with mega-rich economies. It all came down to economic scale. In terms of liquidated assets, the Englishmen were each worth something in the order of four-million pounds, at least half of their worth tied up in their large, detached houses. Affluent gamblers could claim an equivalent worth of at least ten times that, and much higher value real estate holdings. Whence they intended to meter their gambling pastimes proportionally at the Casino Barriére.

Passing through the opulent foyer of Montreux's premier gambling house, the trippers felt the panache and brio of the high life engulf them. Visceral in its effect, they figured the ambience had been purposely generated to induce and seduce punters into hovering to the gambling tables and parting with all their allotted stake money. Deciding to reconnoiter the joint to catch the flavour of gaming before placing any bets, after garnering three double *Chivas Regal*'s from the bar, they meandered around the roulette, blackjack, baccarat, poker and craps tables.

"You see that guy in the gold lame turban playing baccarat," Fraser articulated.

"What about him?" Anderson enquired.

"That's the Maharaja of Indore. He's a client with The Firm's Asia-Pacific operation."

"You know him?" Richmond inquired.

"No. But I recognise him from our publicity pictures. He has trans-continental credentials and substantial investments."

"If most of these players can claim a similar status, we are truly out of our depth," Anderson put forward.

"Ahh, he is probably in the minority," Fraser enumerated. "The core of casino gamblers tends to be less well-heeled, but with expectations of becoming rich. Of course, few if any do. They make up the casino's bread and butter business baseline. Punters like the Maharaja can produce additional bluebird earnings if they lose a bundle."

"You seem to know what you're talking about, Roger," Richmond complimented.

"It's because of taking uber-wealthy clients to the London Playboy Club casino for The Firm. Some have told me about the casino business-model. Candidly, it relies on furnishing games of chance where the house has a built-in advantage, ensuring profitability. However, analysis of the demographics illustrates that most casino punters come from the worldwide middle-classes and the *nouveau-riche*. Relative to the super-affluent, jet-set gamblers, they chance hundreds perhaps thousands of pounds, but they represent at least ninety-five percent of casino gamblers. Hence this stratum accounts for the casino market bedrock base."

"And they are transparent from the prosperous dynamos because all casino gamblers are attired in the same dress style," Anderson proposed.

"Quite." Opening his arms, he labelled, "Without knowing our true financial status, in our penguin suits we could be either high-flyers or just stock punters."

"Mmmm, I take your point," Richmond accorded. "Supposedly that lack of transparency afforded by common dress style invites scope to the criminal fraternity?"

"You mean to con the house?"

"Indeed."

"It does happen. But the confidential nature of the casino business ensures that the fleeced gambling house does not go public. And as you may know from your Vegas trip, casino's employ uncompromising security personnel to recover funds gained illegally without any police involvement."

Trying their hand at blackjack and roulette, the Cheshire boys lost all their stake money in less time than it takes to play the Beatles *Sergeant Pepper's Lonely Hearts Club Band* album. Resigned to the loss before they started, they reviewed the deprivation over more *Chivas Regal* at the bar.

"I was up for all of two minutes playing blackjack," Anderson stipulated. "Then I got over-confident betting too much on the turn of a card and ended up with nothing."

"How did you fare, Colby?" Fraser pumped.

"Just as bad as Gavin. I lost everything by becoming ambitious at the roulette table. After two one-to-one wins on the bounce by backing the right colour, I bet a series of column numbers at two-to-one and promptly lost my original stake and meagre winnings."

"Mmmm, I fared no better at the baccarat table. I'd like to say with practice that the odds begin to benefit the punter, but luck is really the only determinator."

"Yes," Anderson sanctioned. "Independent of whether you stick or play at say blackjack, it all comes down to how the next cards fall."

"Ahh well, it's only a bit of low-cost fun," Fraser qualified. "We knew that in advance."

"Have you guys noticed the amount of exceptionally, ravishing women either playing at or hovering around the tables?" Richmond raised.

"Indeed," Anderson supported. "I judged the female quality at the Casino de Monte-Carlo was outstanding, but the Casino Barriére is equal to it. Most of them take after silver-screen stars or fashion models."

"This location is very much a playground for the jet-set, isn't it?"

"Oh unquestionably. On the previous occasions I've been in Lausanne and Montreux, it has been festooned with high rollers."

"I wonder if we're going to meet any of them."

"Well, Colby, you'll just have to wait and see."

"Incontestably this place has a buzz about it," Fraser observed. "It reeks of the kind of setting described in Chandler's detective stories and Fleming's spy sagas."

"Mmmm, with that in mind, perhaps we will happen on some mysterious characters," Anderson forecast.

"Hah, wishful thinking, Gavin," Richmond contradicted. "We're just three ordinary Englishmen out on a jaunt. Who or what could possibly get us embroiled in something enigmatic?"

"Yep," Fraser supported. "Such a lark would be way out of the ballpark, and personally, I've had more than my fair share of chillers through my trouble-shooter role at The Firm."

"Maybe it's wishful thinking on my behalf," Anderson revised. "It's just this junket seems to have opened me up to the possibilities."

"Could be middle age hankering for the thrills undertaken in your youth," Richmond put forward.

"Yeah, you're right, Colby," he conceded. "It's just a runaway imagination. Nothing unusual is going to happen."

~ * ~

Shimmying into the local chandlers the following morning for some miscellaneous items, the men from Cheshire clapped their peepers on a rather large gentlemen, attired in lederhosen breeches suspended from his shoulders, knee-high white socks, leather Haferl shoes, a chequered shirt, and a Tyrolean hat with a proliferation of German beer badges embedded in it.

"Jesus, he looks like he's come straight from the Bavarian Oktoberfest," Richmond quipped under his breath.

"Either that, or he's a doppelganger tribute act for Auric Goldfinger in the Bond film of the same name," Anderson offered.

"I wonder if he's got a man servant named Odd Job?"

Serving several sassy customers at once, the refugee from German beer central appeared slightly flustered by their demands, his demeanour signalling they tested his patience.

After their forerunners had exited, leaving the seller mopping his brow, the Englishmen sauntered up to the counter, Anderson leading.

"*Guten morgen, mein herren,*" the Swiss welcomed. "*Was kann ich für dich tun?*"

"Roger," Anderson prompted.

"*Guten morgen,*" Fraser reciprocated. "*Konnten sie bitte Englisch sprechan?*"

"Ah, you are English."

"Indeed, and I've just about run out of my German language capability."

"As a courtesy, I vill speak English."

"Thank you."

"I am Herr Griswald, proprietor of zhis establishment. My apologies for keeping you vaiting. Ve are a bit short on resources today."

"Well, get staffed," Fraser mildly suggested, tongue-in-cheek.

"Vot?

"Get staffed," he reiterated, simpering. "Employ more helpers."

"Ahh, you are making ze English joke," Griswald replied, reciprocating the smile. As if resetting the dialogue, he clapped his hands once. "Now, how can I help you?"

"Gavin, can you give Herr Griswald that list of sundry items we need."

After transacting the business and leaving the premises, Anderson jested, "I wonder if Herr Griswald has got a bondage fixation with all that leather he wears?"

"You mean Herr Greaseball," Richmond nominated.

"What?"

"Didn't you notice the excessive perspiration on his face and hands?"

"Now you come to mention it, yes."

"Maybe he'd just had a sadomasochism session with Frau Griswald," Fraser donated.

*

Clearing Port Lausanne-Ouchy under the Argonaut's diesel motor, helmsman Anderson then instructed Richmond and Fraser to raise her sails using electric winches. Picking up speed enabling the diesel to be disengaged, the schooner navigated east-southeast, parallel to the shoreline and towards Bourg-en-Lavaux. With the pleasures rendered by the lake beckoning the crew, they became instilled with a sense of bravado, the machismo of adventure filling them from napper to foot.

Though aware they all stored stress resultant from work and domesticity, it was only when it gushed out of them under the influence of sailing that they truly realised the therapeutic qualities bestowed by the holiday. Not having indulged in a frolics-only furlough since their teens, the impact of responsibilities had gradually filtered into their bodies producing latent pressure. Being aboard Argonaut under favourable sailing conditions coupled with the glorious setting and wonderful weather unleashed their strain valves. Laughing and joking, the comrades felt like young warriors again, able to take on anything before them.

"My God," Richmond drawled. "I can feel decades of pent-up trauma draining from me."

"Yes," Fraser bolstered. "The same sensation is happening to me. Though I love my family dearly, they can be a source of much aggravation. Here with you two in this paradise on Earth, there are no pressures, no one pecking or hectoring. It's such a relief."

"Glad you're both suitably tranquillised," Anderson applauded.

"It must be the same for you, Gavin," Richmond intonated.

"In every way. It's one of the key criteria behind me suggesting this break. Like you two, I'm even-tempered with my family, but they do cause me some torment at times. I suspected a lad's jamboree over a two-week duration could provide both an antidote, and an opportunity to re-charge the batteries for all of us."

"Very smart, Gavin," Fraser complimented.

"We've just got to make the most out of the occasion. Like all holidays, it will be over before we know it."

Coming prepared for a floating lunch, the crew downed sails and dropped anchor opposite Veytaux, a few clicks past Montreux. Their appetites sharpened by the refreshing Swiss air, they munched their way through a luxury hamper of British and continental goodies including *foie gras*, truffles, smoked salmon, cognac flavoured pork liver pate, Dundee fruit loaf, strawberry and clotted cream biscuits and mature stilton, all washed down with *Chablis Grand Cru Les Clos Louis Michel*, fifty-years old tawny port and gourmet coffee. Spaced out after the sumptuous repast, Argonaut's crew splayed themselves on her superstructure like beached sea life to catch some sunrays. With the boat gently tugging at her anchor against a faint wind, it produced a rocking cradle effect, driving them further into a soporific state.

"Wow, I could really get used to this," Fraser consigned.

"For sure," Anderson abetted. "What sets sailing apart from other recreational activities is you can get away from the madding crowd. Just choose a spot on a lake, and invariably it's yours without interruption. I've tried some other pastimes, but for pure relaxation nothing beats achieving the horizontal position on a moored sailing vessel."

"Yep, and some R n R pursuits can be very frustrating."

"For example?"

"Golf," he identified, with a hint of vexation. "Whereas excellence in rugby is accomplished via dedication and practice, the same principle does not in my case lend itself to golf. Professedly I don't play very often, but when I do, my score card is all over the place. Sometimes I can do four to six good strokes on the run, followed by just as many disasters. There's little scope for even the minutest of errors resulting in single, double and triple bogies."

"Couldn't agree with you more, Roger. I've had more centuries at golf than Geoff Boycott has accrued at cricket," Richmond threw into the melting pot. "During my Marconi university sponsorship, one of the sales and marketing managers urged me to take up golf when I graduated, on the basis that more business deals were closed on the golf course than in the boardroom. And like you, my seldom manifestations on the golf course have been littered with more ignominy than glory. True, some business opportunities were and still are progressed and even closed during golfing sessions, clients often suggesting I let them win to get the contract, but really, they triumph because they are much better players." Dallying, he then annexed, "I even take part in the golfing sessions at company annual quota achiever club events, but it's the same story. My shots are haphazard.

"One time during a quota club with IBM in Montserrat I hit a tee-shot with a draw trajectory. The ball flew over the fence of the club I played at, over the fence of an adjoining golf club, bounced down its clubhouse driveway, through the open clubhouse French doors, and into a stack of cocktail glasses on the bar, then crashed into an array of cut-glass decanters. By definition I didn't know about the calamity until finishing the round and moseying over to the adjacent club to make my apologies. Being handed a bill for five-hundred East Caribbean dollars, about a hundred and forty-five pounds, took the sheen off the day!"

"Ohh, Christ, Colby," Fraser blathered between chortles. "I've had some bad golfing goofs, but all pale before your catastrophe."

"That plus the 200 East Caribbean dollars green fees turned out to be the most expensive round of golf I've ever had!"

"Gives a whole new meaning to the phrase, 'getting a round in'," Anderson ascribed, also laughing. "The equivalent of buying drinks for the entire membership of the afflicted clubhouse."

More tales of woe on the golf course and during other recreational activities followed, the Englishmen having no hesitation in recounting sporting gaffs and blunders under the liberating luncheon alcohol coupled with the clement weather and mutual camaraderie. With every passing moment, the accumulated stress of twenty-first century living seeped out of them, laying waste to latent anxieties, niggles and pressures, the Cheshire boys becoming refreshed and reinvigorated by the sojourn.

Sometime later they heard the low-pitch roar of a motor yacht approaching, then dropping anchor no more than a hundred-metres from their position. Curious as to the new arrivals, they craned their attics up to scope the craft — a sleek cruiser christened, Leonie, with dazzling white superstructure — one woman and two men aboard.

"Seems our space is going to be invaded," Fraser remarked to Anderson.

"Yes. How unusual. Vessels normally steer away from an already occupied anchor."

"Wow, she smacks of film star crossbreeding," Richmond extolled. "An amalgam of Grace Kelly and Jane Fonda in their prime."

"Whereas her male companions," Fraser added, "have the appearance of lesser minions."

"She's probably a rich heiress out for a day's sailing with her servants," Anderson tendered.

"Well, whatever she is," Richmond updated, "she has a touch of class about her. That head held high, mane of golden waves and slinky shape marks someone with regal credentials."

"You can see all that from here?" he queried, wrinkling his nose in disbelief.

"When it comes to the female form, Gavin, nothing escapes me. Besides, I still have good distance eyesight."

"What about the manservants?"

"One is as tall as us with dark hair and an equally dark Van Dyke beard and mustache. The other is shorter, possesses a wrestler's build and has adopted the Yul Brynner look."

"You describe them like Munster family members."

"Mmmm," Richmond began, facing Anderson. "That would make the woman Lily Munster, but she's far from a vampire. Irrefutably my senses detect a vamp, however, I suspect that is a minor part of her character. I'd bet she's much more the glossy, calculating type. Someone not to be underestimated."

"Ohh, she's peeking in our direction," Fraser observed. "In fact, she's withdrawing field glasses from a case."

Sitting up, the Cheshire boys stared in the direction of the Leonie.

Raising the binoculars to eye level, the woman then waved at the Argonaut, her crew reciprocating the gesture.

A little later, Fraser observed, "That tall fellow must have gone below. Only the woman and the wrestler are in the stern."

"Yes," Anderson approved, then cackled, "no, maybe not. There's a noodle just bobbed up beside the cruiser's bows."

"Has it got a Van Dyke beard and mustache?" Richmond asked, eyes still closed under the mid-afternoon sun.

"I do believe it has. It's also got a mask, and if my eyes don't deceive me, a snorkel coupled to an air tank."

"He must have been examining the lake's fish life."

"Mmmm," Anderson murmured, generating a puzzled countenance, his brain cogs beginning to engage and rotate — the likelihood of Lake Geneva's aquatic life being surveyed by tourists, remote.

Chapter Six: Stephanie Nightingale

In the early evening, the holidaymakers changed into tuxedo attire, then drove to the Casino Barrière. Deciding to plump for the French style brasserie to be followed by a gambling binge, they made their dinner order at the bistro bar and sipped on gin and tonics.

"Say, have you kept up with contemporary music trends?" Richmond asked Anderson.

"Oh, after the advent of grunge and Britpop in the 1990s, my curiosity waned. Apart from frequenting Rolling Stones concerts and buying revised and remastered CDs, I've not kept abreast of goings-on in the derivative rock sphere."

"Roger?"

"Much the same as Gavin. An expert in masterly inactivity, whilst crashed out on the lounge sofa, my son James used to subject my ears to the most appalling rubbish spewed by the Arctic Monkeys and the Killers. But one day, and I'm still to work out just why, he saw the light, proclaiming the Stones and Led Zeppelin to be the grandmasters of rock, and promptly ditched his former gods.

"However, answering your question more directly, after the kids came along, it became near to impossible for me to listen to rock, jazz or classical music without being interrupted on some minor pretext. On the odd occasion I have the house to myself, I let loose the volume on my twin stereo speakers system set up in the lounge, and drift away to Hendrix, the Doors, Miles Davis and a host of others. It's always short-lived, but during such *rare* moments I become blessed with an inner glow." Tarrying, he then enumerated, "The last top-rate gig Charlotte and I attended was Jeff Beck at Ronnie Scott's in November 2007. Page and Plant were in the audience."

"Impressive," Anderson flattered.

"I suppose, I'm much the same as you two," Richmond confessed. "Whereas during my educational years I played music every day, since entering the workplace and domesticity with their unforeseen demands, my consumption has trailed off. Howbeit, I do get to gigs occasionally whilst on extended business junkets. I remember being taken around the Seattle rock clubs by a couple of Boeing engineers in 1989, and quite by chance coming across the mighty Nirvana. But more recently, well about eight years back, I was in Sacramento getting down to the vinegar strokes on an IBM business partner agreement. Their CFO took me to see a Led Zep tribute act called, Zepparella, at the Sacramento Roundhouse. I'd seen Zep tribute bands in England and expected the usual male stereotypes, but this troupe were an all-girl outfit, and boy could they play. Zepparella were note-perfect on every song, guitarist Gretchen Menn, a faultless Jimmy Page impersonator, her *Gibson Les Paul* sound mirroring his licks flawlessly. Quite frankly, she's the best guitarist I've heard since Television's Tom Verlaine and Richard Lloyd. And she's knockout, incontrovertibly gorgeous. You should checkout Gretchen and Zepparella on You Tube."

"Really that good?" Fraser queried.

"Yep."

Following the lavish meal, they made their way to the gambling rooms, determined to make a better fist of their bet selections. Alas, after roulette and blackjack sessions, Anderson was ninety Swiss francs down on his original stake, Richmond also considerably down, but miraculously, Fraser up by thirty Swiss francs. Following their betting spree, they retired to a table opposite the ornate bar sipping on *Courvoisier* cognac.

"Just goes to show," Anderson foreshadowed, "as Roger indicated last night, routinely the house comes out on top."

"Yes. If I'd continued to play blackjack, my gains would have evaporated," Fraser confided. "As a comparator, in my financial analyst arena, it all comes down to understanding market statistics, and based on the comprehension, making the right decisions. Admittedly, Colby's world of software applications has improved predictions, but nothing remains implicitly foolproof. However, contrast that with gambling, and placing a bet is about best guess."

"You mean luck?" Anderson investigated.

"Assuredly."

"Hey," Richmond began, "look who's just walked in."

Flanked by her presumed two servants, the dashing blonde they had seen on Lake Geneva glided into the casino. Dressed like diamonds in a full-length, off the shoulder, shimmering, pearl-white evening gown, hugging at her upper torso, with her cornflower-blue eyes, generous lips and delicate features highlighted with cosmetics, and a deportment presented in the style of a catwalk model, she embodied all the regal facets of someone with significant standing.

She reminded Anderson of Colette Babineaux, executive director at Moreau-Roux, a French pharmaceutical producer based in Montpellier. An unalloyed pleasure, he'd had to meet with the French sorceress several times during licensing talks for Oxalite products, some ten years before the Lausanne trip. Remorselessly robed to the nines for either formal business meetings or social events, she had left her mark on him as a high-powered company emissary with exceptional tuned-in business savvy, and a capacity to entrance all before her with her vampish mannerisms. Though he'd met many talented women holding positions of authority in both the petrochemical and pharmaceutical industries, and most were older than him and possessed an abundance of university qualifications, by a long chalk Colette Babineaux stood above them. Her innate insight to see business potential and her capacity to persuade ensured the longevity of a very productive career. When they first met, she was thirty-five. Anderson, forty-two.

Used to mainly negotiating with men sitting on the opposite side of the table, his surprise at squaring off against the French pharmaceutical industry's answer to Brigitte Bardot had him lost to make constructive speech for the opening moments of their rendezvous. A failing he had not previously encountered. After gathering himself, he entered into his usual business etiquette, but detected Colette pinpointed she had floored him. Afterwards, when he got to know her, he shared the shortcoming during a cocktail soiree held by the Moreau-Roux board of directors in Montpellier to celebrate the licensing settlement. Ever the diplomat,

Colette convinced him his reaction to her was by no means unique, and he had recovered his concentration quicker than most.

When she visited Oxalite at Welwyn Garden City, she nearly brought work to a standstill during Anderson's guided tour of the plant, everyone he introduced her to bewitched and beguiled. It came down to a concoction of intrinsic femininity and heartfelt humility. Even Francine adjudged her as special, when the Andersons accompanied by other senior Oxalite staff and their wives took Colette to dinner at Brocket Hall, a five-star grillroom on the outskirts of Welwyn Garden City.

As Anderson gazed at the debonair blonde, he wondered if she'd be anything like Colette Babineaux.

"Hot damn, some entrance," Fraser acclaimed. "She really is a corker."

"Older than I first calculated," Richmond corrected. "I'd now guess she's in her mid-thirties, but she's taken care of herself, and she's in *lovely* condition."

"I don't believe it," Anderson chirped. "She's coming over."

As she neared with her aides, the Englishmen couldn't help but stare at her.

"Good evening, gentlemen," the siren called, her husky voice drenched in mystique. Ever courteous, they stood. "Glad to see you successfully negotiated your way back to port. Allow me to introduce myself. My name is Stephanie Nightingale." She glanced towards the beard, then the wrestler. "And these are my companions, Andrey Sorensen and Nostro Kravets."

"Good evening, Miss Nightingale," Anderson responded, recording no ring on her left hand third finger. "My name is Gavin Anderson, and these are my chums, Colby Richmond and Roger Fraser."

"Can we offer you some refreshments?" Richmond volunteered.

"Thank you, a chilled daiquiri, if you please."

"And your escorts?"

"They do not drink."

"Won't you take a seat, Miss Nightingale?" Fraser invited, as Richmond summoned a waiter and made the cocktail order.

"Thank you."

She sat opposite the Cheshire boys, Sorensen and Kravets standing behind her.

"I assume you are on vacation?" she ventured.

"Indeed," Anderson confirmed. "Taking a break from our professions and domesticity."

Little did the Englishmen realise it, but out of their eyelines, exclusively focused on Stephanie, two groups had congregated at the bar. One comprising three men and two women, the second, one man and two women. All peering in the direction of Miss Nightingale, they then exchanged waspish sneers at each other, the opposing women in particular casting disparaging gawks as if about to engage in a Christians verses lions set-to at the Colosseum.

"Are you enjoying Lake Geneva?" Stephanie delved.

"Well, that was our first voyage today," Anderson apprised. "We intend to take in as much of the lake as possible, plus explore Lausanne over our remaining thirteen days. We might even travel further afield, if time permits."

"Indeed. You could take in the city museums and visit some of the outlying villages to the north of the city. They are very quaint."

"Do you have any advice about interesting lake locations?"

"From what I gathered from the Port Lausanne-Ouchy Sailing Club, Saint-Prex and Prangins on the Swiss side of the lake, and Plage di Vindry and Evian-les-Bains on the French side are worth visiting."

"And what were your impressions of these places?"

"Oh, we are yet to experience their undoubted delights. Besides—" She peeped at her minders. "We have other fish to fry."

Continuing with small talk without becoming personal, the Cheshire boys entered a cosy regime with the exotic Miss Nightingale, mutual simpers flying off faces, a hint of laughter resultant from the odd witty comment, a sense of camaraderie building.

Then one man from each of the two watching groups circled the bar area in opposite directions. Both came to rest adjacent to pillars separated by some twenty metres and a cluster of nighthawks behind the Cheshire boys. Registering the men, Sorensen bent forward and whispered in Stephanie's ear.

Beaming at her newfound companions, she proposed, "Why don't we play a little roulette? I fancy I might be lucky this evening."

"Sure," Anderson complied.

With Stephanie cocooned between the Cheshire boys, and Sorenson and Kravets to her rear, the ensemble strolled towards the gambling area. So consumed in bliss, Anderson did not notice Stephanie extract a small envelope from her dainty purse and slip it into his left-hand jacket pocket before they reached a surfeit of people surrounding the roulette table.

"Oh dear," Fraser began, "there's only one spare seat available. You take it, Stephanie, and we'll watch."

"Very gracious," she opined, sparkling. "Thank you."

She did much better than the Cheshire boys, accruing 680 Swiss francs in chips within half an hour, leaving Anderson wondering what their newfound playmate did workwise to fund her gambling habit. Not satisfied with her earnings, she became more ambitious with her betting strategies, in due course leaving the roulette table 945 Swiss francs to the good.

"You seem to be able to read the roulette wheel with some exactitude," Anderson commended.

"Hah." She gleamed. "Tonight, yes. It will make up for the losses I made previously."

She spied about as if searching for someone, the Englishmen refraining from being curious.

"Come," she coaxed. "Let's retire to the Lord Byron bar for cocktails."

Engaging in more small talk and generalities over mixed drinks, the Cheshire boys spent an hour or so with the fetching Miss Stephanie Nightingale, their mutual cordiality taking a further upwards swing. Now able to assess the lorelei more fully, Anderson determined that indeed she did bear all the hallmarks of Colette Babineaux. He computed that beyond the charming front she projected, lay a highly intelligent, business-like crackerjack equipped to deal with anything requiring invention and perseverance. She also possessed a modicum of charisma management, her aids willing and quick to respond to her calls. It all begged the question, what was she really doing in Lausanne? There had to be more to her schedule than just sailing and gambling, but what?

Towards the end of the evening, she enquired, "Where are you staying?"

"The Mövenpick Hotel Lausanne on Avenue de Rhodanie," Richmond informed.

"Will you be out on the lake tomorrow?" Anderson canvassed.

Before she could reply, Sorensen whispered in her ear.

"Regrettably, I'll be away for the next few days" she explained. "However, no doubt we will meet up again on my return."

~ * ~

On return to the Mövenpick, Fraser suggested, "Let's have a nightcap before turning in."

"First class idea, Roger," Richmond applauded.

Making their way to the hotel's main bar, they went for *Courvoisier* then stood nursing their cognacs.

"A great evening," Fraser praised. "Meeting Stephanie has added verve to our sojourn."

"Yep," Richmond supported. "She's definitely put some zip into proceedings."

"Indisputably," Anderson endorsed. About to add more to his salutation, he casually slipped his left hand into his jacket pocket. "Hello, what's this?" Grasping an unfamiliar object, he hauled it out, his physiognomy becoming a mixture of startlement and intrigue.

"It appears to be a small envelope," Fraser classified.

Gently squeezing the sheath, Anderson proclaimed, "There's something solid inside it."

Opening the unsealed container, he pulled out a small piece of yellowed paper and a key.

"Well, well, well. Someone is playing games with you," Richmond declared.

"What does it say?" Fraser probed.

Blinking at the text, he enlightened, "Something written in

German. Here, you take a gander."

He handed Fraser the paper containing the message; *Oh verfolger_sucher nach einem riesigen vermögen and der quelle des liches_was sie suchen, liegt bei 46251452 und 6554296_78740.16 zoll von der — ostküste entfernt. 2094.*

"My German is rusty, and…its joined-up writing." He winked at Anderson. "Not sure I can handle that." Hesitating, he then advised, "I half-recognise some of the words, but translating the entire sentence is beyond my capability." Facing Richmond, he challenged, "How about you, Colby?"

"Foreign languages were never my strong suit at school. Sorry, I can't help."

"I wonder what this key is for?" Anderson quizzed, twirling it between his fingers, as Fraser gave him back the paper.

"Judging by its discolouration, it must be very old," Richmond conjectured. "Might be for a casket or a trunk."

"And the numbers? What can they mean?"

"Could be anything from the combination to a safe to a lottery number."

"Here, let me take another squint," Fraser requested.

Anderson handed over the paper.

"I think *verfolger* translates as chase or chaser, and *liches* is light. That's all I can make out, but—" Raising his head, he blazed. "I know a man who inherently does know German."

"Oh, who?"

"*Obergruppenführer* Heinrich Metzer, based at The Firm's Frankfurt office. He's director of manufacturing investments for the German-speaking parts of Europe. I'll give him a bell in the morning."

Chapter Seven: The *Obergruppenführer*

Early the next day, Fraser telephoned Metzer from his hotel room, only to be told he was holidaying at his schloss in Waldshut-Tiengen. Not put off, Fraser then called the schloss number given to him by Metzer's PA, Anderson and Richmond standing behind him with bated breath.

"Hello, Heinrich, its Roger Fraser."

"Roger, how good it is to hear from you. I often reminisce about zhat business ve did in Dublin vith Ricky Henshaw und Milton Crossman, not so long ago. I very nearly convinced Milton to climb into ze jack boots and ze lederhosen."

"Quite," Fraser interrupted, cutting off Metzer's daydream. "Tell me, Heinrich, do you have a fax machine at the schloss?"

"A fax machine, vhy?"

"I'd like you to translate a German document."

In the background, Fraser heard a high-pitched scream emanating from the schloss.

"What was that, Heinrich?"

"Just an irritant. Nevermind. Obviously, you are not in London. Vhere are you?"

"In Lausanne."

"Zhat is less than three hours from Waldshut-Tiengen, und I need to exercise my *Mercedes Benz C63 AMG*. Far better I examine ze document in person, vouldn't you say?"

"Well, if it's no trouble."

"Not in ze least"

"I'm staying with friends at the Mövenpick Hotel Lausanne on Avenue de Rhodanie."

"I know zhat hotel. I vill be vith you by midday."

"Many thanks, Heinrich. We'll take you out for lunch."

Ending the call, Fraser announced, "Right, we're on."

*

"I must apologise for ze lateness of my arrival," Metzer imparted, as he shook hands with Fraser in the Mövenpick lobby. "Roadwerks on ze E25 north of Bern delayed me."

"A familiar refrain. Never mind, Heinrich, it's happened to me many times."

Slender with sunken cheeks, piercing ice-blue eyes, swept back dark hair and decked out in a black pinstripe suit with a buttoned-up, double-breasted jacket, pristine white shirt, fraternity tie and ultra-shiny black brogues, Metzer cut a formidable figure. His sharp, no-nonsense voice tone added to the impression. As the German spoke to Fraser, Anderson and Richmond swapped wary glimpses.

After introducing his comrades to Metzer, Fraser briefed, "We've booked a table at the Brasserie La Riviera just around the corner from the hotel."

"I hope it serves good sauerkraut," Metzer joshed.

"*Oh*, it's a French eatery."

"I vos only making ze joke, Roger. French is fine for me."

"I see you're wearing your Frankfurt Westend gentlemen's club tie."

"Yes, I have taken to donning zhis tie for important occasions. Judging by ze tone of your voice during our telecom, I deduced zhis vould be such an occasion."

"I remain very impressed from that time you took me to the Westend, when I came to Frankfurt on The Firm's business."

"Excellent. Ze club is intended to have zhat effect. Vhen my Uncle Albrecht sponsored me for its exclusive membership, I vas in awe. You see, ze Vestend in ze splendid halls of ze Villa Bonn with its red carpets, vood-panelled valls, red-marble fireplace, chandeliers und deer antlers, has a traditional outlook going back to 1855 in ze reign of Emperor Francis Joseph I. Ze atmosphere of an elite men's association is palpable. Our membership has always included industrialists, bankers, lawyers, academics und artists.

"Frankfurt Mayor, Petra Roth, vas ze first voman allowed into our ranks in 1995. Zhat was a vatershed change for us, Roger. It marked ze advent of liberalism and inclusivity. Nonezeless, since zhen zhere has not been another voman accepted into ze club."

"Tradition trumping a progressive theme?"

"Quite."

After consuming a smorgasbord of salads and *poissons* flushed down with *Domaine Servin Chablis*, Metzer pressed, "Are you going to show me zhis paper?"

"Of course," Anderson replied, retrieving the envelope from his jacket pocket.

Opening the sleeve, Metzer pronounced, "A key as vell as a piece of paper." Attaching a monocle to his right eye, he studied the inscription. "Zhis is a combination of German and Prussian. It must be incredibly old."

"Yes, but what does it say, Heinrich?"

"Vell, ze grammar needs something to be desired, but I vill give you my best translation…Oh chaser seeker of a vast fortune and ze source of light vhat you seek is at 464207 and 69286_78740.16 zoll from the — east shoreline. 2094."

"Ahh," Richmond began, "when I learnt to fly at Marconi, I got used to navigation. Those numerals after 'is at,' could be map coordinates?"

"Very good, Colby. Vot do they translate as?"

"Could I borrow your smartphone, Heinrich?"

"Gladly."

Picking up Metzer's *Apple iPhone 5*, Richmond notified, "I just need to find a decimal degree to degrees, minutes and seconds application." A few moments elapsed, everyone else glued to the smartphone while Richmond worked his magic. "Ahh, here we are. Now it will only make sense if I apply a decimal point after the first two digits of the first number, and a decimal point after the first digit of the second number." Keying in the first reference, he then reported, "Forty-six degrees, fifteen minutes, 5.2272 seconds, North." After the second keying, he acquainted, "sixty-five degrees, thirty-two minutes, 34.656 seconds, East."

"Very precise numbers," Metzer observed. "Whoever composed zhem, must have been intent on absolute accuracy."

"Now, let's plug these coordinates into Google maps on your iPhone."

After Richmond applied the two scalers, the map application zoomed into Veytaux, less than two clicks south of Montreux and adjacent to the east shore of Lake Geneva.

"Mmmm, we could really do with a hard copy ordnance survey map," Anderson put forward. "That will provide a blown-up, more inclusive view of the area."

"Yes," Metzer agreed, "Zhese café's usually keep ordnance survey maps for tourists. I vill muster ze vaiter."

Snapping his fingers, the cracking noise caught a waiter's attention.

With closing time imminent and all their clientele gone apart from the Anglo-German coterie, the La Riviera staff were making preparations to clear the lunchtime tables and re-lay them with evening dinner accoutrements.

Miffed, the waiter came over to the source of the summons.

"Zir," he gabbed, his accent clearly bearing a Bavarian twang.

"Ve need an ordnance survey map," Metzer specified.

"Ze restaurant is shutting, zir. You vill have to leave."

"Ve just need a few minutes, und zhat ordnance survey map."

"No, you have to leave now, mein herr."

Not used to being pressured by presupposed underlings, Metzer took in the waiter, his right eye beginning to twitch. "Are you Sviss, or German?"

"German."

"Vere you in ze *Wehrmacht*, I mean ze *Bundeswher*?"

"Yes, mein herr."

"Vot rank?"

"Corporal, mein herr."

"Vell I vas a colonel in ze SS, I mean ze *Whermackt*, I mean ze

Bundeswher." Issuing him a menacing demeanour, he ordered, "You vill come to attention vhen you speak to me. Is zat clear, insulant dog?"

"*Jawohl*, mein herr," he replied, clicking his heels.

"Zhat is better. Now, ve need on ordnance survey map of ze area. I vant you to go to ze bar manager and ask for such a map."

"*Jawohl*, mein herr."

"Off you go," he pushed, waving a dismissive hand at him.

"That's much clearer," Anderson assigned, after the waiter gave Metzer a high-resolution ordnance survey map of the area centred on Lake Geneva.

"Yes," Metzer supported. "Ve can now see the coordinates clearly."

"What about the, '78740.16 zoll from the — east shoreline'," Fraser prompted. "And what is zoll?"

"Zhat is an old Prussian vord, Roger. Ze zoll, generally rendered inch in English, vas ze Prussian unit of length or distance prior to 1872, vhen ze German Empire vas formed. Ze zoll is vone-twelfth of a fuzz. An imperial foot is near-equivalent to a fuzz. So—" Selecting a distance convertor on his *iPhone*, he then recorded, "78740.16 zoll or inches equals 6561.68 feet, vhich in turn is equivalent to two kilometres."

"Thereby, the message reads," Anderson began, "Oh chaser _seeker of a vast fortune and the source of light_ What you seek is at forty-six degrees, fifteen minutes, 5.2272 seconds, North, sixty-five degrees, thirty-two minutes, 34.656 seconds, East, and two kilometres from the — east shoreline. 2094." Pausing, he then affixed, "I wonder what 2094 signifies?"

"Well, it's not related to the coordinates," Richmond ascribed.

"No," Fraser upheld. "Must link to something else."

"Now," Metzer began, "let us see vhere zhese coordinates intersect on ze map." Tracing the north reference with his right index finger and the east denotation with his left, they intersected on Lake Geneva not far from the eastern shore at Veytaux. "Mmmm, not vhat I expected."

"Perhaps the coordinate translations are wrong."

After re-checking them, Richmond heralded, "No, they're

correct."

"*Wait a minute*," Anderson yapped. "We dropped anchor opposite Veytaux yesterday, before that cruiser containing Stephanie Nightingale and her two minders moored between the Argonaut and Veytaux, about two kilometres from the coastline. And—" Suddenly catching on, he smiled. "It must have been Stephanie who slipped that envelope containing the paper and the key into my jacket pocket when we were at the Casino Barrière Montreux."

"Extrapolating your conjecture, Gavin," Fraser opened, "do you recall The Beard – Andrey Sorensen, disappeared from our view for quite some time before his noodle bobbed up beside the Leonie?"

"Yes, I do." Stopping, he became fired up. "Now here's a leap of faith. Could it be that Sorensen donned diving gear to audit the lake bottom for something?"

"Possibly," Richmond supported. "But what? And why did Stephanie secrete the envelope on your personage?"

"Vell, gentlemen, it seems like you have a mystery on your hands," Metzer detailed. "If I can be of any further service, Roger knows vere I vill be."

~ * ~

After Metzer had driven off in his *Mercedez*, the Cheshire boys strolled down to Port Lausanne-Ouchy.

"Your pal Heinrich is quite a character, Roger," Anderson observed. "Vas he really a colonel in ze SS, I mean ze *Whermackt*, I mean ze *Bundeswher*?" he asked, mimicking Metzer.

"No," Fraser retorted, tickled by his friend's impression. "The *Obergruppenführer* was a professor in psychopharmacology at Heidelberg University before joining The Firm in 2002." Tongue in cheek, he ascribed, "He's my kind of manager — brutal, vicious, psychotic. A nemesis to delinquent stock traders. Huh…I heard a scream in the background when I phoned him at his schloss. Probably it came from a Frankfurt office trader he had under torture for incurring his displeasure."

"Not a man to cross then."

"No. Though he is not of large stature, nonetheless he possesses a sinister personality, and his voice tone packs a foreboding punch."

"He really eviscerated that waiter."

"That's because the waiter is German. Heiney only does it to his own kind."

"Changing the subject," Richmond posed, "I wonder if Stephanie is out on the lake, off Veytaux?"

"Ahh, she said, she'd be away for a few days," Fraser recollected.

"Maybe it was a ruse?"

"Well, there's only one way to find out," Anderson nominated.

Quickly readying the Argonaut for sailing, soon the companions were steering east-southeast towards the map coordinates translated from the yellowing paper, Fraser at the wheel in the stern, Anderson and Richmond forrad in the bows. As they approached the location where they had moored for lunch the previous day, they saw another schooner had dropped anchor more or less at the same spot where Stephanie's cruiser had stopped.

Examining the vessel with binoculars, Anderson relayed, "I can see two men and one woman, but it's not Stephanie and her minders."

"Surely, it can't be coincidence that schooner is rooted at the same position we saw the Leonie," Richmond remarked, as he and Anderson scooted back to the stern. Spying into the lake north and south, he adjoined, "There's no other shipping in this part of the lake. Therefore, the likelihood of that craft stopping at the identical location is extremely remote. I'm beginning to smell a rat."

"Maneuver to starboard, Roger," Anderson requested. "If that is a nefarious bunch, we don't want to make them curious about us."

"Aye, aye, Captain," Fraser responded, re-setting Argonaut's course to a due south direction.

"There's some alchemy at work here," Richmond tagged. "Something which is yet to become transparent to us. We can see some fragments of reportage, but they hide a profusion of mysteries." Suspending, he then enumerated, "What is at the cross-section of the map coordinates? Who is Stephanie and her minders? And—" He gaped back at the schooner. "Who is onboard that vessel?"

*

Later, the Cheshire boys recapped on the day's events over refreshments in the Mövenpick's bar.

"It appears that the vim Stephaine has added to our sojourn is accompanied by a maze of uncertainties," Anderson defined. "The question is, do we welcome it?"

"Oh, I don't see why not," Fraser parried. "As Heinrich said, it's a mystery, a paradox, something yet to become lucid to us. That is, if we care to pursue it."

"What do you think, Colby."

"Much the same as Roger. At the most, I'd classify it as a perplexity containing several apparently disconnected elements – Stephanie Nightingale, the envelope contents, and an unknown schooner moored at the same location where we saw the Beard diving."

"So you both have no reservations about staying the course?"

Unreservedly, Richmond and Fraser answered in the affirmative.

Swinging over to the Casino Barriére in the evening, the compadres scoped about hoping in vain to find the enigmatic Miss Nightingale, but they drew a blank. To all intent and purpose, she and her minders had indeed left the locale for a few days, as she had told them the previous evening. Why they imagined they'd see her persisted as unclear, other than wishful thinking, and some sort of speculation that she cavorted in a game as yet to coalesce into definable constituents before the Englishmen.

Playing detective as part of all their workplace functions when the obscure and the inscrutable defied business logic, had nurtured their capacities to dig deep, use lateral thinking, and be tenacious until transparency distilled on the incomprehensible. It had filtered into their private lives, the Cheshire boys utilising the talent when things transpired not to be what they seemed. A trait particularly pertinent with their children, and sometimes their wives. Such gremlins called for the gentle touch, diplomacy, or both, to settle the problem.

Based on the elements they had aggregated; they intrinsically knew resolution of whatever Stephanie had become involved in could open a Pandora's box of as yet to be established posers. Just how that could be dealt with lingered as an unknown. Would their tried and tested methodology be sufficient to help her, if indeed she needed help, or could it be completely out of kilter with whatever plagued her?

It all came down to probabilities and possibilities crystalising into fact, thereby allowing a direction to be taken. Even so, with minimal data accrued, any determination triggering a settlement remained flaky and hugely qualified with assumptions. Somehow, they had to discover more factors, meaning more material, and crucially, all of the interested parties.

Chapter Eight: Stephanie Returns

Expecting to encounter Stephanie Nightingale's cruiser again, the next day the Cheshire boys were out on Lake Geneva heading east-southeast. Albeit the only vessel coming into Anderson's binocular's view was the schooner they'd seen the previous day, once more moored at the navigational position identified on the yellowing paper. As soon as he verified the boat, Argonaut veered away south, her crew eyeing the suspicious target and pondering what to do next as she ploughed through narrow waves caused by a breeze from the south-east towards Port Valais.

"Whoever they are, they're up to no good," Anderson professed. "Like an iffy business proposition, I can feel it in my bones."

"Mmmm," Fraser began, "whatever is to be found at that location is drawing some determined forces. Obviously, Stephanie and co are playing a close hand, and that schooner crew manifestly come across as resolute."

"Based on the 'seeker of a vast fortune and the source of light' line, it must be something unbelievably valuable," Richmond supposed. "However, if its say gold bullion and worth millions, it'd be contained in a fairly large housing, such as a crate or even a safe.

"Further, such a receptacle would be easily spotted in these clear waters by a diver, but it appears that neither of the scouring parties can locate it. Plus, to haul such a container onboard a vessel from the lakebed needs a sturdy winch. Neither the Leonie nor that schooner has such a facility."

"So, Colby," Anderson queried, "are you saying whatever is at the location, is small?"

"Yes, and that might be the reason why it has not been found yet."

"Hhmm, I suppose a valuable cache could be housed in a small container."

"Diamonds or perhaps bonds is a possibility," Fraser anticipated. "Coming from the world of finance, occasionally I get a bird's eye view of valuable commodities. Often, they are not large in size."

"For instance?"

"Well, a few years back, The Firm were involved in the resource's sale of a fashion house that had bellied up after over-extending its loans to fuel the design of new *haute couture* clothing. To our everlasting surprise, the CEO had converted the company's pension fund and other liquid assets into a cache of diamonds, valued at thirty-million-pounds."

"So this CEO intended to defraud the company and flee with the stash when bankruptcy occurred?"

"Possibly."

"Why only possibly?"

"Before any subterfuge could take place, the banks foreclosed under the Insolvency Act 1986, and the receiver seized all company assets, including the diamonds. There is nothing prohibiting a company from investing in commodities. So although the authorities suspected the CEO's motives, nothing could be proved."

"Why diamonds?"

"Unlike electronic money transfer which leaves a paper trail, and nine times out of ten is detectable, commodities such as diamonds, or come to that high-value metals, are much easier to remove from a bank by the registered account holder without raising a hue and cry. In this case, certified company officers, meaning the chief financial officer or the CEO."

"What does thirty-million-pounds worth of diamonds equate to in physical size?"

"Put it this way, you could tuck them into your jacket pockets without making the pockets bulge too much."

"So such a haul could be stored in a relatively small receptacle?"

"Oh yes. A six-by-six-by-six-inch casket could effortlessly store the chattels."

Staring at the schooner moored at the location point designated on the yellowing paper, Anderson voiced, "I wonder if they are after a similar-sized bonanza?"

~ * ~

A complete surprise to the Cheshire boys, when they returned to the Mövenpick, Stephanie and her minders intercepted them in the hotel lobby.

"*Stephanie*," Anderson babbled. "We weren't sure if we'd ever see you again."

"I have much to tell you." She scanned around as if scoping for possible assailants. Bemused, the Englishmen mimicked her action. "Can we go to your room? It's too public here."

"Certainly."

With Stephanie sitting in a chair in Anderson's room, and her minders standing behind her, the Englishmen eagerly awaited her explanation.

"Where is the envelope?" she calmly enquired.

"You mean the one you secreted in my jacket pocket at the Casino Barriére?" Anderson replied.

"Yes."

"It's in my room wall safe."

"Good. You must have wondered why I took the action?"

"Well, it's true to say, its contents have had us guessing for the last few days."

"Can I trust you?" she requisitioned, sitting forward, her customary cool interposed with a dab of anxiety.

"I think you've made that commitment already."

"Yes, you're right," she conceded. "I have a sensitive nose. While we were talking in the casino, it didn't detect any malevolence in the three of you. You all came across as what you English call good eggs, so I took a chance."

"But why, Stephanie?" Richmond interjected.

"I will come to that, but first I have to tell you about the circumstances bringing me to Switzerland." Cultivating a sincere mien, she unmasked, "My real name is, Countess Antoniya Katerina Kulikovsky. I am descended from Russian Romanov royalty. My great grandmother was Grand Duchess Olga Alexandrovna of Russia, younger sister to Czar Nicholas II, and the youngest daughter of Czar Alexander III.

"Olga married Colonel Nikolai Kulikovsky. Their second son, Guri Nikolaevich Kulikovsky, was my grandfather. After the October 1917 Bolshevik revolution, the Kulikovsky family escaped to Denmark in 1919, then Canada in 1948. Guri and his Danish-born wife, Ruth Schwartz, had two children — Xenia and Leonid. Leonid Nikolaevich Kulikovsky married my mother of Danish descent, Eva Christensen. They currently live in Darwin Australia where I was born. My father Leonid inherited the key and the letter."

"How?"

"The abdication of Nicholas II on 15 March 1917 as a result of the February Revolution ended 304 years of Romanov rule and led to the establishment of the Russian Republic under the Menshevik controlled Russian Provisional Government. When it became clear to the Czar that the usurpers intended to strip the Romanovs of all their possessions, he ordered a trusted elite detachment of guards from the Saint Petersburg Winter Palace, led by General Losif Bodrov, to take the personal Romanov valuables, meaning a huge stockpile of gold rubles and customised Fabergé eggs out of Russia."

"Good god," Fraser leaked. "Reputedly, that king's ransom was enormous in value."

"Indeed. Not just because of its liquidity worth, but who owned it."

"So what happened?" Anderson pushed.

"The Bolsheviks got word about Bodrov, Lenin despatching agents to recover the nuggets. They pursued the Bodrov contingent through Ukraine, Czechoslovakia, Austria and Liechtenstein before he ended up in Lausanne. Along the way, the communists caught up with them in Bratislava, where over half the detachment were killed in a gun battle. Bodrov was wounded, but he managed to escape their clutches, and fled to a Romanov family supporter in Vienna, who removed a bullet from his upper left arm. After a few days of recuperation, patrolling members of the detachment recognised Lenin's henchmen in the

Stephansplatz.

"Knowing they would be found, Bodrov and his men left Vienna under moonlight, the communists intercepting them in Innsbruck, giving rise to another exchange of fire. Fortunately, the Austrian Police intervened, closing in on Lenin's brigade and arresting them, allowing Bodrov and co to escape. In the long run, they ended up depositing the treasure somewhere in the Lausanne locale, then returned to Russia."

Tarrying, she rose to her feet, crossed the room to the window and ogled Lake Geneva. "Bodrov composed the note in that envelope and gave it to the Czar along with the key. Then in August 1917, when it materialised that Menshevik chairman, Alexander Kerensky, intended to send Nicholas II and his family into exile at the Siberian town of Tobolsk, the Czar gave the envelope to Colonel Nikolai Kulikovsky for safekeeping.

"Later in the October Revolution, the Bolsheviks ousted the Provisional Government, and in April 1918, the Romanovs were moved to the Russian town of Yekaterinburg in the Urals. On the night of 16–17 July 1918, the entire central Russian Imperial Romanov family, along with several of their retainers, were executed by Bolshevik revolutionaries, most likely on the orders of Lenin. Though Lenin became heavily involved in the creation of the communist state, he sent Bolshevik agents to ferret out other Romanov family members.

"Fortunately, the Kulikovskys avoided their grasp. Over the subsequent years with division in the Bolshevik Party caused by Stalin opposing Supreme Soviet policies, Lenin relented on pursuing escaped Romanov family members. When Lenin died in 1924, Stalin came to power. Though he mainly focused on his totalitarian regime and liquidating political opponents in the USSR, even so he reenacted the Romanov persecution, State agents despatched to either kill extended family members or return them to the Soviet Union for a show-trial. Thankfully, most of the surviving Romanovs managed to dwell incognito.

"And so it went on until the Berlin Wall came down in 1989, and the Soviet Union was dissolved." Refacing the Englishmen, she disclosed, "I became aware of the envelope earlier this year, my father telling me how it had been handed down from generation to generation of

Kulikovskys."

"So presumably, he tasked you with recovering the Romanov heirlooms?" Anderson speculated.

"Indeed."

"Does he want the prize for personal gain?"

"In part, but he intends to mostly use it to refresh the Romanov name, and any recovered baubles are to be put on display in a museum."

"We decoded the message contained in that envelope, giving the map coordinates of whatever you're hunting for," Richmond advised. "Are you aware there is another camarilla investigating the pinpoint location in Lake Geneva?"

"Yes, and that brings me to the troublesome part of my saga." She sat and faced the Englishmen. "When Eastern bloc communism dissolved soon after the Berlin wall came down, rumours started to circulate about Romanov precious objects on the international treasure trove market. Adventurers began to unearth such claims, most ending in nothing but talk. In the early 1990s, some well-known personalities became clandestinely involved in forming alliances with shady characters. Some ended in tragedy.

"Meanwhile, my father gathered together a group of Romanov loyalists including Andrey and Nostro, their aim to keep a watching brief on godsend seekers as they went about the business of tracking down supposed Romanov riches. All of the enterprises failed. The searchers found nothing. By 2012, most of the gem chiseller groups had given up and were focusing on other jaunts.

"It was then my father told me about the envelope and sent me on my mission. Notwithstanding, he didn't realise one particular cartel had been monitoring his activities in Australia. When I left for Switzerland with Andrey and Nostro, we were stalked by this group."

"Hence the unknown schooner at the map reference?" Fraser speculated.

"Quite."

"Who are they?" Anderson enquired.

"The Austerberg syndicate. My father gained intelligence about the gang whilst they pursued Romanov bullion rumours. Their ruthless

Clive Radford

but charismatic overseer, Julius Fyodor Austerberg, is known as, The Mincer. Of Russian and German descent, he is an ominous maven with an imperious deportment, angular features, and a glass eye. During his forty-plus years in the plunder purloining business, he has been suspected by a plenitude of law enforcement agencies worldwide to have disposed of many of his competitors.

"His 2IC is Claudette Ducal, a ravishing and cunning operator with a penchant for getting men to do what she wants. The balance of his team are martial arts maestro Kim Lindberg, another man-wrecking enchantress, and ex-Russian Mafia enforcers in exile, Viktor Zinchenko and Stanislav Greshnov, both ruthless killers."

"Why did you slip the envelope into my pocket?" Anderson pumped.

"Because Andrey saw them in the casino the night we met, and I didn't want to chance them getting hold of the envelope. Hoping they'd think we had solved the location of the hot goods riddle, the following day we led Austerberg and Ducal on a fool's errand up to Bern. Par for the course, it was a ruse."

"So the two men and one woman on the schooner, we saw at the map coordinates point on Lake Geneva were Lindberg, Zinchenko and Greshnov," Fraser put forward.

"Yes, Austerberg couldn't be sure we had sussed out the enigma, so he must have dispatched them to examine the reference point."

"What is it you suspect is submerged in the lake?" Richmond queried.

Shrugging her shoulders, she replied, "That's the big question. We don't know. Originally, we surmised it was the placement of the capital. However, because the horde is large and would be contained in several trunks, it should stand out visually. But we found nothing on the lakebed."

"Mmmm, and since the competition has been at the spot for the last two days, it may be safe to assume they have not succeeded either."

"Huh, on the button." Lowering her cranium, she confessed, "I'm beginning to think the hoard has already been found."

"But surely that would have made worldwide news," Anderson proposed.

"Not necessarily. Most collectors do not seek publicity and want to exist incognito. Many priceless artefacts gone missing over the centuries have ended up with private collectors, never seeing the light of day again."

"So how did Austerberg root you out?"

"My father set up a false trail to put him off the scent while I travelled to Switzerland with Andrey and Nostro. Regardless, he quickly saw through the deception, and using his array of influential contacts established we were in Lausanne. We had only been reconnoitring Lake Geneva for one day before he arrived and intercepted us at the Port Lausanne-Ouchy quayside. He knew we'd hired a launch and diving equipment from local proprietors, and made it clear he wanted the Romanov bijou. Though he came across as eloquent and sophisticated, he made no secret about after monitoring our endeavours, he intended to take the booty from us."

"And so far, your excursions into Lake Geneva have revealed absolutely nothing?"

"Not a sausage. Either we are missing something, or the evidence we have *vis-à-vis* the whereabouts of the prize is incorrect."

"Gavin," Richmond began, "let me see that paper again."

"Sure."

Retrieving the envelope from his room safe, Anderson gave it to Richmond.

Gathering around him, everybody watched as he re-examined the yellowing paper.

"You see that hyphen in the line *6554296_78740.16 zoll von der — ostküste entfernt* which we know via Roger's associate, translates as two kilometres from the — east shoreline?"

"Roger's associate!" Stephanie echoed, frowning.

"Don't be concerned. He can be trusted," Fraser assured.

"Please continue, Colby," she requested.

"Well, it could be that General Bodrov added a further layer of esoteric security to the message, so as not to make it too easy to fully decode. That hyphen might in fact be a negative operator, meaning an inverse logic sign. If that rings true, then the real location point is two kilometres from the *west* shoreline."

Her jaw dropping at the punch of the proclamation, she heralded, "We've been looking in the wrong place!" Pinpointing Sorenson, she entreated, "Andrey, go get that ordnance survey map of the Lake Geneva area from your room." Turning to the Cheshire boys, she said, "We're also staying at the Mövenpick."

When Sorenson returned, he spread the map out on a tabletop.

"Let me see," Richmond began. "We're questing for a point opposite the west shoreline on the forty-six degrees, fifteen minutes, 5.2272 seconds north latitude. That is a landfall opposite Veytaux." As the assemblage spectated, his finger snaked along the parallel west from Veytaux until it hit Lake Geneva's western shoreline. "Ahh, here we have it," he pronounced. "Gland."

"So we need to comb the lake bed two kilometres east of Gland?" Stephanie solicited.

"Well, since nothing has resulted from your exploration off Veytaux, it's patently worthwhile giving it a shot."

"Yes, but we still have the Austerberg obstacle to contend with."

"You're going to need another diversion," Anderson stipulated.

"Will you help us?"

Glancing at Fraser and Richmond, they made affirmative nods. "Yes."

"What do you suggest, Gavin?"

"Well, it's going to need a dash of stardust applying to it, and perhaps some timing finessing."

"How?"

"We must make Austerberg think that the east coast is still the correct location. I suggest you take the Leonie to the point off Veytaux tomorrow morning, and have Andrey continue his lake bed probe. Either Austerberg will follow you in his schooner, or he will be at the site already. If he is, assume an observation position to keep him occupied.

"Meanwhile, using Argonaut's navigational system, we will take the schooner to a point in the lake two kilometres off Gland. I'll hire some scuba diving gear from Port Lausanne-Ouchy and make the dive."

"Do you have scuba-diving experience?" Stephanie queried.

"Some." Delaying, he then turned to Sorensen. "How deep is the lake, two kilometres from the Veytaux shoreline, Andrey?"

"About ten to twelve fathoms. The lake is seventy-three kilometres in length and fourteen kilometres wide. Its maximum 164 fathoms depth is symmetrical about its midpoint. So I'd assume that two-kilometres off Gland will also be ten to twelve fathoms in depth."

"Right, I think I can manage that," Anderson guaranteed.

"Very well," Stephanie approved. "If you find anything, I'll take a dekko at it in the Mövenpick."

"In the meantime, do you want me to keep the envelope and its contents in my room wall safe?"

"Indeed."

Chapter Nine: The Countess's Legacy

Way before the Cheshire boys embarked on their careers, Stephanie's parents had settled down under. Thinking they had landed on their feet after buying a 3,000-acre fruit farm at Howard Springs, a few miles south of Darwin, disaster arrived for the Kulikovskys on Christmas Day 1974. Cyclone Tracy struck Darwin, killing seventy-one people and destroying over seventy percent of the city's buildings, including many old stone buildings such as the Palmerston Town Hall, which could not withstand the lateral forces the winds generated. After the disaster, 30,000 of the 46,000-population including the Kulikovskys were evacuated in the biggest airlift in Australia's history. Thereafter rebuilt with newer materials and techniques during the late 1970s by the Darwin Reconstruction Commission, the refurbished town boomed with new businesses and an influx of workers from other parts of Australia.

Though the cyclone wiped out their fruit crop, fortunately Leonid had the foresight to insure the farm, the couple able to re-activate farming when the insurance company coughed up. Surging back into the chipper and breezy lifestyle they had prior to the catastrophe, the Kulikovskys quickly got over the disaster, their fruit produce blossoming and anchoring their economic future. A very happy event for the Kulikovskys, Eva gave birth to their daughter, Antoniya Katerina, in 1979, the happening giving rise to unbridled contentment for her parents. After the worries and anxieties regarding detection by Soviet agents they had braved in their formative years, everything had fallen into place, the arrival of Antoniya in their lives, the crowning glory of their endeavours.

Growing up in Australia, Antoniya underwent an entirely different kind of life compared to her ancestors. With security and anonymity as their bywords, after migrating to Canada, Nikolai and Olga Kulikovsky went out of their way not to publicise their origins for fear of assassination by Soviet agents. Returning to Denmark, Guri Nikolaevich and Ruth

Kulikovsky adopted the same safeguard. Likewise, Leonid Nikolaevich and Eva Kulikovsky made it a family policy not to refer to his illustrious lineage when they took root at Howard Springs.

Inheriting the necessary obscurity regime, at her kith and kin's insistence, the very young Antoniya positioned herself as a first-generation Australian of Russian and Danish descent to everyone she met. She had a happy upbringing, her parents ensuring she wanted for nothing, the trials and tribulations Leonid had undergone in his own adolescence not impinging on his daughter, Darwin providing a cogent and non-threatening environment. Easily making friends within the local community, Antoniya thrived, her pre-school life mainly comprising of playing with other farm children and picnicking with her parents. She also liked helping her father and his workers to tend to the fruit crop, extensive matrix rows of citrus, mangos, figs, avocados, bananas, guavas and rambutan plants and trees providing an Aladdin's Cave backdrop for fun and games.

Needless to say, other than her parents' nationalities, Antoniya had no idea about her family background. Blissfully unaware of what had happened to the Romanovs and the possibility of assassination by Soviet agents, she grew into an effervescent, contented girl, with a keen interest in geography and wild animals.

Building on the instruction given by her mother, Antoniya quickly attuned herself to the three-r's — reading, writing and arithmetic — at Howard Springs Junior School. A naturally inquisitive pupil, never short of fielding questions to her teachers, it became clear to them that she bore all the necessary hallmarks for success in the educational system. Flowering in leaps and bounds, when her contemporaries were still coming to terms with long-division and words containing more than eight letters, Antoniya was tackling trigonometry and reading Hardy's *Far From the Madding Crowd*. Not content with the school curriculum, she spent many hours in the Howard Springs library digesting data sources on a wide variety of motifs. And whilst at home, she asked her father to teach her how to play chess. She even got curious about driving his tractor. Astounded by their daughter's evolution and advancement, her parents began to think nothing would daunt Antoniya in the years to come

*

After her eighth birthday, Leonid launched into telling his daughter about her volcanic heritage, including her full title — The Countess Antoniya Katerina Kulikovsky. She took it in, but did not really understand its significance until several years later, when Leonid began recapping family members going back to her great grandparents, Nikolai and Olga Kulikovsky.

Now fascinated by her lineage, she often asked her father to recount the family chronicle and to tell her something new, Leonid relaying to her the great Romanov dynasty and what had happened after the 1917 Menshevik and Bolshevik revolutions. To the juvenile Countess, it seemed like a fairy tale gone tragically wrong, the pomp and splendour of Russian royalty abolished and eliminated, communist Russian history officially beginning in 1917, and the Romanovs expunged from the record. Asking her father to review the reasons behind the overthrow, he held nothing back, his narrative stark and uncensored.

"When Colonel Nikolai Kulikovsky married Grand Duchess Olga Alexandrovna, younger sister to Czar Nicholas II," Leonid told her, "He was under no illusions as to the imminent danger to the Romanovs from a gathering pace general Russian revolt.

"The 1905 Russian revolution was a major factor contributing to the cause of the revolutions of 1917. Bloody Sunday, a series of events on Sunday 22 January 1905 in Saint Petersburg, when unarmed demonstrators were fired upon by Imperial Guard soldiers as they marched towards the Winter Palace to present a petition to Czar Nicholas II, triggered nationwide protests and soldier mutinies. The resultant chaos produced a council of workers called the Saint Petersburg Soviet. While the 1905 Revolution was conclusively crushed, and the trailblazers of the Saint Petersburg Soviet arrested, it laid the groundwork for the later Petrograd Soviet and other revolutionary movements during the leadup to 1917. It also led to the creation of a duma or parliament, later forming the Provisional Government following the February 1917 revolution.

"Russia's poor economic performance in 1914-1915 prompted

growing complaints directed at Czar Nicholas II and the Romanov family. A short wave of patriotic nationalism ended in the face of defeats and poor conditions on the World War 1 Eastern Front. By taking personal control of the Imperial Russian Army in 1915, a challenge far beyond his skills, the Czar made the situation worse and was held personally responsible for Russia's continuing defeats and losses.

"In addition, German born Czarina Alexandra, left to rule while the Czar commanded at the front, created suspicion of collusion, only to be exacerbated by rumours relating to her relationship with the controversial mystic and holy man, Grigori Rasputin. His influence evoked disastrous ministerial appointments and corruption, resulting in a worsening of conditions within Russia."

"What about trade, Papa? Surely mother Russia could call upon trading partners in her hour of need?"

"After the entry of the Ottoman Empire on the side of the Central Powers – Germany and Austria-Hungary – in October 1914, Russia was deprived of a major trade route to the Mediterranean Sea, worsening the economic crisis and the munitions shortages. Substandard conditions during the war resulted in a devastating loss of morale within the Russian army, and the general population, commonly apparent in the cities, owing to a lack of food in response to the disruption of agriculture.

"You see, daughter, food scarcity had become a considerable bugbear in Russia. But the cause of this did not lie in any failure of the harvests, which had not been markedly altered during wartime. The indirect reason lay in order to finance the war, the Duma printed millions of rouble notes, and by 1917 inflation had made prices increase up to four times what they had been in 1914. Consequently, farmers were hit with a higher cost of living, but with a slight increase in income. As a result, they tended to hoard their grain and revert to subsistence farming.

"Thus, the cities were constantly short of food. At the same time, rising prices led to demands for higher wages in factories, and in January and February 1916, revolutionary propaganda, in part aided by German funds, led to widespread strikes. This incited a growing criticism of the leadership, and an increased participation of workers in revolutionary parties.

"Meanwhile, socialist revolutionary front-runners in exile plotted to overthrow the Czarist regime. Lenin rejected both the defence of Russia, and the cry for peace. He advocated that World War 1 must be turned into a civil war of the proletarian soldiers against their own overlords."

Breaking off from his review, Leonid's complexion became ashen.

"I know this is difficult, Papa, but please go on. I have to know everything."

"Very well, daughter." Mustering his innermost strength, he took a deep breath. "Social causes prompting support for a Russian revolution can be derived from centuries of oppression of the lower classes by the Czarist regime. A paltry one-point-five percent of the population owned twenty-five percent of the arable land.

"Further, the rapid industrialisation of Russia had propelled urban overcrowding and poor conditions for industrial workers. Due to the bottleneck in the cities, the rank and file were much more likely to protest and go on strike than the peasantry had been in previous times. The poor conditions only aggravated the injustice, with strikes and public disorders rapidly increasing in the years shortly preceding World War I.

"When hostilities did kick-off they added to the chaos, and conscription across Russia sparked unwilling citizens being sent off to war. To fuel the conflict, the vast demand for factory production of war supplies and workers brought about many more labour riots and strikes. Unsurprisingly, military enlistment stripped skilled workers from the cities. Replaced with unskilled peasants, product quality suffered proportionally. When famine began to hit due to the poor railway system, workers abandoned the cities in droves seeking food.

"Finally, the soldiers on the Eastern Front, afflicted by a lack of equipment and protection from the elements, began to turn against the Czar. Mainly because as the war progressed, many of the officers loyal to the Romanovs were killed during battle and replaced by discontented conscripts from the major cities having little devotion to Nicholas II. A deeply conservative ruler, he maintained a strict authoritarian system. Individuals and society in general were expected to show self-restraint, devotion to community, deference to the social hierarchy, and a sense of duty to the country. Religious faith helped bind all of these tenets together as a source of comfort and reassurance in the face of difficult conditions, and as a means of political authority exercised through the clergy. Perhaps more than any other modern monarch, Nicholas II attached his fate and the future of his dynasty to the notion of the ruler as a saintly and infallible father to his people.

"This illusory vision of the Romanov monarchy left him unaware of the state of his country. With a firm conviction that his power to rule was granted by Divine Right, Nicholas assumed that the Russian people were devoted to him with unquestioning loyalty. Whence, this ironclad belief rendered him unwilling to allow the progressive reforms that might have alleviated the misery of the Russian people."

"Even after the 1905 Revolution?" Antoniya probed.

"Yes, though that episode drove the Czar to decree limited civil rights and democratic representation, he worked to limit even these liberties to preserve the ultimate authority of the crown.

"Since the Age of Enlightenment – an intellectual and philosophical movement that occurred in seventeenth and eighteenth centuries Europe, originating global inclines and effects, including a range of ideas centred on the value of human happiness, the pursuit of knowledge obtained by means of reason, the evidence of the senses, and ideals such as natural law, liberty, progress, toleration, fraternity, constitutional government and separation of church and state – Russian intellectuals had promoted Enlightenment ethics, inclusive of the dignity of the individual and the rectitude of democratic representation. Russia's liberals championed these values most vociferously, although populists, Marxists, and anarchists also claimed to support democratic reforms. Accordingly, a growing opposition movement began to openly defy the Romanov monarchy well before the turmoil of World War I.

"One of the Czar's principal rationales for risking war in 1914 was his desire to restore the prestige that Russia had lost amid the debacles of the 1904-1905 Russo-Japanese War. Nicholas also sought to foster a greater sense of national unity with a war against a common and old enemy. Ostensibly, the Russian Empire was an agglomeration of diverse ethnicities that had demonstrated far-reaching signs of disunity in the years before the First World War. Nicholas believed in part that the collective peril and tribulation of a foreign war would mitigate the social unrest over the persistent issues of poverty, inequality, and inhumane working conditions. Instead of restoring Russia's political and military standing, World War 1 led to the slaughter of Russian troops and military defeats that undermined both the monarchy and Russian society to the point of collapse."

"So the abdication of the Czar became inevitable?"

"Indeed, daughter. Those forces rallying against Nicholas left him with no other option."

"I see." Resting, she then cultivated a big-eyed visage. "Tell me about my great grandmother."

"Grand Duchess Olga Alexandrovna of Russia was raised at the Gatchina Palace outside Saint Petersburg. Her relationship with her mother, Empress Marie, the daughter of King Christian IX of Denmark, was strained and distant from childhood. In contrast, she and her father, Emperor Alexander III of Russia, were close. He died when she was twelve, and her brother Nicholas became emperor.

"Aged nineteen, in 1901 she married Duke Peter Alexandrovich of Oldenburg, privately believed by family and colleagues to be homosexual. Though their marriage of fifteen years abided unconsummated, at first Peter refused Olga's request for a divorce. Because the couple led separate lives, their marriage was eventually annulled by the Emperor in October 1916. The following month Olga married your great grandfather cavalry officer Nikolai Kulikovsky, with whom she had fallen in love several years before. officer,

"During the First World War, Olga served as an army nurse and was awarded a personal gallantry medal. At the downfall of the Romanovs in the 1917 Russian revolutions', she fled with her husband and children to Crimea, where they lived under the threat of assassination. As you know, her brother Nicholas and his family were shot and bayoneted to death by revolutionaries."

Becoming morose, he halted, as if recounting the murders of distant family members plagued his sensitivities.

"Please go on, Papa," she encouraged, lovingly kissing him on his forehead.

"Olga and Nikolai escaped revolutionary Russia with their two sons, Tikhon Nikolaevich, and your grandfather, Guri Nikolaevich, in February 1920. Fleeing to Denmark, they joined her mother, the Dowager Empress. While in exile, Olga functioned as companion and secretary to her mother and often was sought out by Romanov impostors claiming to be her relatives.

"After the Dowager Empress's death in 1928, Olga and Nikolai purchased a dairy farm in Ballerup near Copenhagen. She led a simple life, raising her sons, working on the farm, and painting. During her lifetime, she painted over 2,000 works of art providing extra income for both her family and the charitable causes she supported.

"On 9th April 1940, neutral Denmark was invaded by Nazi Germany and occupied for the rest of World War II. Olga's sons, Tikhon and Guri served as officers in the Danish Army. They were interned as prisoners of war, but their imprisonment in a Copenhagen hotel lasted less than two months.

"Other Russian émigrés, keen to fight against the Soviets, enlisted in the German forces. Despite her sons' internment and her mother's Danish origins, Olga was implicated in her compatriots' collusion with German forces, as she continued to meet and extend help to Russian émigrés fighting against communism. After the surrender of Germany in 1945, the Soviet Union wrote to the Danish Folketing accusing the Grand Duchess of conspiracy against the Soviet authorities. At the end of the war, Soviet troops occupied the easternmost part of Denmark. Fearful of an assassination or kidnap attempt by Joseph Stalin's forces, in 1948 Olga decided to move her family across the Atlantic to the relative safety of rural Canada, a decision with which the Colonel complied. The Kulikovsky immediate family relocated to a farm in Campbellsville, Ontario, Canada.

"With advancing age, Olga and Nikolai moved to a bungalow near Cooksville, Ontario. The Colonel died there in 1958. Two years later, as her health deteriorated, Olga moved with allies to a small apartment in East Toronto. She died aged seventy-eight, seven months after her older sister, the Grand Duchess Xenia. At the end of her life and afterwards, Olga was widely labelled, the last Grand Duchess of Imperial Russia.

"Your grandparents, Guri Nikolaevich and Ruth, then moved back to Denmark with my sister, Xenia, and myself, in 1952. Later when they returned to Canada, I stayed in Denmark, met your Danish mother, Eva Christensen, and we moved to Australia in 1967."

~ * ~

Gradually, the Kulikovsky name became known further afield, Russian émigrés and Romanov sympathizers from other parts of Australia making themselves known to Leonid, including Andrey Sorensen and Nostro Kravets. Many had a Russian White Army heritage, and as such were monarchist supporters. By the time the Berlin Wall came down, Leonid had nurtured a network of over fifty Russian émigrés, feeding him data pertinent to how the Russians currently perceived Romanov descendants, and sharing information about booty hawker exploits to exhume supposed Romanov riches.

Behind Leonid's fruit farming business, in the background he kept abreast of Russian goings-on and activities related to the Romanovs, his growing band of monarchist supporting exiles also supplying him intel. Since the death of the Czar and his immediate family, rumours circulated in adventurer cliques worldwide with reference to the possibility that some of the Romanov trinkets had been spirited out of Saint Petersburg by agents acting on behalf of Nicholas II. Many of the sagas and legends came to the attention of surviving Romanovs, including Olga and Colonel Nikolai Kulikovsky and their sons Tikhon and Guri. Naturally, they discerned most of them to be folklore.

When it became crystal to Nicholas II that the communists would arrest him and his inner family, he gave the envelope containing the note and the key to the Romanov cache given to him by General Bodrov, to his younger sister, the Grand Duchess Olga Alexandrovna of Russia and her husband Colonel Kulikovsky for safekeeping, also telling them the hiding place for the kitty lay in Switzerland. As soon as Olga and Nikolai received word that the Czar and his closest family members had been murdered, they kept the envelope in a secure location on the basis that

Bolshevik agents would continue to hunt down Romanovs and in the process gain the envelope, and thereby the Romanov bonanza.

Because of sustained anti-monarchist policies conducted in Stalin's reign coupled with the impact of World War II, Olga and Nikolai did not chance breaking cover and going after the horde, their stance hardening when the Iron Curtain partitioned Eastern Europe to the Soviets at the end of World War II, signalling the onset of The Cold War.

Commensurate with Guri Nikolaevich and Ruth moving back to Denmark, Olga and Nikolai entrusted them with the envelope on the basis they would dwell nearer Switzerland, and if the opportunity arose could mount an expedition to claim the Romanov inheritance. Similarly, when Guri Nikolaevich and Ruth returned to Canada, the envelope passed to Leonid.

Though Nikita Khrushchev and subsequent Soviet autocrats took the Romanovs off the political agenda, nonetheless, hardline members of the KGB executive-level, especially those seeing action in the October 1917 Russian Revolution, maintained an anti-monarchist stance. Perturbed by the decimating news, the Kulikovskys and other satellite families with Czarist connections often heard about the liquidation of Romanov descendants and their supporters. It was only when Gorbachev came to power, fathering glasnost and perestroika, bringing about the end of totalitarian communist rule in Russia did Leonid consider it might be safe to retrieve the Romanov property.

Soon becoming clear to Leonid from intelligence fed to him by monarchist sympathizers worldwide that other parties were intent on going after Romanov treasures, he put the brakes on the endeavour, knowing no one else beside him and his wife Eva knew about the envelope. Several well-publicised stories came out in the 1990s centred on Romanov artefacts coming to light and being sold at Sotheby's or Christie's auctions for astronomical amounts of money. Additionally, the émigré pipeline picked up info apropos failed attempts to trade-in or uncover more Romanov valuables, some involving well-known celebrities from the world of publishing and commerce. No matter how Leonid sliced and diced his options to excavate the Czar's stockpile, nothing equated as foolproof. There were just too many initiatives in play from loot nimrods, most bearing the hallmarks of criminal masterminds.

Worse still, his band of supporters reported that some had shadowed him and awaited his action to retrieve the Romanov wealth before relieving him of the find. Subsisting ambivalently, Leonid hoped as time passed, the foes would lose interest and pursue other sugar trailing ventures.

~ * ~

When Antoniya matriculated to Palmerston City High School and obtained the required entry qualifications to study chemistry at Charles Darwin University, she had become adept in many academic disciplines, her continuing education bringing out further scholarly talents including an aptitude for foreign languages. Post graduation, she embarked on a physical chemistry research career with conglomerate, Turner-Martin Enterprises, in Sydney.

During her senior educational period, Antoniya had blossomed into a ravishing honey with smouldering looks. Her long, wavy blonde hair, teal-blue eyes and curvy figure distinguishing her as a young woman not short on attracting male attention. Several summers down the track at Turner-Martin, she married fellow research scientist, Ryan Lambert, an affable Englishman who had migrated to Australia from the Turner-Martin UK headquarters in Berkshire. Five years later, whilst in New Guinea on behalf of the company, Lambert was killed in a road accident, leaving Antoniya heartbroken.

By now, she'd moved into a management role, displaying all the necessary leadership characteristics for one of the top slots in the corporation. Well-liked, her subordinates did her bidding under the influence of her magnetism, rather than delegated authority. Soldiering on at Turner-Martin in Sydney, for a while, she lost herself in her work as an antidote to her loss. Then at some point she lost all interest in her career, quit her profession, and returned to the Kulikovsky fruit farm.

Acutely sensitive to their daughter's trauma, Leonid and Eva went out of their way to accommodate her, never over-taxing her about her husband's death, and providing a stress-free habitat for her recuperation.

Losing herself in fruit farming work, gradually Antoniya put the tragedy into perspective, the pain of loss melting, her preoccupation with tending to the farm rejuvenating her being. Occasionally, old school and university pals visited her at the farm, including a few eligible bachelors clearly intent on wooing Antoniya, but she diplomatically rejected their loving cup proposals. Ryan had gotten under her skin, and she just didn't feel comfortable engaging in another romance.

Time passed, and with-it Antoniya's sense of gamble reignited, her farming duties no longer making her boat float. Her parents became profoundly aware she longed for something to test her.

After sensing the change, one evening after supper, Leonid said to her, "Come and sit out on the porch with me, daughter. I've got something to tell you."

Retiring into two rocking chairs, Antoniya stared at her father under a luminous, southern hemisphere, late autumn night sky, crickets filling the backdrop with their chirping cacophony.

"What is it, Papa?"

"Your mama and I have detected your restlessness. We think you need a challenge to give your life direction and purpose."

"Oh, Papa, it's just a phase I'm going through."

"It's the sixth anniversary of Ryan's death this November. I know you have stopped grieving, but I see no signs of you wanting to form another relationship."

"True."

"You need a substantial distraction to get you out of yourself."

"Hah —" She beamed at him. "Know you of such an exploit?"

"As a matter of fact, I do. Earlier today, I retrieved an article from my bank safety deposit box."

Producing an envelope from his jacket inside pocket, he held it in his right hand at an oblique angle, intending to inflame curiosity in his daughter.

"What's that?"

"To paraphrase from Dashiell Hammett's *The Maltese Falcon* – *the stuff that dreams are made of.*"

Going on to recap the Kulikovsky family history pertaining to their duty in respect of the Romanov treasure and General Losif Bodrov's creation of the envelope contents, Antoniya became dumbstruck by Leonid's narrative. Not in her wildest imagination had she ever conceived that beyond the lurid tale of the Romanov family demise lay a boodle waiting to be claimed.

"This is incredible, Papa. You've really surprised me. I'd always assumed all of the Romanov proceeds had been confiscated by the communists."

"That is the legend we like to propagate."

"What about the Anastasia folklore?"

"The Grand Duchess Anastasia Nikolaevna of Russia?"

"Yes. Isn't she the rightful inheritor of Romanov treasure valuables?"

"That is a complex story, daughter. Rumours have endured over many decades that the youngest daughter of Nicholas II, Anastasia, and the younger sister of Grand Duchesses Olga, Tatania and Maria, had escaped from Yekaterinburg before the primary Romanov family killing by Bolsheviks on 17 July 1918. Such persistent tittle-tattle of her get away circulated after the mass murder, fueled by the fact that the location of her burial was unknown during the epoch of communist rule. Howbeit, the abandoned mine serving as a mass grave near Yekaterinburg holding the acidified remains of the Czar, his wife, three of their daughters and three of their servants was exposed in 1991. These carcasses were put to rest in 1998 at the Peter and Paul Fortress, the original citadel of Saint Petersburg. The bodies of their valet, Alexei Trupp, and the residual daughter - either Anastasia or her older sister Maria - were discovered in 2007, her purported survival conclusively disproved. Scientific analysis including DNA testing confirmed that the leftovers are those of the imperial family, showing that all four grand duchesses were killed in 1918.

"Over time, several women falsely claimed to have been Anastasia - the best-known impostor being Anna Anderson. Anderson's body was cremated upon her death in 1984. DNA testing in 1994 on pieces of Anderson's tissue and hair showed no relation to the Romanov family. In 1925, Olga and Colonel Kulikovsky travelled to Berlin to meet Anna Anderson, who claimed to be Olga's niece, The Grand Duchess Anastasia Nikolaevna of Russia. Anderson insisted that with the help of a man named Tchaikovsky, she had escaped from revolutionary Russia via Bucharest, where she had given birth to his child. Olga refereed the story as 'palpably false', since during her entire alleged time in Bucharest, Anderson made no attempt to approach Queen Marie of Romania, first cousin of both of Anastasia's parents."

"So, Papa, are the Kulikovskys the only existing descendants of Nicholas II?"

"There are others splattered across the world, but it is only we that know of the Romanov belongings in Switzerland."

"What do you want me to do?"

"I'm far too old to become involved in an overseas forage for gilded ornaments. Using the envelope contents, I want you to retrieve the heirlooms. Huh—" Grinning, his phiz filled with optimism. "It may even give you the opportunity to use your French and German language skills. Howbeit—" Rising from his rocking chair, he wandered along the veranda before turning to face his daughter. "It will not be a simple exercise. Groups of fortune seekers have been questing for Romanov family members since the 1920s by probing rumours regarding Romanov legacy finds. Independently, they have been responding to hearsay about such bonanzas, and currently there are plenty of gold digger coalitions rummaging around all five continents. Several Russian émigrés have told me that one innately sinister group led by Julius Fyodor Austerberg, known as The Mincer, have traced me, and have been keeping tabs on the farm for the past six months. Andrey Sorensen and Nostro Kravets have reciprocated the watch, keeping an eye on them."

"Is that why more monarchist sympathizers came to work on the farm?"

"Indeed. Those we took on are also acting as security officers."

"Because Austerberg knows about the envelope?"

"No. I don't think so because only your mother and I, and now you, know of the envelope. But, he must suspect I have something that can steer him to our Romanov birthright. Hence my fear is, if you depart for Switzerland, he will get to know and follow you."

"So we need a diversion to take Austerberg off the scent while I travel to Switzerland."

"Mmmm, quite right. Laying a false trail might do the trick. Here is what I propose. I will make flight reservations for Stephan Azarov, Fyodor Galkin and Kirill Dubinin to fly to San Francisco drawing Austerberg's attention. Apparently, he is preeminent, so he will find out about the reservations, and arrange to be on the same flight. Your mama and I will see off the dummy crew from Darwin Airport, giving credence to Austerberg's assumption that I have despatched them on an estate-quarrying mission. As soon as the Frisco flight leaves, Sorensen, Kravets and you will fly to Geneva on the first available flight. I've already done some auditing. There is an American Airlines flight to San Francisco on 28th June at 07:45, and a Qantas flight to Geneva at 21:15 the same day."

"How about if Austerberg leaves some of his resources in Darwin to monitor the farm?"

"My understanding is that despite his reputation as a practised and fearless paladin, he prefers to have all of his clan in the same locale as himself."

"Do you know why?"

"In his nascent spoils-dogging career, he split-up his outfit in a campaign to find an irreplaceable Aztec handicraft effigy in Mexico. A competing consortium seized the moment to take him out of the game and found the prize. Since, Austerberg tends to move *en bloc*."

"I see." She shuffled in her chair, charged with excitation at the prospect of an electrifying quest." Just one question, Papa. Why now?"

"For a long time, I was happy to let the endowment rest in Switzerland, but of late I've developed a notion that whatever it is, should be put on display in a Darwin Museum for the whole world to see."

"So, we're talking about majestic objects, such as jewels."

"Maybe. No one knew precisely what the stash contained, apart from the Czar and General Bodrov. Your great grandparents and grandparents determined it might be a mix of customised Fabergé eggs and gold coinage, but they could have been wrong, and it might indeed be precious jewels."

*

Before leaving for Geneva, Leonid explained his interpretation of the envelope's yellowing paper to Antoniya, saying the coordinates outlined in the text fixed a point off the east coast of Lake Geneva, and Andrey Sorensen had been selected for the mission because of his diving knowhow, whilst both he and Nostro Kravets would act as her protectors.

When the confederacy arrived at Geneva-Cointrin Airport, they hired a *Range Rover*, drove to Lausanne and checked-in at the Mövenpick Hotel, the Countess Antoniya Katerina Kulikovsky using the *nom de deplume*, Stephanie Nightingale, so as not to arouse curiosity in connection with her presence in Lausanne, the pseudonym reflected on her passport arranged by Leonid from a specialist forger in his émigré entourage.

Early the following day they hired the cruiser, Leonie, and diving gear at Port Lausanne-Ouchy, navigated to the setpoint defined on the yellowing paper and began a seabed trawl for something – maybe a large casket or a smaller container, but Sorensen found nothing. Backtracking to the Mövenpick, the desk clerk told Stephanie someone had telephoned her from home and to return the call. Intrinsically knowing the caller to be her father, she and her bodyguards retired to her room to telephone Darwin.

"Papa, it's Antoniya."

"The subterfuge team in San Francisco has contacted me. Beware, daughter, Austerberg is on his way to Switzerland."

"What! How does he know where I am?"

"Seems that he *did* leave a man behind in Darwin to monitor my goings-on. When Austerberg landed at San Fran International, there was a message waiting for him from the man about your flight to Geneva. Caught in two minds as to which of my groups was the real deal, he decided to pursue Azarov, Galkin and Dubinin for twenty-four hours. They led the gang on a wild-goose chase around Frisco, Austerberg intercepting them at gunpoint. To cut a long story short, without having to resort to violence, he surmised Azarov and co were a ruse, and that you were the genuine article. Then rather flippantly and flamboyantly, he said to Azarov, he may tell his master, meaning me, that his daughter would be receiving visitors in Switzerland."

"So Austerberg is probably still in transit?"

"Yes, but he will arrive in Geneva by dawn tomorrow, and from his linkages, he will quickly establish you are at the Mövenpick." Dwelling, he then asked, "How is your underwater search going?"

"Andrey has found nothing, Papa."

"Keep on exploring. I have every faith that General Bodrov's letter is fully credible."

~ * ~

At sunrise, the following day Stephanie Nightingale and her minders sailed across Lake Geneva to the original demarcation point and dropped anchor, Sorensen going below to continue the underwater pursuit. Unbeknown to them, a man monitored their activity with a powerful telescope from a high vantage point at the Château de Chillon in Veytaux. Though Sorensen extended his scan area, repeated dives continued to bear nothing, Stephanie beginning to think the dowry had already been found. By midday, with the diver exhausted, they had lunch aboard the Leonie then set off for Port Lausanne-Ouchy.

Nearing the cruiser's allotted berth, they clocked a tall, elegantly dressed man, forward of two shorter bulkier men, and two women, one blonde, one brunette. Apart from the lead man, all wore sunglasses. As the Leonie docked, the group came forward.

"Good day, Countess," felicitated the tall, elegantly dressed man, blazing like a predator about to devour its prey. "Please allow me to introduce myself. I am Julius Fyodor Austerberg, and these are my companions, Viktor Zinchenko, Stanislav Greshnov, Claudette Ducal and Kim Lindberg," he revealed, indicating to each of them as he reeled-off their names. "I am of German-Russo descent, and a major player in the treasure hunting guild. Viktor and Stanislav are my enforcers." Glinting devilishly, he disclosed, "They are ex-Russian Mafia operatives in exile, and very turned-on by riches. Claudette is my 2IC. An exceptionally talented lady, and an excellent interrogator. Kim is our martial arts expert. She is also an excellent interrogator."

"I guessed who you were as we came along the quayside," Stephanie responded. "Your fabled glass eye corroborated my suspicions. I also know why you are here."

"Good, then let us get down to business. In return for your lives, you will hand over the Romanov legacies that you seek."

"There is no treasure."

"Come, come, Countess—" Smirking, he then shone at his troupe before confronting her again. "I hope you're not going to be tiresome. Surely you don't expect us to believe that you have given up on finding the curios already?"

"You can imagine what you like."

"Very well. Plainly a civilised policy with you is going to fall on stony ground. So let's have no more niceties," he insisted, his upbeat countenance giving way to assertive features. "I know you are foraging Lake Geneva. While your man servant was diving, Viktor observed your cruiser from a high point on Château de Chillon in Veytaux. He relayed to me what you were doing by mobile phone. Now, what have you discovered?"

"Nothing."

"*Hah.*" The smirk returned. "Now why is it that I don't believe you? Viktor, Stanislav."

Zinchenko and Greshnov began moving towards Stephanie and her minders, only to halt in their tracks at the crack of a nearby car door closing.

About turning, Austerberg registered a man standing behind his group, flanked by one other man and two women.

"Patrice," he welcomed, "it's been some time since our paths crossed." Facing front again and then at the new arrivals, he declared, "Allow me to make some introductions, Countess. This is Patrice Devereux, from the Swiss Federal Office of Culture, and his illustrious acolytes, Marco Brunner, Nicole Steiner and Zoe Weber. They are also here to relieve you of whatever you may find under the provisions of the Swiss treasure trove act."

"That's quite enough, Julius," Devereux insisted. "As yet you have not broken any Swiss laws. I would suggest you retire from this street drama and allow me to conduct my official business with the Countess."

"Of course," he graciously accepted. "We have no wish to interfere with Swiss State workings." Peering at the Leonie crew, he said, "*Au revoir*, Countess, until the next time we meet."

As Austerberg and his pack sauntered off, Devereux came forward. "You are the Countess Antoniya Katerina Kulikovsky?"

"Yes, I am."

"Yet you entered Switzerland with a false passport, using the name, Stephanie Nightingale."

"Indeed. You are well-informed, Monsieur Devereux."

"The Swiss Federal Office of Culture has close workings with our immigration and passport control authorities. When Austerberg, a well-known artefacts and treasure hunter, often operating outside the law, entered the country, his arrival was flagged up to my department, prompting the question, why is he here? We examined the registry of arrivals over the past forty-eight hours. Using biometrics for identification, we established that your passport photograph matched that of the Countess Antoniya Katerina Kulikovsky, yet you were using the alias Stephanie Nightingale.

"You are the daughter of Count Leonid Nikolaevich Kulikovsky and descended from the Romanovs. We put two and two together deciding that your entry into Switzerland closely followed by that of Austerberg was no coincidence. You are in pursuit of Romanov commodities. Austerberg intends to relieve you of what you might find."

"You have a very vivid imagination, Monsieur Devereux. My friends and I are merely vacationing."

"Then why the alias, and why has Austerberg got an interest in you?"

"Wanting to stay out of the limelight, I'm incognito, and as to why Herr Austerberg curries my company, I cannot imagine."

"Be warned, Countess," he advised, his manner betraying both prudence and dread. "Austerberg eats innocents like you for breakfast. He might come across as a sophisticated buccaneer, but believe me, he is ruthless. The Mincer, as Julius Fyodor Austerberg is known in treasure angling circles, has been operating both inside and outside the law for forty years. He is both clever, and inordinately lucky. No law enforcement agency worldwide has ever managed to catch him in the act. But we know he has been responsible for purloining articles worth hundreds of millions of pounds, dollars, Euros, and Swiss francs. And though not proven, the killing of those who get in his way. I have gone head-to-head with Austerberg in the past, so I know the nature of the beast." Pausing, he then appended, "I will neglect the fact that you have entered the country under a false name. But I warn you, if you do find Romanov possessions, you must notify me or face the possibility of imprisonment. Under Swiss law, treasure trove not claimed by the rightful owner after fifty years belongs to the Swiss State."

*

"Devereux will use you as a source to find the bonanza, and as bait to nail Austerberg," Sorensen warned Stephanie, after the Swiss officials had departed. "That's why he's not had you deported for holding a false passport."

"Yes, Andrey, I also figured that out." Staring across the lake reflectively, she then conceded, "This exploit is going to need some very careful management. Somehow, we have to uphold our drive to unearth the sugar whilst keeping Austerberg at bay, and not incurring the displeasure of the Swiss Federal Office of Culture."

"Indeed, but how?" Kravets interjected. "It's an enormous balancing act. We are caught in a pincer movement by two interested bodies. One is out to steal the lucre from us, the other to put us in jail."

"My gray matter is swimming in a concoction of the possibilities," Stephanie admitted. "All we can do is carry on, play it by ear, and hope something occurs to ensure we fulfill my father's mission."

Chapter Ten: Devereux's Warning

After Stephanie and her cohorts had left Anderson's room, Fraser voiced, "Are you sure about making the dive, Gavin? Wasn't just bravado, was it?"

"Yeah, I was thinking that." Richmond supported.

"No. I've scuba-dived off the Bahamas a couple of times. Besides—" Rubbing his chin, he divulged, "I can't resist a bit of thrill-seeking, and Stephanie's caper has got me fired up."

"Well, I must admit," Richmond began, "I too wouldn't mind an adrenalin-stirring spree. I'm not complaining, but my domestic and professional lives have become extremely predictable. After the riptides that engulfed me during my university years, little anxiety has caused my pulse rate to rise since marrying Carolyn and settling into the work environment. Yes, there are the usual difficulties to overcome in the I.T business, and they can be intoxicating, but it's nothing to stretch me. The only excitement I get on a regular basis is in the bedroom with Carolyn. Thereby, all things considered, like Gavin, I find this situation mightily stimulating."

"Despite the knowledge that Austerberg and his crew are probably killers?" Fraser articulated.

"Alright, Roger, I will admit that is disturbing."

"Have either of you ever had a loaded heater pointed at you?"

"We know you have."

"Yes, and I nearly soiled my trousers during the showdown." Dwelling, he then added, "Though my trouble-shooter role at The Firm is immensely invigorating, that uncomfortable occurrence in Grand Cayman has made me wary when it comes to facing off against brigands and gangsters."

"So, it's true that the investment banking fraternity transacts with outlaws and desperadoes," Anderson lightly gibed.

"If you have that impression, Gavin, it is fostered on myth and sensationalist news copy. That Caymans incident was a rarity and came about because The Firm were put under pressure by the security services to help break up a money-laundering cartel. Usually, my trouble-shooting escapades centre on resolving investment disputes."

"Like the one in Guatemala, when your agent got shot," Richmond reminded him.

"That, my dear Colby, was an accident. It was not intentional. All the same, it did illustrate that when conflicting forces shed energy, the unforeseeable can happen."

"Just returning to the Romanov affair," Richmond rejoindered. "Do you gauge there's a possibility that Stephanie exaggerated the Austerberg syndicate threat as a means of giving us a get-out card?"

"You mean," Anderson interpreted, "she wants us out of the picture once the kitty has been discovered, just in case the clash turns nasty, and we are put at risk?"

"Yes. Obviously, she trusts us, or she wouldn't have agreed to tomorrow's action. Could it be her sense of responsibility towards us that prompted that - Austerberg disposes of his competitor's comment?"

"Well, gentlemen, it's decision time," Anderson asserted. "Are we in or out?"

"In," Richmond allocated.

"Roger?"

"In."

~ * ~

Intending to dine in the hotel, the three Cheshire boys were making their way through the lobby towards the restaurant when a smartly dressed man intercepted them.

"Mister Anderson," he challenged.

"Yes," he replied, surprised that a stranger apparently knew him.

"My name is Patrice Devereux. I'm an inspector with the Swiss Federal Office of Culture working on behalf of the Musée d'Art et d'Histoire in Geneva." Taking in the Englishman as if trying to assess him for credence, he then flashed his identity card.

"How can I help you, Monsieur Devereux? Better still, how do you know my name?"

"I know all your names from Swiss Immigration, after you landed at Geneva-Cointrin Airport." Facing the others, he acknowledged, "Mister Richmond. Mister Fraser."

"You've been clandestinely photographing us and comparing the images against our passport photos held by Swiss Immigration," Anderson put forward.

"Indeed."

"Why?"

"We have a mutual acquaintance."

"You're barking up the wrong tree." Eyeing his confederates, he insisted, "Come on chaps, let's go get some dinner."

As the threesome began to move away, Devereux unveiled, "It concerns the activities of the Countess Antoniya Katerina Kulikovsky a.k.a., Stephanie Nightingale."

Halting, they then turned and pouted at the Swiss civil servant.

"Come and meet my colleagues in the bar, gentlemen," Devereux seduced, pushing out a guiding arm. "We can then tell you what you've got yourselves into."

"Do we have a choice?"

"Not if you want to stay out of jail."

Leading them to a table at the far edge of the bar, remote from gaiety hubbub, Devereux introduced, Marco Brunner – studious demeanour and wearing spectacles the Cheshire boys observed, Zoe Weber – dark in appearance, tall, lean and projecting an air of menace, and Nicole Steiner – definitely the entrapment agent in the team, her blonde waves, ocean-blue eyes and curvy superstructure zinging loudly at the Englishmen.

"What exactly do you want from us, Monsieur Devereux?" Richmond posed.

"We want you to help us recover the Romanov stockpile. As I notified the Countess, under Swiss law, treasure trove not claimed by the rightful owner after fifty years from deposit in a Swiss bank, belongs to the State. When this property is recovered, it will be displayed in the Musée d'Art et d'Histoire."

"Why do you think we can help you accomplish your objective?" Fraser queried.

"Because the Countess has taken you into her confidence."

"As I said, Monsieur Devereux, you are barking up the wrong tree," Anderson insisted. "Sure, we have met the Countess, as you call her, but we know nothing about a bonanza."

"Huh." Squinting at his counterparts, Devereux then posed, "Has she promised you a share of the loot in return for helping her?"

"Since we know nothing about this wealth, how could she? Now if you don't mind, we're very hungry, so we'll be on our way to the restaurant."

As the Cheshire boys made to leave, Devereux cautioned, "You are playing with fire, Mister Anderson. The Countess is not the only party pursuing the cache. If you participate in assisting her, you will come across The Mincer, one Julius Fyodor Austerberg, a professional booty chaser, and his lieutenants."

"Your competition?"

"Let's just say, our interests do not coincide. They clash diametrically. Austerberg has a huge ego. Big enough to ensure he rarely if ever gets beat. Be warned, his faction is not to be trifled with. Many have tried and perished because they underestimated The Mincer. Austerberg has stayed one step ahead of international law enforcers because no wrongdoing has ever been proved. Among other trades, he is a paid procurer for members of the Illuminati."

"A supposed confederation of mega-rich families descended from the Medici, Hapsburg and Capetian dynasties," Fraser clarified, "purporting to run the entire world's economy and political structures, above national governments and international organisations such as the UN."

"Quite correct, Mister Fraser. No doubt your investment banking career has furnished you with hearsay about the Illuminati."

"Obviously you know I work for The Firm."

"Indeed. In itself, *The Firm*, as it is euphemistically called in financial circles, has come under the beady eye of international law enforcement officers over the past hundred-years. However, we will not go into that."

"How do you know that Roger works at The Firm?" Anderson pumped.

"We know where all of you work, where you live, the names of your immediate families, and your histories going back to birth. Since coming across you three whilst keeping tabs on the Countess, we have concluded your combined occupations could be used for criminal activities."

"That's absurd," Richmond repudiated.

"Is it, Mister Richmond? You're a high-flying businessman with Brunswick Scorpio. Mister Anderson is an executive with foremost pharmaceutical Oxalite. Put that together with Mister Fraser's trouble-shooting role at The Firm, and you have a powerful conglomerate for potential unlawful activities. Especially the disposal of priceless artefacts and valuables."

"Your imagination is running wild," Anderson condemned. "We're friends by way of mutual business connections enjoying a spell of sailing on Lake Geneva and gambling at the Casino Barrière Montreux."

"That might be so, but whether you admit to it or not, you have become involved with the Countess Antoniya Katerina Kulikovsky, and thereby a drive to deprive the Swiss State of treasure trove. Hence, we have investigated your backgrounds and concluded you have the wherewithal to engage in criminal activities." Tarrying, he then appended, "Probably you don't know this, but the other night when you were at the casino, Austerberg's men were about to pounce on you, and the Countess, until my lineup intervened. Their very presence prevented what could have been a provocative confrontation. We may not be in the same vicinity if Austerberg makes a further attempt to entrap you."

"Have you quite finished, Monsieur Devereux?" Anderson coolly enquired.

"I see you and your compañeros are going to shoulder a classic

English machismo attitude. *That* is a big mistake. You will be juggling with your lives." Motioning to his brethren, he affixed, "We will be tracking you, as will Austerberg when he realises you are involved with the Countess. Be very careful what you do next."

~ * ~

Patrice Devereux began working at the Swiss Federal Office of Culture following ten years in the Swiss Air Force and five years with the Cantonal Police Corps. His grandparents, Alain and Colette Devereux, had left France with their two sons and one daughter after the 1940 Nazi invasion. An aero-engine designer, Alain worked for Clerget-Blin on diesel radial engines installed in French Air Force aircraft. A staunch republican, he saw the writing on the wall before Hitler's blitzkrieg on Warsaw, and reckoned after the tyrant turned his attention to France, his skills would be filched by the Nazis for the German war machine. Offering his services to the Swiss Federal Constructions Works in Zurich, manufacturer of fighter and ground attack aircraft, the Swiss Federal Assembly granted the Devereux family Swiss citizenship. Following in his father's footsteps, Patrice's father, Emile, joined Pilatus Aircraft after graduating from the University of Bern with a degree in aeronautical engineering, and setting up home at Lucerne with his wife of French descent, Sophia.

Influenced by his family heritage and republicanism, young Patrice quickly took on an orthodox outlook, wanting to serve the country giving refuge to his grandparents. In the wake of joining the Swiss Air Force, aged eighteen, and after flying training, he became assigned to *Dassault Mirage IIIS* and *Northrop Tiger F-5E* fighter squadrons, their role, to patrol Swiss airspace and prevent incursions from hostile aircraft and illegal airborne activities. With five-years' service under his belt and after attaining the rank of major, he left the air force for a police career.

Flowering a penchant for antiquity as a schoolboy, he had visited over a dozen Lucerne museums, the interest gaining momentum throughout his air force and police career. Supremely familiar with the fabulous artefacts on display in Bern, Zurich and Geneva museums, Devereux's engrossment became well known in senior police circles.

Employing his usual drive and determination to succeed, he'd reached the rank of chief inspector when he applied to the commissioner of police to be transferred to the Swiss Federal Office of Culture. Granted, Devereux was appointed superintendent, then chief superintendent, for the Swiss Federal Office of Culture, first based at Berne then at Geneva.

Before the Romanov affair, he'd established a strong reputation for unmasking exclusive, often illegally obtained artefacts, and pursuing the adventurers intent on pilfering them. In so doing, many of them had been imprisoned conditional on international cooperation with other culture policing agencies worldwide, Devereux establishing his credentials to both co-workers and the criminal fraternity.

Several times he had locked horns with one particular soldier of fortune, Julius Fyodor Austerberg, but never assembled sufficient evidence to have him put away. A wily fox possessing high intellect, cunning, and a forensic focus on his objective, invariably Austerberg kept just on the right side of the law, dupes and pawns sacrificed to the authorities when the going got tough. Devereux had pursued him around Europe and further afield, never quite getting to the point whereby he could catch The Mincer in the act or lay sufficient proof with the courts to send him to jail.

The closest he had got to imprisoning his foe happened when he arrested the Austerberg gang after they had stolen priceless artefacts from a collector's den. In the long run they were released on a technicality, Devereux knowing the Illuminati's sway had been at work in the highest echelons of the Swiss establishment. Not so much a vendetta, more of a want for policing excellence, Devereux harboured musings that one day Austerberg would overstep the mark, and he could arrest him without any scope for a legal appeal culminating in a heavy prison sentence.

~ * ~

"This is far more serious than I had foreseen," Richmond confessed, as the Englishmen sipped on their pre-dining aperitifs at the hotel restaurant's bar.

"*Ohh*, Devereux is just trying to scare us off the playing court,"

Anderson insisted.

"Well, if Austerberg and co are working for the Illuminati," Fraser opened, "they'll have imperious empowerment against lawful constraints."

"How do you mean, Roger?"

"If Illuminati folklore is to be believed, Austerberg will have been issued a get-out-of-jail-free-card, meaning if he is caught in the act of lifting the Romanov hoard, in due course the authorities will release him."

"Hhmm, I wonder if Stephanie is aware that Austerberg may be working for the Illuminati?"

"Well, before the Russian Revolution," Fraser began, "the Romanovs would have been related in some way to the Illuminati. Perhaps by means of the Frankish Capetian dynasty because of the cosy relationship between Russia and France, notably after it became clear that the Kaiser intended to open up a war front against Russia at the outbreak of World War One. Thereby, it can be assumed that knowledge of the Illuminati filtered into the post-Czar Nicholas II Romanov generations and distilled onto Stephanie. Whether she thinks Austerberg is working for the Illuminati is a matter of conjecture. I got the impression, even if she does, that will not deflect her from carrying out her father's delegated task of recovering the fabled Romanov treasury."

"Then again," Anderson insisted, "Devereux could be posturing, first with official Swiss authority threats, then with the possibility that Austerberg has been engaged by the Illuminati and thereby has exemption from lawful prosecution."

"Either way," Richmond initiated, "are we still in Stephanie's caper?"

"Professionally, we are all in the risk business," Anderson mandated. "We make judgments based on known facts, and on that foundation, agree on a go, no-go decision. Perhaps we should view the Romanov affair in the same context."

"But unlike business," Fraser argued, "aren't we merely feeding our egos in the pursuit of excitement?"

"Roger is right," Richmond backed. "Despite becoming stimulated by the monkeyshine, I'm beginning to temper it with justification motivators, and how our families and careers might be adversely affected."

"Let's sleep on it," Anderson promoted. "Then give our decision to Stephanie in the morning."

"We'll need a relaxation for the rest of the evening," Fraser forwarded. "After dinner, let's go waste some more of our hard-earned cash at the casino."

~ * ~

Though they appraised the feeling to be psychosomatically induced, amid their gambling session, the three amigos had the distinct impression that Devereux or one of his team were close by, monitoring them.

From his business dealings, Anderson had long been a believer in if the senses detect something, then it is so, the faculty enabling him to root out suspicious goings-on and counter accordingly. He also discriminated that Richmond and Fraser possessed the same aptitude. None of them made assertions about being shadowed, but each of them sensed the others were plagued by the spied upon notion.

At one point, Richmond thought he saw Nicole Steiner, but in the few seconds taken to alert Andrson and Fraser, the apparition had disappeared. His buddies put it down to nagging auto-suggestion implant.

Chapter Eleven: Austerberg and Co

Despite trying to concentrate on gaming at the Casino Barriére, besides notions of being observed, the minds of the Cheshire boys became consumed in a mixture of certitude tempered by misgivings apropos the Romanov episode. Decidedly they were hungry for stimulation, but after becoming fired up by Stephanie's account, the inevitable bringing down to earth by Devereux's salutary review produced ambivalence.

When it came to important matters, like his streetwise book-smart comrades, Gavin Anderson had acquired the knack of careful consideration before pressing the activate button. In the business domain it came down to risk versus reward, the binary decision rarely coated in ambiguity. Certainly, during the assessment period, when he and other associates could be stalling for time or even be missing in action, it allowed for all the determinants to coalesce into an immutable entity exhibiting recognisable peculiarities, thus allowing a rational decision to be made. Though family and domestic related matters came under the same scrutiny template, nonetheless emotional elements often obscured authenticity and sureness, love dissipating common sense, and often bringing about a decision saddled with consequences, some lifelong.

There had been occasions when he'd given into Francine, Michelle or Wyatt, knowing either their want would turn sour, or downline other factors could scupper their fancy. Now and then he adjudicated, maybe better to let them find out the hard way. And true to form, he didn't elude fallibility himself, some of his own household resolutions bellying up. Like for Fraser's investment banking analytics world, despite multi-order crunching of the known facts, it always left over a trivial residue of uncertainty, the tiny snippet ultimately responsible for impacting on decisions if circumstances changed just slightly, or a new factor never considered at the outset came into play.

As the Englishmen made their bets, such machinations percolated into Anderson's noodle. He also distinguished the same thorny conjectures would be happening to Richmond and Fraser.

Sometime into the amusement, whilst at a blackjack table they heard a feminine voice, its owner standing behind them. "Herr Austerberg would like to see you."

Swiveling about, the Englishmen were faced by a dazzling blonde with Tiffany-blue peepers, and a curvy body encased in a full-length evening gown.

"My name is Claudette Ducal."

She had a major beef against the establishment because they had destroyed her father, Antoine Raphael Ducal. He had publicised the truth about the threat to Europe from African, Middle Eastern and Asian invaders masquerading as refugees and immigrants. That had happened in the late-1990s when she was a teenager. A prominent professor of history in the French university stratum, Antoine Ducal became castigated, vilified and hounded by the European powers that be for presenting irrefutable facts supporting his observation. Though a strong man, the sheer severity of the harassment by the police and secret service sparking arrests on trumped-up charges had a catastrophic debilitating effect on him. One day, Claudette returned to their home in Lyon to be told her father had been carted off to an asylum, because the authorities adjudged him to be mentally ill.

Enraged by the false determination, she vowed to oppose the state for the rest of her life. Austerberg had taken her under his wing, when it came to his attention, she had hatched a plan to raid the *Musée d'Orsay*. Impressed by her bravado, he told Claudette there were easier pickings to be had elsewhere to get her own back on the status quo. Persuaded by his rhetoric, she joined his coterie, eventually becoming his 2IC.

"Good evening, Miss Ducal," Anderson cautiously responded. Gawking at Fraser and Richmond, he then probed, "What does Herr Austerberg want to talk to us about?"

She gleamed at them, her perfect pearly whites to the fore in her entrancing puss. "We both know why he wants to engage with you. Little goes unnoticed in our trade, and it has come to our attention that you have formed a friendship with a competitor of ours."

"And what specifically is your trade?" Richmond pushed.

"Wealth realisation, Mister Richmond. Something that your investment banking ally, Mister Fraser, intimately knows about."

"You appear to know our names," Anderson intonated.

"Indeed, Mister Anderson. In our market, we make it our business to be well-informed."

"And if we are not inclined to powwow with Mister Austerberg?"

"Then we will use more persuasive means of getting you to the summit."

"I see."

"Mister Austerberg has hired the casino's *Le Corbusier* Suite for the evening. Come." Her twinkle broadened. "I'm sure you will find the exchange enlightening and beneficial."

After receiving approving nods from Fraser and Richmond, Anderson okayed the invitation.

Like iron filings attracted to a magnet, the Cheshire boys followed Claudette out of the gaming area and along a corridor to the meeting venue, their pulse rates rising in anticipation of what could be a dangerous confab.

~ * ~

Born to *Reichsritter*, meaning Imperial Knight, Christoph Florian Von Austerberg of Heidenheim, and his Russian wife, Anoushka Lana Vysotsky, Julius Fyodor Von Austerberg entered the world at a time of turmoil and uncertainty. Ancillary to the nuclear arms race, the United States and the Soviet Union prepared for Armageddon, and the Korean War kicked off when communist forces from the north invaded South Korea heightening global tension between the Western allies and the communist bloc.

When Hitler achieved absolute power in the 1930s, the Von Austerberg's chemical plant at Heidenheim was seized by the Nazis after they refused to supply the Third Reich. Stripped of their German citizenship, the Von Austerbergs moved to Geneva and ploughed their offshore savings into fragrance company, Chuit and Naef, Christoph

Florian Von Austerberg designated as a non-executive director. At the termination of World War Two hostilities, the Von Austerbergs returned to Germany opening a chemical plant at Rosenheim, manufacturing a variety of refined products for industrial and agricultural use.

With the German economy booming in the mid-1950s, the Von Austerbergs were able to send their son to the Landheim Schondorf private boarding school at Schondorf am Ammersee. Viewed by his teachers to be intelligent but congenitally crafty, in tandem with excelling at his studies, the sheer charisma of the young Julius Fyodor Von Austerberg's personality attracted fellow pupils into his clique of mischievous non-conformity. Whenever the sect was caught engaging in forbidden activities, Julius always managed to persuade one of his acolytes to take the can, a trait he'd develop later in his life to ensure he remained at liberty when law enforcement agents were on his tail.

By his mid-teens, he had morphed into a calculating schemer, the finished article just over the horizon. Always in pursuit of get-rich-quick stratagems, he ignored his father's plea to join the family business or go on to university when he matriculated from the Landheim Schondorf upper school. Instead, the late-teenage Julius told his parents he intended to be a multi-millionaire by becoming a treasure hunter. From the very start he vowed to himself he'd form his own gang and never be a subordinate in someone else's outfit.

Deciding precious artefacts including fine gems and priceless works of art would be his domain of choice, he surprised his parents by announcing he had gained a place at Heidelberg University to study antiquity. During his stint at university, his treasure-chasing ambition crystallised into discernible constituents as he conceived plans and methods to fulfill his aspirations. In his perverse mind, he foresaw it'd be like reaching up into the night sky and scooping up a hatful of stars.

Reaching his twenty-first year, he had grown to over six feet in height, possessed a lean but powerful physique, and character had been added to his innate splendour. Post-graduation he dropped the Von in his surname, and set off on a life of skulduggery, shady liaisons and extortion to reap inestimable masterpieces and valuable jewels. When opposing hotshots got in his way, he had them dealt with by one of his band of hoodlums. If the going got tough, he willingly sacrificed partners of convenience to the law or conflicting cadres. Mercy, goodwill and loyalty were anathemas to him. Hence his attributed nickname - The Mincer, a codename *nom-de-plume* awarded to him by Interpol.

His glass eye came about after he went toe-to-toe with a South American cartel in pursuit of priceless Inca gems. Clashing in the ancient city of Cusco, high up in the Peruvian Andes, Austerberg's left eye received a blow from a gaucho wielding a digging pickaxe, irrevocably damaging the cornea, iris and optic nerve. Subsequent to surgically removing the fatally damaged organ he donned an eyepatch, but soon realised it made him standout for easy identification by his victims. Thenceforth, he adopted a glass eye to match his teal-blue right eye.

Ten years into his illegal career, Austerberg came to the attention of the Illuminati, the overarching world order engaging him on an *ad hoc* basis to do their bidding. Realising Illuminati backing could make him virtually immune to national and international laws, he made sure he delivered on whatever they desired. Though he had become a millionaire resultant from his private ventures, his Illuminati fees boosted his income by a factor of ten enabling him to set up multiple residences in countries with faint regard for international relations and no extradition treaty.

By his fortieth birthday, Austerberg had achieved a high profile with just about every law enforcement agency worldwide, but had evaded their shackles courtesy of Illuminati supremacy, a passel of good luck, and by sacrificing puppets to the authorities. Pretty much fire-proof, he continued his questing *modus operandi*, gaining a reputation for gusto, flair and even humour thrown into his meticulous operations to relieve rightful owners of their valuables.

~ * ~

As the Englishmen entered the ornately decorated *Le Corbusier* Suite, three men and another woman came into their lines of sight.

"Welcome, gentlemen," a man at the centre of the group with aristocratic features, opined. "My name is Julius Fyodor Austerberg, and these are my confederates, Miss Kim Lindberg, Mister Viktor Zinchenko and Mister Stanislav Greshnov. Miss Ducal you have met already."

Also formally dressed in evening attire, to the Cheshire boys, the Austerberg bloc appeared more like professional gamblers than supposedly cold-blooded agents of the Illuminati.

"What can we do for you, Mister Austerberg?" Anderson canvassed.

"Please, call me Julius. This is not a formal meeting, more a forum to exchange views and familiarities."

"About?"

"Hah." He shone at them. "Gavin, if I may address you by your Christian name, don't be coy. We both know why I invited you to this tête-è-tête."

"The Romanov affair."

"Yes, the Romanov affair. An enterprise I have devoted many cycles to, and one which I prognosticate will yield a great deal of reward." Dwelling, he then stated, "I won't fence with you. We know you Englishmen have an alliance with the Countess Antoniya Katerina Kulikovsky, a.k.a., Stephanie Nightingale. Obviously, she has told you about her claim on the Romanov cache, which is to be found somewhere not too distant from where we are now. But has she told you about other Romanov artefacts that have come onto the market since the Berlin Wall came down?

"Did you know, for example, that a certain billionaire media-magnet who went missing in 1991, had been in pursuit of a passel of priceless Romanov artefacts?"

"You must mean—" Anderson began.

"No, don't say his name. Best to let the dead rest in peace, if in fact this high-stakes player is actually deceased! However, Mister Fraser, er Roger, you're an analyst and trouble-shooter for The Firm, recall the condition of the communications market in the 1980s and early 1990s, if you please."

"How do you know I'm with The Firm?"

"Like Patrice Devereux and his interfering band of Swiss officials, I know everything about all three of you. Mister Colby Richmond, you are director of global sales for Brunswick Scorpio. And Gavin, you are operations director for Oxalite."

"How do you know all this about us?" Anderson gabbled.

"Huh." As if he'd had to explain the nature of his intel capacity many times before, a wry smile spread across his face. "In the execution of my trade, we know everything about everybody coming across our bows and making waves, but more of that later. Roger, can you please oblige us?"

"Communications, essentially meaning the print media, especially newspapers underwent a massive boom in the 1980s. The er, person to which Mister Austerberg refers, became one of two major players in the UK market." Pivoting to face Anderson and Richmond, he testified, "I'm sure you can work out who the other one is. Anyway, let's call this deceased media magnet, Mister X. Mister X was excessively ambitious. Over the course of just a few years, he procured a whole host of comms companies to add to the Mirror Group." Gaping at Austerberg, he sought, "Is it permitted to say Mirror Group?"

"Yes."

"The acquisition assault got to the point whereby the vast majority of Mister X's money was ploughed into more procurement investments. This was fine so long as his core Mirror Group empire was self-sustaining in terms of covering daily operational costs from customer base sales. But by 1989, the UK media market had become swamped by a spate of newspaper competitors reducing the Mirror Group's revenue stream. With meagre liquidity to cover fixed operational costs across the Mirror Group and the rest of his media publications, Mister X went to his banker, Nat West, for a loan. Notwithstanding, Nat West had done their homework and could see the writing on the wall *vis-à-vis* Mister X's core business failing in an exceedingly competitive market. Thereby the bank refused the loan. It forced Mister X to sell many of his companies to bankroll his core business. However, the rate at which most of his companies were losing sales revenue outstripped his garage sale, the cash from those sales quickly consumed in operating costs to keep the leftover businesses alive.

"Then it got to the point of no return. He went missing, presumed dead, and it quickly came to light when auditors examined Mirror Group finances that there was a five-hundred-million-pound hole in the pension fund. Soon thereafter a body was fished out of the Atlantic off Las Palmas and identified as Mister X by family members. However, behind ceremonial scenes, some observers speculated that Mister X had faked his death, the recovered body a like-for-like duplicate, and Mister X had got away with the five-hundred million."

"Right," Austerberg intervened, "and here is where the story crossed over into Romanov artefacts territory. Five-hundred-million pounds is a lot to conceal, and even through money laundering using the UK offshore banking system in Switzerland and the Caribbean, it is easily brought to light by financial regulators. I'm sure you'd agree with that appraisement, Roger?"

"Quite."

"Mister X needed to exchange the loot privately for a different commodity – one not so visible and trackable."

"Romanov gems," Richmond guessed.

"*Precisely*, Colby, and a lot of other priceless gems that had come to the attention of Mister X, including irreplaceable works of art purloined by the Nazis during their invasion of Europe, which had found their way into secret private collections. However, let us not get entrenched in this side issue. It is the Romanov squirrel away that concerns us." Halting, he stared at the Cheshire boys as if attempting to decipher their inner beings. "Stories about several Romanov possessions had been circulating in pathfinder circles since the mid-1920s. Most were folklore generated by self-interested parties, meaning the descendants and followers of Czar Nicholas II, to put treasure seekers off the real scent.

"Nothing was ever discovered until retired Russian White Army General, Yaroslav Maxim Gruzinsky, crossed the Armenian border with his family, and set up house in Istanbul. Without delay, rumours began to circulate that the Czar had put a quantity of customised Fabergé eggs and other fabulous gems into his guardianship, and that after the execution of the Romanovs, the General intended to clandestinely sell the wealth. One Richard Goldsworthy, known as slithering Dick, an American living in exile in Tangier, and wanted by the FBI for money-laundering, bought the entire horde from the General. He then marked it up and re-sold most of it piecemeal to speciality collectors. Many years later, when Goldsworthy was down to his last million, he put the surviving articles on the black-market. Egyptian billionaire, Gamal Abdelaal-Sharaf, bought the stash. And with him they stayed until 1965, when his Cairo villa was burgled by an international league of professional safe crackers, the thieves making off with the Romanov items and other gemstones.

"The story then went flat until 1990, when it emerged that some Fabergé eggs, surmised to be from the Abdelaal-Sharaf heist came onto the market. Mister X as er…Roger has branded him, sent agents to make purchasing enquiries." Pausing to ensure continuing preciseness, he then supplemented, "Make of it what you will as to the relationship between Mister X's apparent passing, and his intended acquisition of the Romanov jewels. Suffice to say, he was not the only party intent on pocketing them. Such high-value objects attract, shall we say, permanent measures to disengage competitors."

"You mean, instead of getting away with feigning his death, he *was* actually killed?" Richmond postulated.

"Very possibly…Colby. I was also pursuing that particular prize, but a competitor, who will remain nameless, beat me to the draw." For a split-second, Austerberg's demeanour darkened like he intended to be careful metering out his endgame to them before he resumed business-like physiognomy. "This neatly brings us on to the latest Romanov spoils, calculated to be in the Lake Geneva locale." Advancing towards the Englishmen, he disseminated in an uncompromising tone, "My organisation has been in pursuit of Romanov booty since Gamal Abdelaal-Sharaf came onto our radar. Apart from one item recently spirited away from a zillionaire Arab, we missed out on the General Gruzinsky loot. Unlike in 1990, we're *not* going to be disappointed this time around. It is my intention to acquire this latest Romanov haul, by either fair means or foul.

"Let me be clear, gentlemen, I do not intend to let another raider stop me from accomplishing this goal. However—" Beaming, his glass eye refused to cooperate in an otherwise radiant visage. "Let's not get too maudlin. I'm sure you understand the syntax of my warning and will do nothing to stop me achieving my objective."

~ * ~

Back at the Mövenpick, the Cheshire boys nursed balloon glasses of *Corvoisier* in the main bar whilst reviewing their encounter with Austerberg and co.

"Did you notice Austerberg's two molls, Claudette Ducal and Kim Lindberg, peered at us continuously throughout that conclave?" Fraser tested.

"They were assessing us," Richmond offered.

"Assessing us for what?" Anderson queried.

"Male weaknesses."

"As a means of exploiting us?"

"Uh-ha. The female of the species, and distinctly those blessed with vampish credentials, abidingly stake out and observe their prey before striking."

"You've had such a baptism?"

"Before Carolyn, I became embroiled in some out-on-the-rim sexual exploits with sirens and enchantresses. Be assured, such man-wreckers possess the necessary qualifications to accomplish their objectives, first among these – assessing their mark."

"And you think that's what Ducal and Lindberg were doing?"

"I do."

"So, taking it to the next stage, Colby, would you care to tell us what they might do?"

"Patently, Austerberg is going to keep tabs on us. Should he adjudicate, we can assist him in his endeavours, he might deploy Ducal and Lindberg to make it happen."

"You could be right," Fraser conceded. "Albeit I'm more alarmed about those Russian Mafia enforcers in exile – Viktor Zinchenko and Stanislav Greshnov. They both bore the stamp of terminal violence."

"You mean, liquidators?" Anderson pushed.

"Yes. During my career in investment banking, I've interfaced with private investor billionaire clients who employ their own praetorian guard. Mainly ex-military Johnnies who have seen a lot of action in the interdictor zone and will do anything to ensure the security of their master, including wasting his enemies. Zinchenko and Greshnov had the same glassy, cold stare, and implacable body language."

"Mmmm, clearly, we have to treat Austerberg seriously. Though he appeared measured, even pleasant, the semantics in his discourse conveyed the message – don't play in this game if you value your lives."

After a moment of mutual silence, Richmond positioned, "This Romanov affair has become inordinately convoluted. What began as a plea from a damsel in distress for help has blossomed into a multifaceted rats nest of intrigue, and danger."

"Yes, what Colby says is right," Fraser concurred. "Unequivocally, we are out of our depth with no real incentive to continue other than keeping our word to help Stephanie."

"It's a paradox," Anderson positioned. "If we don't execute the subterfuge plan tomorrow, Austerberg will outflank the Countess, and-or Devereux will arrest her attempting to smuggle treasure trove out of Switzerland."

"It's not as if we really know her, let alone have some kind of inherited obligation to help her out," Richmond stationed. "It could turn out to be very bad for us."

"Yes," Fraser favoured. "We could get shot by Austerberg or sent to jail for aiding and abetting by Devereux."

"It's more than a tricky one, it's a possible life-changing conundrum," Anderson prompted. "But perhaps there's a halfway house."

"Go on," Richmond encouraged.

"Well, the subterfuge is relatively risk free. We won't be breaking the law, and if it goes to plan, Austerberg will be on Stephanie's tail at the original search spot on Lake Geneva. It's if we find something on the lakebed and then consult with Stephanie that the net will start to close.

"So we need to modify the plan in such a way that neither Austerberg or Devereux sees us with Stephanie, and I think I've got an idea to achieve that aim. Let's go to my room and call her on the hotel internal phone system."

Chapter Twelve: The Deep Dive

A crystal-clear day greeted the intrepid Englishmen as they wound their way to Port Lausanne-Ouchy, then weighed anchor in the Argonaut for the two-kilometre demarcation point, east of Gland on Lake Geneva. Stephanie and her minders had already departed for the original point, two kilometres west of Veytaux, in the Leonie. Before scurrying down to the jetty, Anderson had scoped the area with binoculars from a distant point, his scan confirming the schooner used by the Austerberg-set had departed from Port Lausanne-Ouchy. Also scouting for Devereux and his cohorts, he breathed a sigh of relief when none of the Swiss functionaries came into his field of regard, though that did not preclude they were concealed, monitoring Stephanie, Austerberg, and the Englishmen.

As Argonaut ploughed along the lake surface on a 210 degrees course using the on-board GPS navigation system to find the two-kilometre mark off Gland, the crew began to mentally prepare themselves for the risky mission. As Anderson inspected his scuba diving gear and a fully-waterproof, underwater metal detector, Richmond and Fraser spectated with more than a hint of uneasiness for their shipmate's forthcoming dicey dive. He had hired the equipment from Herr Griswald's chandlers before they set sail, the supposed German beer enthusiast with a suspected appetite for sadomasochism advising Anderson about the equipment, and to be aware of underwater hazards, principally seabed's of thick vegetation capable of entrapping unsuspecting divers. On reaching their signposted setpoint, Fraser downed the schooner's sails with the electric winches, and Richmond heaved to by bringing her tiller to midships, whilst Anderson loosed the anchor.

After finalising his diving preparation, Anderson apprised, "I'll be down for no more than thirty minutes."

Slipping over Argonaut's stern into the water, he turned on the metal detector and checked for full function in the submerged state, a diode emitting a glowing red light authenticating operational availability. Though the air temperature had hit a blistering seventy-seven degrees Fahrenheit, despite donning a wetsuit he sensed a sharp temperature differential with Lake Geneva's clear water, its colder climate making him shiver until he acclimatised to the change.

Bobbing around beside Argonaut, he gave the thumbs-up before placing his air mouthpiece and headed down, his buddies watching him disappear beneath the surface.

Significantly different from his recreational schemes in the Caribbean, Anderson found the twelve-fathoms space between the surface and the lakebed to be filled with a sparsity of freshwater marine life. When he dived off the Bahamas, brightly coloured surgeon fish and midnight cowfish filled the mid-water level in great quantities. Vast shoals of angelfish and blue parrot fish nosed into coral reef crevices, and a profusion of groupers scoped the reef gullies in pursuit of small fry. Oppositely, Lake Geneva's game and common fish were grouped in much smaller numbers. A smattering of rainbow trout went after invertebrates, batches of white bass fed on crustaceans, and the odd carp harvested aquatic vegetation.

Diving slowly so as to acclimatise to the increasing depth pressure, when he finally came to rest on the lakebed, initially he perused for an obvious manmade object or objects without success. Glancing at the metal detector, it registered nothing. Deciding to set about a methodical approach, Anderson mentally mapped out a forty-by-forty metre section directly under Argonaut and began a back and forth swim of each forty-metre by one-metre rectangle.

Above, Richmond and Fraser exchanged agitated gestures, apprehension for their friend increasing. Constantly consulting their wrist watches, time for them seemed to travel through treacle, the second hands artificially appearing to be moving much slower than normal adding to their anxiety.

By Anderson's thirty-fifth trawl nothing had come to light, the metal detector's gauge needle still tarried stationary. He began to think Richmond's interpretation of General Bodrov's instruction was a blind alley. Then just beyond his selected matrix, he caught sight of something partially encrusted in curly-leaf pondweed glinting against sunlight refracted through the water. Pointing the metal detector in the direction of the target, its needle swung to a mid-dial position, annunciating the object to be metallic.

Kicking his flippers hard, he quickly reached the source of the reflection, establishing it to be a stainless-steel box approximating the size of a lady's jewel case. Sweeping about the immediate area he reconnoitred for more same-sized boxes, but nothing came into view, the sensor device echoing the single box to be the only canister in the area. Whatever the General had concealed at the datum point, Anderson envisioned the single receptacle had to be it. Picking up the box, he slowly rose to the surface, stopping for thirty-seconds every two fathoms to avoid the bends. When his napper popped up behind Argonaut's stern and he held the box aloft, Richmond and Fraser rushed to help him aboard.

"It's too small to hold a substantial treasure," Fraser asserted, as the Cheshire boys glued their eyes to the box set on the stern deck. "It's got to hold another clue."

"Yes," Richmond consented. "You brought it up, Gavin. You should have the honour of opening it."

Remarkably, when Anderson took hold of the box and applied pressure to its lid, it hinged open with little effort, ninety-odd years of immersion in water not impairing its stainless-steel construction. Swimming around in the water that had seeped into the box interior, the Englishmen discovered a scaled, water-tight, plastic pouch.

"Good god," Fraser blathered. "There's a piece of rolled-up paper in that pouch."

"Yes, it's definitely another clue," Anderson maintained. "Let's see if we can penetrate the pouch to extract the paper using the Swiss Army knife in Argonaut's tool chest."

After retrieving the cutter, Anderson carefully broke the plastic surface of the pouch, then sliced it to extract the paper.

"Oh, Christ," Fraser gushed, "I hope it's not written in Prussian. If so, we'll have to call on the *Obergruppenführer's* services again."

Laying the rolled paper flat on Argonaut's saloon table, Anderson then read, "8461XXXX, N. Romanov. Banque Cantonale Vaudoise, BCV, Placé Saint-François 14, 1001 Lausanne."

"Has to be an account number," Fraser prescribed.

"Yes," Anderson approved. "But the last four digits are missing."

"Wait a minute," Richmond spouted. "If I recollect correctly, there were four numerals tagged on to the first message."

"That's right. Put the two messages together and we have the full account number."

~ * ~

When Anderson called Stephanie the previous night, he had told her, when she returned from the original Lake Geneva dive location to evade Austerberg by instead of meeting the Cheshire boys at the Mövenpick, to rendezvous with them midday at *Le Musee Olympique* on Quai d'Ouchy 1, not far from the hotel.

Returning to his room after Argonaut docked at Port Lausanne-Ouchy, Anderson retrieved the envelope, and with the latest clue, the Englishmen took the *M5* to the *Le Musee Olympique* with Fraser at the wheel, while Richmond and Anderson monitored for Devereux and his associates.

"Well," Richmond began, during the short journey, "if the Swiss authorities are keeping tabs on us, they're good at remaining in the shadows. I've got a mental image of Devereux and his crew, but I can't see them anywhere."

"They're professionals, "Anderson qualified. "I'd expect nothing less."

Glimpsing into the rearview mirror, Fraser supported, "The good news is, since leaving the Mövenpick, no vehicles appear to be tailing us."

Only recently re-opened after extensive renovation work, Anderson had arranged to tie up with Stephanie on level two of the museum, a floor focusing on sporting equipment displays. Browsing out of a panoramic window array onto Quai d'Ouchy, the Cheshire boys saw her and her minders alight from a taxi and rush into the museum.

"What happened out on the lake?" Anderson queried, when

they joined the Englishmen.

"Austerberg was already at the demarcation point when we arrived," Stephanie reviewed. "And one of his band had gone below." Pursing her lips, she snarled, "The bastard had the nerve to smirk and wave to us."

"So he still thinks there is something at the point off Veytaux?"

"Indeed. However, when we left to return to Port Lausanne-Ouchy, he followed us to the port, and back to the Mövenpick. We all went to my room, then left via the fire escape onto Avenue Frédéric-César-de-la-Harpe, and hailed a taxi. Austerberg thinks we are still in my room."

"Good."

"Did you find anything off Gland?"

"*Indeed,* we did," Anderson upheld.

Fervently he showed her the strip of paper retrieved from the plastic pouch.

"8461XXXX, N. Romanov. Banque Cantonale Vaudoise, BCV, Placé Saint-François 14, 1001 Lausanne," she read aloud, then gawped at him. "Are those first four digits part of an account number?"

"Yes, we think so, and referring to the first message—" Pulling out the envelope from his jacket pocket, he withdrew the yellowing paper. "2094 must be the last four digits of the account number."

Scanning both pieces of paper, Stephanie fused the numerals together. "Account number 84612094 at the Banque Cantonale Vaudoise."

"Yes."

"*Then we have it,*" she excitedly trilled.

"Well," Fraser alerted, "you will note the second message contains the name, N. Romanov, most probably meaning Nicholas Romanov, the Czar. It may be that the bank is only authorised to allow the named account holder to access the account. However, if family provenance can be proved, that is to say you are a descendant of the Czar, then the bank will allow you access."

"I see." Dwelling, she then illuminated, "I believe my father has inherited some documentation." She reached into her bag and withdrew a smartphone, then peeked at her wristwatch. "It's nine-thirty in the evening back in Darwin. I'll ask him to email the documents to my laptop, then we can print them out."

"I doubt that the Banque Cantonale Vaudoise will accept copies," Fraser forecast. "They will need originals."

"Damn, that means I'll have to fly back to Australia. In round terms, with stopovers, that's a five-day there and back trip. How long will you be in Lausanne?"

"Until the weekend after next," Anderson replied.

"So can I rely on your further assistance with the bank when I return?"

"The worst is over, so yes."

"Thank you." Making a note of the bank details, she then begged, "Please keep both pieces of paper in your room wall safe."

"Will do."

Calling her father, Stephanie established he had inherited the family provenance documents. She then booked the Geneva to Darwin flights for herself and her minders with Qantas.

"No doubt Austerberg will follow you to the airport," Anderson predicted. "And maybe he'll think you have given up the prowl and gone back home."

"I'm not that lucky," she replied. "Besides, with his contacts, he will soon suss out that I've made return flights."

When the Englishmen accompanied the down under bound travellers to Geneva-Cointrin Airport, a metallic-lime-green *Mercedes Benz 600 Grosser* followed the *Range Rover* and *M5* cavalcade. Leaving the departures terminal after the Darwin flight had taken off, the Cheshire boys saw Austerberg and his accomplices lounging against the *Grosser*, the gang's leader raising a hand in acknowledgement at them and glowing as if he'd worked out exactly what was going down.

~ * ~

"If someone had told me we'd become embroiled in the hunt for a priceless heirloom whilst in Lausanne, I'd never have believed them," Richmond professed, when they returned to the Mövenpick.

"For sure," Fraser ratified. "It does bear all the hallmarks of the implausible."

"I suppose these things do happen," Anderson wagered. "Howbeit, it's not over yet, and I think Stephanie may have to negotiate more hurdles before she gets her hands on the Romanov haul."

"Yes," Fraser supported, "There's always the chance that the Banque Cantonale Vaudoise will not accept her credentials, and they put the entire matter in the hands of the Swiss authorities."

"Is that likely, Roger? I mean what sets Swiss banks apart is their reputation for preserving client anonymity."

"True, but once they see Romanov provenance documents, it could result in them calling in the police at the very least."

"Mmmm, best to keep that to ourselves. We don't want to deflate the Countess before she even sees the curios."

Chapter Thirteen: *The Pit and the Pendulum*

With the fine weather continuing to top up their suntans, the Cheshire boys resumed their holiday intentions sailing Argonaut over the Lake Geneva Swiss French border to Evian-les-Bains and Yvoire. In moments of awe after witnessing something spectacular on the lake or ashore, momentarily they forgot about the Romanov episode, their absorption refreshed and their excitement at happening upon the new turning them into regular tourists. Inevitably, when it did resurface, the caper seemed so far-fetched as to be unreal, a vast figment of their combined imaginations.

Whilst aboard the schooner taking their usual exotic luncheon, they even began joking about the larger-than-life characters involved in the escapade. The ever silent in their company Peter Lorrie doppelganger, Nostro Kravets, Zoe Weber's projected menacing air, and the feline entrapment tentacles of Claudette Ducal.

"It has all the necessary ingredients needed for a mysterious thriller novel by Agatha Christie," Richmond positioned. "If we weren't secondary players in the cliff-hanger, I'd find it difficult to credit its authenticity."

"Categorically," Anderson underpinned. "Although I've come across some macabre dignitaries during my plus-three decades in the petroleum and pharmaceutical industries, all pale before the members of Stephanie's coterie, Devereux's enforcement squad, and Austerberg's cabal."

"Perhaps they're all in line with the territory we find ourselves involved within," Fraser put forward. "Every circle, whether it be business or domestic, tends to possess a brand of unique characteristics, including prototypical personalities."

"How do you think the balance of the drama is going to play out from a banking angle, Roger?"

"Mmmm." Raising his eyebrows, he responded, "Being money driven, the thing about banking and the financial services industry in general, is that despite regulation and monitoring by external agencies, often we tend to make it up as we go along, our eye never deflecting from the primary objective."

"To make a profit," Richmond interjected.

"Quite, and to do that, we bend and shape-shift to accommodate whatever factors are in play governing the opportunity. Relating to investment banking, sure there is a baseline business model we adhere to for stock trading, mergers & acquisitions and a host of other services. Even so, due to market peaks and troughs causing volatility, we are constantly redefining our go-to-market strategy in-line with business drivers, and the ever-pervasive effect of monetary regulation. Consequently, creative measures are needed to nourish market position and client confidence in our abilities. When a bluebird comes along — that is the opportunity to make a lot of money without too many sales cycles — we jump at it."

"So are you saying the Banque Cantonale Vaudoise might take advantage of Stephanie's precarious position?" Anderson categorised.

"Depends on the nature of the kitty."

"Surely the bank knows that already."

"No. Confidentiality precludes a bank knowing the contents of a deposit left by a client. It will only be when the bank signs-off the withdrawal that they will become aware of what has been lying in their vault since 1917. It's at that point that the bank will make consideration about a business opportunity."

"You mean whether to play ball with the Countess or not?"

"Yes. They could simply choose to be gracious, allowing her to take the cache — no questions asked. However, the Romanov provenance documents will alert them to the substance of the haul, and thereby possible interest from the Swiss authorities."

"So, when I said the worst is over at the *Le Musee Olympique*, that was a false representation," Anderson reviewed.

"Plainly the puzzle is solved, but we're about to enter phase-two of the high jinks, meaning contending with the Banque Cantonale Vaudoise. Plus, Devereux and Austerberg will still be hot on the Countess's and thereby our tails."

"I wonder if these possibilities are going through Stephanie's mind?" Richmond wondered.

"She strikes me as intelligent and astute. I'd bet she is under no illusions."

~ * ~

Taking late afternoon tea, the next day at the Café Renoir in the Place du Port, after another glorious spree on Lake Geneva, the Cheshire boys talked about the delights of sailing the Argonaut followed by human resource appraisal experiences. Freely admitting he found interviewing prospective new staff not to be his forte, Anderson told his companions he preferred to offload the management duty to his subordinates. Similarly, Fraser said on the rare occasions he was called upon to perform the task, he never felt comfortable deciding someone's fate.

"What about you, Colby?" Anderson questioned. "New salesmen assessment must be an integral part of your job."

"True, and a very significant part. You see, selection and training are the cornerstones of a successful sales team."

"So what's your technique?"

"Well, salesmen are fair game for an exacting interview. Long ago, I developed a sure-fire method for finding interviewee true character."

"Go on."

"Verifying C.V claims and references doesn't always unearth the nature of the candidate. In sales, we have to ascertain that the applicant is case-hardened to win business in the most extreme selling environments."

"How do you do that?"

"After twenty to thirty minutes of the interview, when they feel relaxed and think they've cracked it, I hit them with the unexpected to test temperament and inner-being. Assuming a neutral countenance, I table, 'Are you, or have you ever been a practising homosexual?' Shocked, they blurt something like, '*What*! No, never,' in a squeaky voice. So I write something down on the assessment proforma, then ask, 'Do you, or have you ever suffered from premature ejaculation?' '*What!*' they again reply. 'No, never,' their voice tone rising from normal to upper soprano. I make another entry on the form, then sternly ask, 'Are you sure your answers to my last two questions are correct?' '*Yes, yes,*' they invariably bleat, 'I only pork girls, and I never cum for at least ten minutes, then I erupt like a volcano. I'm a normal bloke, honestly. *Aagghhhhh…*'"

Anderson and Fraser burst into laughter.

"And it works?" Fraser tabled, between chortles.

"Well, it certainly separates the wheat from the chaff, the men from the boys."

Caught up in hilarity, they were still chuckling when Fraser suddenly entreated, "*Look,*" his expression dropping into deadpan as he pointed to a man on the opposite side of the strasse. "Isn't that Stanislav Greshnov, one of Austerberg's henchmen?"

"I believe it is," Anderson corroborated. "He's going into that bookstore." Thinking on his feet, he advocated, "Here's our chance to get one up on Austerberg."

"How do you mean?" Richmond asked.

"If we find out where their hideout is. That puts us one step frontwards in the game. Might eliminate the threat of surprise."

"I see what you mean."

"Clearly, he's not been tasked with spying on us, so he must be on some other business. When he moves off, let's follow him."

In due course, Greshnov left the bookstore with a copy of *Die Welt* and *Junge Freiheit*, and made his way east on Place du Pont, the Englishmen following at a discrete distance. Veering left onto Avenue d'Ouchy, the target rambled north for several blocks before wheeling right into Chem. de Brillancourt, across Parc de lécole, and on into the basement door of a large nineteenth-century townhouse on Chem. de Beau Rivage. Observing from a spot giving cover in Parc de lécole, the pursuers decided on a watching brief.

As Anderson surveyed up and down Chem. de Beau Rivage, the Hôtel de Ville where Suzannah Arliss, the model he had sat next to on the inbound flight, said she would be engaged in a fashion photoshoot, came into his sight no more than fifty-metres from the townhouse. Small world he cogitated to himself. Then he recalled she had told him, on one occasion, a group of suspicious-looking characters came out of its restaurant and watched her photoshoot, its apparent group leader, a tall aristocratic grandee with a domineering presence. Must have been Austerberg, he concluded.

Soon, the metallic-lime-green *Mercedes Benz 600 Grosser* drew up outside the house, the Cheshire boys scoping Austerberg and his two female deputies in the back seats with Zinchenko driving. Straightaway Greshnov alighted from the basement door and up a short flight of steps, carrying the German newspapers, then slid into the front passenger seat. Like a shot, the *Grosser* departed at speed.

"Obviously Austerberg is up to something," Anderson surmised. "But what?"

"Perhaps with Stephanie gone, he's making a concerted attempt to find the Romanov legacy," Fraser suggested.

"Possibly." Wrinkling his nose, he posed, "How about if we check out that basement?"

"Bit risky, Gavin," Richmond cautioned. "If we'd brought our mobiles, one of us could monitor for the *Grosser* returning whilst the other two cased the basement. Besides that, there must be a lock on that basement door."

"Maybe a credit card can be used to lift the latch."

"Have you done that previously?"

"There's a first time for everything. How hard can it be?"

"What do you think, Roger?" Richmond ticketed.

"We've come this far. May as well take it a stage further."

"Very well," Anderson accepted. "Since we have no communication devices, we may as well all go."

While his brethren kept watch for the *Grosser*, Anderson managed to unlatch the basement door lock with his *Diner's Club* card. "We're in."

Entering the basement, the men from Cheshire faced a very dark environment only marginally relieved by light penetrating the opaque panes of its door. Fingering about the wall to the left of the door, Anderson made out a switch, threw it and the chamber became illuminated from a series of wall and ceiling mounted incandescent lights. Perusing about, they saw a proliferation of stuffed alpine wildlife — some in showcases, a collection of antique furniture, chandeliers, and a host of porcelain decorative pieces laid out on tables.

"It's far larger than I envisaged," Anderson adjudged.

"What's that pug-ugly beast in the far right-hand corner?" Fraser blurted.

"Could be a yeti," Richmond postulated.

Stepping forward, they never took their peepers off the exhibit.

"What's that growth on its face?" Fraser solicited, frowning at the hideous sight.

"That's its nose, dummy," Anderson verified.

"Looks like Wayne Rooney."

"Oh it's not that bad," Richmond insisted.

Rotating to his left, Anderson inputted, "There's a big hole in the floor on the far side."

Edging over between the menagerie collection, the Cheshire boys stared down at the cavity.

"It's a pit," Fraser labeled.

"Yes," Richmond okayed, leaning slightly over the aperture. "I wonder where the pendulum is?"

"What?"

"Edgar Allen Poe."

"Ohh…yes."

"Maybe it's used to incarcerate Austerberg's adversaries," Anderson nominated.

"Very probably."

Still weighing up its intended use; they heard a groaning dissonance coming from the abyss.

"*Good god,*" Fraser exclaimed. "Someone is down there."

Reaching for a tiffany lamp on a nearby table, Anderson plugged it into a mains socket, then angled its luminescence downwards into the chasm. Sure enough, at least fifteen feet beneath floor level at the pit's bottom they saw a man dressed in an Arabic thawb, sandals and a fez, crouched up as if he'd taken a beating.

"*Hello,*" Anderson called.

"*Please,* no more torture," came the response.

"We're going to help you."

"Help me!"

"Yes."

"You are not Austerberg's men?"

"No." Pursing his lips, he browsed about the cellar. "Roger, see if you can find a rope ladder or even a rope. There must be something to facilitate egress from the pit by connecting it to those two anchor points by its side."

Rummaging around the area adjacent to the cavity opening, Fraser found a coiled-up rope ladder in a large chest. Connecting it to the anchor points, he then rolled it down into the void.

"Can you climb?" Anderson whooped to the prisoner.

"I must."

Taking tentative steps as though his ability to use his legs had become impaired, the captive made his way up the rope ladder, Anderson and Richmond hauling him up the last few rungs.

No more than five-six in height and of slender build, it became clear to the Cheshire boys that the liberated man presented no appreciable threat to the Austerberg cartel.

"Thank you, thank you, effendi," he whimpered.

"Who are you?" Anderson investigated.

Trying to compose himself, he replied "My name is Mustapha Tawfik-Nasseri."

"Why did Austerberg imprison you?"

"Please, we have to get out of here before they come back. They will torture me again just for fun. They are sadists. See what they've done to me." Beetle-browed, he pointed to marks on his body and a gash on his face.

"First, what's your story, Mustapha?"

"That is confidential," he almost whispered.

"We could always put you back down the pit, if you don't cooperate," Richmond threatened.

"Ohh, not that!" Screwing up his countenance, he recoiled, the very notion of more torture chilling him to the bone. "Very well. My master is Sheikh Hadem Kladed-Zainab of Nador in Morocco. He is a good and gracious man, loved and much respected by his people, and a collector of fine antiquity pieces. He has many priceless items in his villas, and…"

"*Get to the point*," Anderson pressed, scowling.

"…He sent me to Lausanne with the express purpose of regaining a priceless artefact that Austerberg took from him by deception."

"What artefact?"

"It came into the Sheikh's possession from a jewel thief combine, who had raided an Egyptian billionaire's horde."

Remembering Austerberg had told them he had spirited away one Romanov item from a zillionaire Arab, procured from an international coalition of professional safe crackers, when items from the Abdelaal-Sharaf heist came onto the market, immediately the Englishmen exchanged shrewd goggles as they made the connection.

"Is this artefact a Fabergé egg from the Romanov collection?" Anderson grilled.

His jaw dropping and his optics opening wide, he shrieked, "*Yes. How could you possibly know that?*"

"Nevermind." Delaying to gather theories, Anderson then speculated, "So you were caught in the act of trying to recover the Fabergé egg?"

"Yes."

"And Austerberg had you tortured when you refused to tell him who your master is?"

"Yes."

"But nonetheless, he got it out of you?"

"I couldn't hold out after those Russian brutes went to work on me. I told them everything, but still they continued…sadistic swine."

"Why has he kept you on ice?"

"I can only assume he wants to use me as a bargaining chip."

"With your master?"

"I have been in the Sheikh's service for over thirty years. He would not like to see my life ended prematurely."

"So the Sheikh has other Romanov items of interest to Austerberg?"

"He does, but after I'd been knocked senseless, I came to and overheard them talking about another hijack, and they'd put me on ice as you call it, until afterwards."

"And it was just you sent on this mission?"

"No. Under the Sheikh's direction, I hired some Arab mercenaries, but when Austerberg closed in on us, they ran away…*bastards*."

Considering for a moment, Andeson said, "What do you think, Roger?"

Shrugging his shoulders, he responded, "He's not in our particular play. We could let him go."

"Colby?"

"If we do that, he might run straight to the Swiss police complicating other matters."

"*No, no*, I won't, effendi," Mustapha pleaded.

"Why not?" Richmond quizzed.

"Because strictly speaking my enterprise is not legal. If I did go to the police, that would lead to my master. I can't let that happen."

"Mmmm," Anderson began, "but can you be trusted? That's the big question."

"Yes, yes, effendi. You can trust me."

"If we let you go, what will you do?"

"Return to Morocco."

"How?"

"The Sheikh has contacts in the Swiss banking community."

"Huh." He rolled his eyes. "Not entirely surprising. Go on."

"As backup, he gave me the name and contact details of such a person in Lausanne. This ally will get me out of Switzerland by tonight."

"Right, let's get that rope ladder back in its trunk," Anderson proclaimed to his adherents. "All being well, Austerberg will conclude that Mustapha climbed out of the pit and escaped." Gazing at the ceiling, he annexed, "I'd really like to take a gander around the upper floors of this house, to see what else we can find that might help us."

Viewing his slim-line *Louis Cartier* timepiece, Fraser forewarned, "We've already been here for over fifteen minutes. Austerberg and co could return at any moment."

"And the last thing we need is to be caught here," Richmond flagged.

Making a concessionary expression, Anderson relented. "Yep, you're both right. We shouldn't test lady luck any further."

As the foursome navigated the basement to the exit door, Richmond saw a large grandfather clock, its swinging pendulum reigniting his earlier pit and the pendulum remark.

"*Jesus*," he blurted. "Look at that."

Suddenly attuned to the click-clank of the chronometer's action, Anderson and Fraser gawked at the large timekeeper.

"I hope that's not an omen," Anderson babbled.

Chapter Fourteen: Richmond Taken

Shaken by the turn of events emanating from their Austerberg lair break-in, the Cheshire boys discussed the happening at the Mövenpick. Evidently, they determined, Austerberg had more than one pillage in play. As well as pursuing Stephanie - their assumed primary objective - his secondary appeared to be reengaging with Sheikh Hadem Kladed-Zainab by using Mustapha Tawfik-Nasseri as a pawn to thieve more treasure. Now that his prisoner had escaped, the second mischief had become null and void, enabling him to focus on whatever turned up at the Banque Cantonale Vaudoise. They also speculated over the purpose of the two German newspapers held by Greshnov. Were they related to the primary or the secondary exploit?

Deciding to park the conundrum, the following day saw them out on Lake Geneva again, the Argonaut trekking parallel to the shoreline off Villeneuve, located in the south-east corner of the lake. Hoping the trip might crystalise their notions pertaining to the relevance of the German periodicals, nothing came to light with reference to Stephanie's assignment, leaving them to arbitrate they must have something to do with the intended assault on the Sheikh's wealth, or something else.

The other item debated concerned the *apparent* escape of Austerberg's prisoner. Spurred on by the portent of more torture, would he believe Mustapha had summoned all his residual strength and guile to somehow climb out of the pit? Probably never done before by previous pit incumbents, it was unlikely Austerberg might persuade himself the captive escaped without external help. Did that put the Cheshire boys in the frame, and thereby they had become subject to a double-jeopardy?

~ * ~

Nighttime saw the Englishmen parade to the Casino Barriére to chance

130

their arms again.

"Hot damn, we may as well be pouring money down the drain," Fraser quipped, after losing five consecutive blackjack hands.

"Yeah," Anderson assented. "Unless you're a professional gambler, all the games are stacked heavily in favour of the house."

"Thank god, it's only pin money," Richmond branded. "If we got hooked, we'd be bankrupt within days."

"Quite frankly, I get more kicks out of watching," Fraser admitted. "Explicitly when it's a cardsharp taking the casino to the cleaners."

"How about we go to the bar and get blitzed on cosmopolitans and screwdrivers?" Anderson advocated.

"Gets my vote," Richmond blessed.

"Mine too," Fraser rounded out.

Strolling over to the bar, the Cheshire boys discussed their sailing plans for the next day, then started into a mass of cocktails.

Sometime later, Richmond excused himself to go to the restroom. Finishing up, he washed his hands, checked his hair and re-straightened his bow tie. About to re-join his pals, out-of-the-blue he was seized by two men, recognising them as Viktor Zinchenko and Stanislav Greshnov, the former pushing a *Smith and Wesson 340PD* pistol into his side.

To the trained eye, Zinchenko and Greshnov were like two peas from the same pod — standard Soviet issue. Crewcuts, flushed complexions masking potato-white skins, and built from grit and tungsten carbide. Products of the Russian mafia, known as the Bratva, it had come to prominence after the dissolution of the USSR in 1991, following Gorbachev's glasnost and perestroika political reform and transparency policies. Both G-men had been in the Soviet army and had bonds as contract henchmen with successors to the KGB, the newly formed FSB. Seeing an opportunity to climb aboard the burgeoning Russian free-market bandwagon, both had independently offered their enforcer skills to the Bratva. Later, Zinchenko and Greshnov met in Bratislava whilst supporting a racketeering operation for an Omsk oblast oligarch. Concurrently, they became aware of Austerberg's set-up and sought him out via a contact in the Slovakian underworld. Mutually arranging to meet at the Spaso-Preobrazhensky Cathedral in Odessa on the north-western shore of the Black Sea, Austerberg interviewed them clandestinely while interviewer and interviewees knelt and prayed in adjacent pews. Making it clear they could add value to his organisation, after machinating on the proposal Austerberg allowed them to join his team.

"Don't make a fuss, Mister Richmond," Zinchenko warned in a deep Slavic accent. "I'd hate to have to shoot you."

"What do you want?"

"Miss Ducal and Miss Lindberg would like a word with you."

"*What*! Who the hell do you think you are, gangsters?"

"*Hah*!" Smirking at his partner, he growled, "Yes, we are. Now are you going to come quietly, or does Stanislav have to put you out for a while?"

Craning to face Greshnov, the Russian leered back menacingly at Richmond.

"Okay, but first I must tell my comrades I have to leave."

"Ohhh," Zinchenko gibbered, chuckling. "You must think we are dimwits, imbeciles. Let me assure you, we are not. *Come*, the ladies await your presence."

First handcuffing him, Greshnov then took Richmond's arm forcing him out of the restroom and down a hallway away from the bar and the gambling area, whilst Zinchenko held the gun to his back. Entering a supplies storage room at the rear of the casino, the camarilla then alighted into the night using its backdoor, previously unlocked by Greshnov with a skeleton key before they enacted the kidnap. Forrad, Richmond saw the metallic-lime-green *Mercedes Benz 600 Grosser* parked across the street, its right-hand back door opening as the Russians pushed him towards it. Pressing his noggin inside, their captive became confronted by Austerberg.

"Good evening, Mister Richmond. Glorious weather we're having."

"What do you want?" he blathered.

"Ahh, it's Miss Claudette and Miss Kim who want to see you." Patting Richmond's arm, after Greshnov pushed him in to sit beside his boss, Austerberg pronounced, "They seem to be far more persuasive than Viktor and Stanislav at getting information without resorting to crippling their victims."

About to retort, Greshnov cut him off with a slap to his face, then blindfolded him.

"Just a precaution," Austerberg justified. "Should you come out of your interrogation with the ladies alive, we don't want you knowing where you've been. Incidentally—" He dallied as if making inward consideration. "Did you and your colleagues help Mustapha Tawfik-Nasseri escape from his confinement in my basement pit?"

"Who?" Richmond bluffed.

"An Arab gentleman I was trying to persuade to assist us in a treasure shadowing endeavour."

"No. Your line of conviction is mistaken and misguided. I have no idea what you're talking about."

"Hhmmm, I wonder."

*

As the *Grosser* accelerated away, Richmond felt himself shifted back on the seat. Kick-starting his mental processes, he wondered if they'd take him to the same large, nineteenth-century townhouse on Chem. de Beau Rivage, where he and his chums had rescued the Arab? Twenty minutes later, the executive carriage came to a stop, the Russians manhandling him out of the car, up a short flight of stairs, through a door, along a corridor, and into a room. Sitting him on an ornate chair, they then removed his cuffs and bound his arms and legs to the chair with rope.

When the blindfold was removed, he squinted under intense light and wriggled in an attempt to free himself.

"Relax, Colby," he heard a soft voice say.

Acclimatising to the luminescence, he distinguished the mischievous features of Claudette Ducal, her head inches away from his, and beyond her, Kim Lindberg lazily leaned against a wall.

Although coming from a well-off family, after leaving the American International School Saltzberg with a high-school diploma, Kim Lindberg recoiled at the prospect of nine-to-five-thirty work as a means of earning a crust. She wanted to get independently rich quick and live the high life. A natural actress to accompany her man-devouring cuteness, she became a con-artist, relieving male dupes of their valuables. Sensitive to the inherent riskiness of her adopted vocation, in parallel she acquired martial arts credentials as a means of defending herself. Notwithstanding, caught in the act by an infuriated Bolivian narcotics baron, she would have met her end if not for the intervention of Austerberg. A guest of the drugs bigwig at the time she pulled the con, he was impressed by her audacity and persuaded the mogul to spare her. Seduced by Austerberg's vision of rich pickings, she joined his illicit baubles-stalking clique.

Richmond clocked that both seductresses were attired in raven-black, eighteen-denier nylons suspended from figure-hugging black and red basques, red panties, and six-inch, high- heeled patent black court shoes — classic dominatrix *femme fatale* outfits. Also logging he dwelt in a Regency-styled room with Louis XVI furniture and accoutrements including two other chairs placed opposite him, eighteenth-century portraits, and highly polished walnut hardwood flooring, he deduced he had been deposited in the Chem. de Beau Rivage townhouse.

"Now," Claudette continued, as she straddled him and pushed her more than adequate traffic stoppers into his chest, her *Eau de Givenchy* perfume wafting into his nostrils, "we can do this the nice way, or the painful way." Glancing at her partner in seduction, she then delineated, "Kim may look like pure eye-candy, and palpably she can please, but behind that girly facade lurks a feline psychopath who loves to torment men."

"What about you?" he impishly quizzed.

"Oh, I can either caress you, or make you suffer as well."

"Really," he curtly replied.

As she dismounted him then stood facing her victim, Kim stepped over to stand next to her partner in sadomasochism. Gleefully sparkling at each other, they then sat on the chairs opposite Richmond, crossed their man-devouring, long, shapely legs, and peered at him like vipers on heat.

"You don't seem to be scared, Colby," Claudette adjudged.

"Might be that's because I'm good at projecting an image."

"Hhmm, you used to be a girl magnet, quite the Don Juan - a judie hunter I believe is the term used in your native Royal Cheshire".

"Of course, you know everything about me, don't you?"

"Everything we can exploit. So…you were a ladies' man?"

"That was a long time ago. I've been happily married for the past thirty-years."

"Is the sex still good with Carolyn?"

"Better than ever," he shot back.

"Huh." She radiated at him. "I do admire loyalty in a man."

"What do you want?"

"We want to know if the Countess has found the clue leading to her Romanov patrimony. We know she has flown home to Australia. We also know she is due back in Geneva the day after tomorrow."

"Got influence at the airport, have you?"

"We have influence everywhere." She turned testy. "Enough jousting. Has she found a clue, and why has she gone back to the Land of Plenty?"

"I have no idea," Richmond refuted. "We know the Countess, as you call her, socially, but beyond that she has not taken us into her confidence with respect to other matters."

"Hah." She glared at him. "Do you take us for amateurs, fools? Do you really think we'd believe such crass lies?"

"Sorry, I can't help you."

"Hhhmm, we'll have to be more persuasive." The smile returned and broadened. "What say you, Kim?"

"Oh yes. This is the part I really enjoy. You'll tell us what we want to know before we've finished with you."

As Kim and Claudette put on lacey black gloves with poke holes to expose their fingers, Richmond wondered what the hell they were going to do - ruffle up his hair, tickle him to death, beat him with feather dusters? It soon became clear that the girls had another method in mind for extracting information.

"When was the last time that you had your wang thoroughly exercised?" Kim inquired.

"That's between me and my wife."

"Well, let's see if some rough handling can loosen your tongue."

Her eyes blooming with eagerness, Claudette released his belt, unzipped and parted his trousers, sprang his hampton holders beneath his scrotum, and liberated his joystick.

"My, oh my, Colby, I've not seen a specimen like that since Julius bought a prize-winning stallion." She glittered at Kim. "There's enough here for both of us to work on."

Candidly the status quo since his early teens, Richmond's Moby had a mind of its own when it came to the feminine touch. No matter how much he tried not to become aroused by Claudette and Kim massaging his member, nonetheless, it extended to its full length under their stimulation.

"Now, Colby," Kim began, "if you want this pleasuring to continue, tell us about the Countess. Has she found out where the Romanov horde is hidden?"

"I know nothing," he insisted.

"Very well," Claudette responded. "This delight will end in pain for you after you have shot your load. Why submit yourself to that ordeal? Just tell us what we want to know."

"I don't think so," Richmond retorted. "Do your worst."

After several minutes of incitement from the vixens, Richmond felt a gushing sensation in his python and shot off man-relish like Mount Vesuvius erupting, all over his dress shirt and bow tie. Not stopping at the summit, Claudette and Kim continued their stroking, the action beginning to distress him.

"*Aaaahhh,*" he agonisingly moaned.

"Oh dear, is that hurting?" Kim asked, pouting. "Tell us what we want to know, and the pain will be over."

Persisting with their torture, Richmond grimaced as the aching increased, his face contorting under the stress as he spat out more cries in response to the torment. Then nature came to his rescue, his spent Excalibur softening and resuming its non-excited dimensions.

"*Damn,*" Claudette blurted. "We'll have to employ more conventional measures. Go get the Tucker, Kim." Addressing a completely dishevelled Richmond, she sought, "Do you know what a Tucker Telephone is, Colby?"

136

"No," he managed to squeak out between deep breaths, trying to recover from the girl's handywork.

"A Tucker Telephone is a torture device based on an old-fashioned crank telephone. The electrical generator of the telephone is wired in parallel to two, twelve-volt dry-cell batteries. When the telephone is cranked, the electrical supply from the batteries is greatly amplified from twelve-volts to many thousands of volts by the generator, dependent on how fast the crank is rotated. The ground wire and the hot wire from the generator output terminals are connected to the victim under torture. I'm sure you get the idea."

Hearing spike-high-heel footsteps on the wood flooring to his left, Richmond turned his napper to see Kim returning with the Tucker Telephone mounted on a trolley. Glowering, he discerned he couldn't hold out for much longer without spilling the beans.

After connecting the ground wire to his deflated hampton and the hot wire to his left ear lobe, Claudette told him, "This is really going to hurt, Colby. If you don't tell us what we want to know, the pain will eventually result in permanent organ damage and mental health problems...even death."

She nodded to Kim to begin winding the torture contraption.

"*Shstop*," Richmond heard from a discernible Germanic voice. Twisting about to the source of the demand, to his everlasting surprise Heinrich Metzer came into his field of regard, pointing a pistol at the antagonizers.

"Who the hell are you?" Claudette burbled.

"You vill release Mister Richmond from his shackles."

Not impressed by having a shooter pointed at them, Kim and Claudette smirked.

"I varn you, I am very good with zhis *45 Auto Luger*, und I vill not hesitate to use it."

Unfazed, the girl's smirks widened as they moved towards the intruder. Equally adamant, Metzer let off a round at a nearby Edwardian-period crystal glass vase in reply. Obliterating it, the girls stopped in their tracks.

"Now, do as I say, or ze next round vill be fired at vone of you."

Spooked, their simpers turned sour. Retreating, Claudette and Kim obliged the *Obergruppenführer* by releasing Richmond from his captivity.

"Now, it is your turn to be bound and gagged," Metzer declared to the tormentors. "Colby, tie zhem into those chairs und gag zhem."

Doing his bidding after pulling up his trousers, Richmond fastened and secured the vindictive dames, then applied gags to them.

Examining the Tucker Telephone, Metzer then leered at the persecutors. "A useful device. I must have vone installed in my schloss." Turning to Richmond, he voiced, "Come on, Colby, let's get out of here."

Making their way out into the street, Richmond dialed Metzer's *Mercedes*.

"Climb in, Colby. I vill return you to your companions at ze casino."

As the *C63* pulled away, Richmond peeked back at the torture residence. Sure enough, it was the same house with a basement containing the pit and the pendulum he and his companions had broken into earlier in the day.

"How much of that circus did you see?" Richmond enquired, acutely aware of the embarrassing humiliation he'd been subjected to by Ducal and Lindberg.

"Put it zhis way, as Roger vill tell you, I am discrete. Do not be alarmed. Wot I saw is commonplace in ze financial services sector."

Raising his eyebrows at the confession, he then asked, "How did you know I'd been taken, Heinrich?"

"After our meeting at ze Brasserie La Riviera, I knew you Englishmen vould be in trouble. So, I based myself at a confidant's apartment in Morges, just a few kilometres from Lausanne. I have been covertly vatching you since."

"So you know about Devereux and Austerberg?"

"I photographed Devereux with my *Leica* camera and powerful telescopic lens combination, vhen he intercepted you at ze Mövenpick. Likevise, I photographed Austerberg vhen he left ze Casino Barriére after your first meeting vith him. Zhen, I sent ze digital images to another affiliate of mine in Frankfurt, who werks for ze *Bundespolizei*. He supplied identification details."

"Did this abettor have anything substantial to say regarding them?"

"Indeed. He said because Austerberg is viewed to be psychotic, you should avoid him at all costs."

"And Devereux?"

"Ahh. He is a man on a mission. He hopes to be Austerberg's nemesis. Again, ze advice is not to get in his vay, or you and ze others could be imprisoned." Tarrying, he then said, "I take it you Englishmen have made some sort of commitment to ze Countess?"

"You know Stephanie Nightingale is the Countess then?"

"I photographed Frau Nightingale vhen you met her and her musclemen in ze lobby of ze Mövenpick a few days ago. I had my *Bundespolizei* associate check-up on her as well."

"But how?"

"Oh, it vas quite simple. Ze *Bundespolizei* have access to ze *Bundesamt für Migration und Flüchtlinge*, zhat is German passport control. Zhey in turn have a reciprocal protocol to share data vith Sviss passport control. Ze photo I took of Frau Nightingale came up under ze registered passport of Countess Antoniya Katerina Kulikovsky." Glancing at Richmond, he added, "I couldn't get you any sooner, because zhose Russian thugs hung around outside ze house for a few minutes before driving off."

"No matter, Heinrich. I'm just glad you showed up."

When the *Mercedes* pulled up at the Casino Barriére main entrance, Richmond asked, "Are you coming inside, Heinrich?"

"No. It is best I remain in ze shadows. Should another mishap occur, be assured I vill be somevere in ze vicinity. Say hello to Roger and Gavin for me."

With that, Richmond closed the *C63* passenger door, and Metzer disappeared into the night.

~ * ~

"Where *the hell* have you been?" Fraser reeled off, as a rumpled

Richmond rejoined them at the casino bar. "We looked for you everywhere."

"I've just had a close encounter with Ducal and Lindberg, Austerberg's feline agent provocateurs. If it hadn't been for your pal Heinrich—"

"Heinrich!" Fraser interrupted.

"Yes, he figured we were in the mire that day he came down to the Brasserie La Riviera and has been keeping an eye on us ever since."

Aghast, Fraser blurted, "Well I'll be damned."

"Seems that there is much more to the *Obergruppenführer* than meets the eye," Anderson observed.

"Doubtlessly," Fraser praised. "I knew he had some military training prior to becoming professor in psychopharmacology at Heidelberg University and joining The Firm in 2002, but I had no idea he was capable of covert operations."

"A powerful piece of manpower," Anderson ranked.

"Quite."

"Anyway, Colby, tell us what happened?"

Subsequent to relaying his abduction, but missing out the fruity part, and his deliverance by Metzer, the Cheshire boys painted Austerberg to be very serious about purloining the Romanov cache.

"As the master criminal told us," Anderson reviewed, "by fair means or foul, he intends to walk away with the spoils, his abduction of Colby proving his point."

"Well, we can't just hide away in our hotel rooms," Richmond injected. "We'll look like lemons."

"Huh, after your intimidating escapade," Fraser babbled, "I'd assumed you'd want to call it off."

"No. If anything, Ducal's and Lindberg's shenanigans have honed my determination to stay with the Romanov episode to its conclusion. All we have to do is steer clear of the Austerberg set until Stephanie returns from down under."

*

Sure that the night had no more unpredictable clashes, nevertheless when the Cheshire boys entered the Mövenpick lobby well after the witching hour, they heard someone call, "Mister Anderson."

Revolving to the source of the appeal, Patrice Devereux came into their field of regard.

"Oh no," Anderson mumbled under his breath. "Not another set-to."

Sauntering over to them, the Swiss official quipped, "I understand that Mister Richmond had a heart-pounding standoff with the Austerberg gang this evening."

"How do you know that?" Richmond blurted.

"Nicole Steiner has been keeping an eye on you Englishmen."

"So she saw me being taken?"

"Yes. It was inevitable that Austerberg would try something. I did warn you that night at the Mövenpick, you were playing with fire."

"And she did nothing about it!"

"Mister Richmond, we are not the police. We have no power to intercept."

"But you could have called for the police."

"Yes, but that would have defeated my objective?"

"And what is that, Monsieur Devereux?" Anderson intervened.

"To allow you to see what you've got yourselves into."

Once more shocked by the act of fate, the vacationers gaped at the government man.

"Do I take that to mean," Anderson resumed, "you will do nothing about Austerberg and co plaguing the Countess and ourselves?"

"Certainly not, you Englishmen and the Countess have become bait. This evening Austerberg took a nibble. Next time perhaps he'll take the entire lure. If that involves contravening the Swiss treasure trove laws, I'll nail him."

"Before that happens," Anderson vociferously countered, "he could nail us!"

"Mister Anderson, the Swiss authorities are not forcing you to assist the Countess." Fanning out his hands in a gesture of surety, he certified, "You are free to leave the country at any time."

Not absolutely sure about their continued wellbeing, after

Devereux departed, leaving the foyer deserted apart from the Cheshire boys, they took soundings from each other apropos the passion play they'd become entangled in. How much of the unnerving rhetoric delivered by the Swiss functionary was designed to make them quit their alliance with Stephanie Nightingale? And how much erred towards a genuine sense of duty aimed at preserving their lives? Without knowing the underlying nature of Devereux, it became impossible to make a clean judgement.

Deciding to sleep on it, the threesome made tracks towards the foyer elevator. Halfway into their trek, they clocked the reflections of Zinchenko and Greshnov behind them in the glass partition between the restaurant and the snoozing night manager behind the reception counter. Closing in on their quarry, the hitmen indicated to them with their *Smith and Wesson 340PD* handguns to head down the ground floor corridor.

Herding the Englishmen through the Mövenpick's rear sliding doors, and into a dimly lit section of its car park, they anticipated their fate.

Chapter Fifteen: Last Roundup Part Two

... "*Wait*," Anderson barked. "You're making a big mistake, Herr Austerberg. Surely you know that Patrice Devereux has us on his radar, and if anything happens to us, you'll be receiving his calling card."

"Quite so, Mister Anderson. But he'll need proof of any wrongdoing, and we're sufficiently versed at covering our tracks to ensure we're not implicated."

Emerging from the night's dimness, Claudette Ducal and Kim Lindberg joined their leader, animosity covering their complexions.

"Go ahead, Julius," Ducal encouraged. "Waste them."

"Is this revenge for evading your torture?" Richmond bellowed.

"Ohh...nothing so base," Austerberg contradicted, as if he'd been insulted. "Quite frankly, it amused me that you managed to escape from Claudette and Kim, with some help from a third party. No, this is the pragmatic way of purging an irritant before it blooms into something less manageable."

"Okay, Julius, you've had your fun," the two groups heard from a source in the shadows.

Stepping forward into moonlight, Devereux, accompanied by Marco Brunner, materialised. "Put your weapons away, and let the Englishmen go."

"Patrice," Austerberg hailed, almost as if greeting a long-lost friend. "How good it is to see you again."

"You can dismiss the civilities, Julius. Just do as I say, then depart."

"You surely didn't think we were going to kill these Englishmen?" Austerberg teased, breaking into a broad grin. "We were just trying to impress upon them the futility of going up against a professional treasure-hunting clique. Come, come, Patrice, allow me a little latitude for putting the competition off the scent."

"We both know if I hadn't intervened, the Cantonal Police Corps would be checking the corpse for identification in the morning."

"Oh, you're being overly dramatic. I can assure you, nothing untoward would've happened to them."

"Enough of the parrying, Julius. We both know what you're playing at." Advancing towards the criminal maestro, he tattled, "Now, if you wish to sustain your freedom, retire and leave, or I will call the police and have you arrested for threatening behaviour."

Opening his arms and pushing his bottom lip forward in a mime of complete innocence, Austerberg then guaranteed, "Very well. We will be away." Sermonising to his clan, he instructed, "Come ladies and gentlemen. I'm sure we can find some distractions to amuse us at the Casino Barriére."

With that they strolled to the *Grosser* parked on the far side of the car park, and were gone within seconds.

"Why didn't you call the police?" Anderson clamoured, clearly annoyed with the Swiss civil servant. "You really *could* have had them arrested on charges of witnessed threatening behaviour."

Smiling, Devereux replied, "I'm sure you can work that out for yourself, Mister Anderson."

Chapter Sixteen: The Bank

Early the next morning, Anderson's room phone rang, bringing him out of slumber.

"Gavin Anderson," he murmured, still half asleep.

"It's Stephanie Nightingale. We're back."

"Earlier than forecast," he trilled, sitting up and fully awakening.

"Fortunately, we were able to catch an earlier flight."

"Will the provenance documentation stand up to scrutiny with the bank?"

"Yes. Andrey has some hereditary credentials. He told my father they are written and-or printed on the pictured water-marked paper and have the necessary wording and signatures."

"Then we're in business."

"Indeed, thanks to you and your friends. Meet me in the lobby in an hour and bring the envelope with you. We'll then mosey on down to the Banque Cantonale Vaudoise."

Assembling adjacent to the reception station, the Cheshire boys met up with Stephanie and her minders. She'd dressed appropriately for the occasion, adorning herself in a black, *Chanel* two-piccc, business suit, cherry-blossom-pink ruffled blouse, electric black pantyhose, patent black, four-inch, high-heeled court shoes, and a flamingo pink, wide brim hat, worn at a jaunty angle.

"You have the regalness of royalty today, Stephanie," Anderson complimented, as he handed the fabled envelope to her. "Or should it be Countess?"

"Thank you, Gavin. I think Countess today." She angled her noodle so she could view towards the hotel entrance. "No doubt Austerberg and Devereux will have us in their sights."

"Probably," he concurred. "Austerberg took Colby last night."

"What!" she screeched, gazing at Richmond. "Did you tell him anything?"

"No. Roger's colleague, Heinrich Metzer, rescued me. He's really become our guardian angel."

"Yes, Heinrich is probably watching Austerberg and Devereux watching us," Fraser supplemented.

"Did Austerberg hurt you, Colby?" she enquired, stepping towards Richmond, an anxious goggle adorning her face.

"Only my ego, and that was by unrequited courtesy of Ducal and Lindberg," he divulged, smiling.

"We also had a close encounter with Austerberg," Anderson exposed. "However, let's not get embroiled in that unwelcome contretemps."

"As well as being smart, I can see my English friends are brave," she replied, complementing with a twinkle. "Okay gentlemen, let's get to the bank."

Climbing into the *Range Rover* and the *BMW M5* respectively, the two parties drove to the Banque Cantonale Vaudoise at Placé Saint-François 14, 1001 Lausanne. Knowing they would be followed, neither coterie bothered to even monitor for the other interested litigants.

An imposing, three-storey, regency-style building in origin, without any close-by neighbouring edifices on Placé Saint-François, the Banque Cantonale Vaudoise location contributed no scope for those pursuing the Countess and her combine to take up hiding positions. When the *Range Rover* and the *M5* pulled up outside the bank, and their occupants alighted, they saw the metallic-lime-green *Mercedes Grosser* stop behind them six car lengths away, and on the opposite side of the *strasse*, a white *Audi A5* saloon came to a halt, Anderson swiftly recognising Devereux in the back seat, intensely gazing at them.

"Come on," the Countess counseled. "Let's do it."

If the exterior of the Banque Cantonale Vaudoise could be classified as distinguished and regal, its inside retreat also fell into the portentous domain. An exercise in financial seduction, it reflected the industry's' universal status quo benchmark, generating the necessary kudos and longevity the bank wished to portray to clients. Everything about the edifice spelt the hallmarks of banking protocol – stability, reassurance, discretion. Anderson noted a very high ornate ceiling on the ground floor, coupled with an oak bank teller counter snaking into an oblong shape denoted the demarcation into the middle office. Marble stairways and eighteenth-century portraits festooned the interior, wrapping up the grand core. Millions of transactions had been processed by generations of tellers for 168 years, their suit sleeves and shirt cuffs shining the service counter into a brilliant reflecting medium. Soaked in ambience and symbology, it represented the same bedrock of commerce he had first seen in London's square mile of eighteenth and nineteenth century buildings housing investment banks when he represented Oxalite, before many of them moved to Canary Wharf.

Walking up to a vacant teller station with her entourage behind her, the Countess felicitated, "Good morning," in a sensuous, cultured voice. "I'm here to collect items in the account number 84612094."

"You are ze owner of zhis account, fraulein?" the teller responded.

A dapper, smallish man with a receding hairline, wavy mustache and dressed in a morning suit, he reminded Anderson of David Suchet's Hercule Poirot portrayal in the T.V series of the same surname, based on Agatha Christie's creation.

"I'm the authorised representative of the inheritor."

"Vhot is ze name on ze account?"

"N. Romanov."

"Ze late Czar?" he tested, his countenance changing from *de facto* bank standard neutral into a slightly more stimulated regime.

"Indeed."

Applying twenty-first-century technology, the teller keyed the account details into a computer terminal, bringing up the account credentials on a monitor.

"Zhis account vas taken out on ze 19th April 1917, by a General Losif Bodrov, on behalf of Czar Nicholas II of Russia."

"Correct. I need access to the account's contents."

"Ahh, I see. In zhat case, you vill need provenance documents and identification. Vot is your name, fraulein?"

"I am the Countess Antoniya Katerina Kulikovsky."

"And your identification?"

She handed over the passport bearing her real identity.

"And ze documents of provenance."

Giving the teller the deeds from Czar Nicholas II, her great grandmother, the Grand Duchess Olga Alexandrovna of Russia, her grandfather, Guri Nikolaevich Kulikovsky, and a letter of authority signed by her father, Leonid Nikolaevich Kulikovsky, witnessed by the manager of the Commonwealth Bank Darwin, he examined the documentation, his pulse rate not varying, as if such claims were a regular occurrence at the bank.

"Zhis all seems to be in order, Countess. My name is Herr Schäfer. I am ze bank's senior teller. Please follow me to ze vault."

Maintaining her cool and not displaying any signs of relief, along with her cortege she followed Schäfer. After keying-in the access code to a security door, he then led them along a corridor, and down a flight of steps into the bank's basement vault chamber. Forward of the advancing troupe, she saw two-armed security sentries standing either side of an outer steel bar matrix containing an integral locked door. Beyond, lay the vault, its giant, circular, high-tensile, reinforced steel door already open, and its vault wall beneath the door width lowered to ground level with a steel plate over the dropped wall, allowing clients access to safe deposit boxes.

Escorting the Countess and her intimates into the much larger than they visualised inner sanctum of the vault, Herr Schäfer indicated to safe deposit box 84612094, then stood in the wings to give her privacy.

Inserting the key from the envelope, she tentatively turned it twice to release the locking mechanism, and pulled the box forward to reveal another envelope fastened with sealing wax and embossed with the Banque Cantonale Vaudoise brand. Taking the sheath, she showed it to Schäfer.

"In all my years at ze bank," he recalled, his peepers opening wide, "zhis is ze first time I have seen a Banque Cantonale Vaudoise brand seal on a client envelope."

"What does it imply?"

"If my understanding is correct, it means ze client has arranged special vault facilities vith ze bank management for votever was deposited in 1917."

"Can I open it?"

"Of course, Countess."

So old, when she applied a little pressure to the seal, it easily sprang open. Extracting the paper inside, she read out its contents.

"This document confirms that Herr Karl Gunther Dietrich, Manager of the Banque Cantonale Vaudoise at Placé Saint-François 14, 1001 Lausanne, has agreed with General Losif Bodrov, client representative on behalf of Czar Nichlas II of Russia, to store the following items deposited in the bank's secure vault annex by General Bodrov.

"One: two chests, each seventy by fifty-five by sixty centimetres, containing unlisted valuables.

"Two: one chest, sixty by thirty by thirty-five centimetres, containing unlisted valuables."

She then removed three small keys from the envelope. Cocking her attic up, she gazed at Schäfer as if seeking guidance.

"Ahh," he knowingly began. "You vill need special permission from ze current bank manager, Herr Sander Lindemann, to enter ze vault annex."

Using the bank's internal phone system, Schäfer called Lindemann from a telephone on the outside of the vault's steel bar line, informing him about the special situation and asking him to lend his presence to proceedings. Shortly thereafter, the Bank Manager materialised in the vault, Schäfer introducing him to the Countess, she reciprocating by making all-round affiliate introductions.

Somewhat larger than Schäfer, but again possessing a receding hairline, wavy mustache and attired in a morning suit, Lindemann emanated an aura of permanence, calm and tact from the off – qualities presupposed by clients. His projected deportment signalled a capacity to grapple with any issue without becoming authoritarian or supercilious, his tone safeguarding premium service without tedious bureaucracy. In short, the very incarnation of the high-powered, low on red tape financial services operator.

"As vell as Herr Schäfer," Lindemann assigned, "zhis is ze first time I have been called upon to grant access to ze vault annex by a client, Countess." Glinting at her, he pronounced, "Zhis is a monumental event in my experience."

"Vhy, I mean why, Herr Lindemann?" she corrected.

"Because usually vhen deposits are stored in ze vault annex, zhey are never reclaimed. Regrettably, zheir owners pass on vithout making settlement for a dependent to inherit." Halting, he scanned around the gathering. "Countess, you appear to have a lot of auxiliaries supporting you."

"Yes, I didn't want to take any chances apropos security."

"Very vise. Now—" He turned to Schäfer. "Can you retrieve ze key to ze vault annex from ze security sentries?"

"At vonce, Herr Lindemann," Schäfer assented, glowing at the prospect of retrieving an item from the vault annex.

Returning with a very large key, Schäfer handed it to the Bank Manager.

"Come," Lindemann dictated, "let us proceed to ze vault annex."

Walking ahead of the convoy with Schäfer at his side, he led them to the front of the inner vault, housing yet another reinforced-steel door. Applying the key to its keyhole, he turned it three times, then pulled the door open by its handle. Reaching inside, he threw a switch, the sacrarium becoming bathed in fluorescent light. At least four times the volume of the previous chamber and housing a collage of boxes, trunks and other receptacles, as she entered, the Countess gasped at its size and numerous contents.

"Now Schäfer," Lindemann instructed, "ve are scouring for items vith ze account name imprinted upon zhem. Everything is stored in account name order, starting vith A on ze left of ze annex. I vould suggest R for Romanov is at ze far right-hand corner."

Going forward, Schäfer muttered the names he came across before finally happening on three chests marked, N. Romanov, Account Number 84612094.

"I have zhem," he called back.

Moving forward at pace and stopping next to Schäfer, the

Countess and her companions eyeballed the three chests as if mesmerised. Dissolving their absorption, Lindemann suggested that the Countess empowered Schäfer to open the trunks on her behalf. After she had handed him the three small keys, everyone craned over the bank teller anticipating something wonderful to be uncloaked.

"I vill begin with ze smallest vestibule," Schäfer stipulated.

Twisting the key and releasing the chest catch, he opened its lid to expose eight sparkling, jewel-encrusted, elliptical gold objects separated by a matrix of soft packaging.

"*My god*," the Countess murmured. "The Czar's Fabergé eggs."

"Let's see vot is contained in ze other trunks," Lindemann directed. "Schäfer, if you please."

Moving in closer, the party awaited the openings with bated breath. When the bank teller completed the actions, everyone stared at the two trunks teeming with gleaming gold rouble coins, appearing like they had been freshly minted the same day.

Overcome with the scale of the find, the Countess requested a chair, Schäfer obliging her with one of the chairs used by the vault security contingent.

"This haul is far larger both in value and weight than my father had envisaged," she testified. Raising her eyebrows at Anderson, she subjoined, "It could present a logistics and security bane withdrawing the treasure from the bank."

"Indeed." Facing Fraser, he asked, "What are we looking at in terms of monetary worth, Roger?"

"I'd have to check the today gold trading value. As for the Fabergé eggs, they could be worth millions."

"You werk in banking, Herr Fraser?" Lindemann catechized.

"Yes, I'm director of market analysis and trouble-shooter with The Firm in London."

"Ahh, ze fabled Firm, an investment house vith as much mystery surrounding its dealings as Goldman Sachs. Banque Cantonale Vaudoise has an association with ze Firm."

"Quite. I'm aware of the alliance."

"So," the Countess intervened, "what value would you put on the eggs, Roger?"

"The last time I examined the Fabergé egg market, they were valued between three to twenty-two million U.S dollars, dependant on the design and its provenance. I'd have to compare each egg with the latest Fabergé catalogue to gauge a more precise worth per egg."

"How about the gold coins?"

"Before coming out to Switzerland, the last trade value I saw in gold on the London Stock Exchange was about 823 pounds per imperial ounce, and falling."

"Falling!"

"Yes. This time last year, gold was trading at about 1,035 pounds per imperial ounce."

"Why the drop?"

"Gold's decline has been accelerated by a record-breaking bull run in U.S stocks. A string of stronger economic data soothed worries about wealth preservation and encouraged investors to seek greater gains in equities, considered riskier than gold, but nonetheless exhibiting higher trading yield."

"And the trend?"

"Based on historic factors, most probably, gold will continue to decline throughout the year and into 2014."

"I see." Turning to the Bank Manager, she requested, "Can you please have the gold coins counted and weighed, Herr Linderman?"

"Oh, most surely, Countess. Schäfer, see to it."

Two hours later, the bank's staff had counted and piled 550,967 coins from the two chests, each coin weighing 0.3086 ounces, with a summed weight of 170,028.41 ounces, equivalent to 139,933,389 pounds sterling based on 823 pounds sterling per imperial ounce.

In parallel, Fraser had requested Lindemann to provide him with a laptop with an internet connection enabling him to access a website citing current values of Fabergé eggs. On inspection, all the items turned out to be customised Fabergé creations never catalogued, the great artisan's stamp on each of the masterpieces signifying their uniqueness. As a comparator to judge their value, Fraser examined pages on the Third Imperial Easter Egg valued at twenty-million pounds, the Imperial

Coronation egg, valued at ten-million pounds, the Winter egg, valued at eight-million pounds, and other lesser-valued Fabergé eggs. All were housed in museums.

Overwhelmed by his examination, he excitedly advised the Countess that the probable value of each customised egg to be at least nineteen-million pounds, making a trading total of 152 million pounds.

"That means," she estimated, after the bank staff had summed the gold coins value, "the Romanov property is worth something approaching 292 million pounds."

"Shoot, your father could buy a pretty good Premier League football club for that amount," Richmond observed.

Completely going over her dome, the Countess's mind swam in a crucible of conflicting notions. How would her father react to the kitty value? More essentially, how could it be transported to Darwin without either Austerberg or Devereux intervening?

Gathering herself, she said, "Herr Linderman, I need time to consider what to do with the riches. Can we please retire to your office?"

"Certainly, Countess."

*

Still overpowered by the value of the Romanov fortune, the Countess sat in a deep-pile chair in the bank manager's top-floor opulent office, Sorensen and Kravets comforting her, leaving the Cheshire boys deep in discussion about the find, and Lindemann and Schäfer fervently dreaming up schemes to benefit the bank by offering services to the Countess.

Coming out of her entrancement, she adduced, "Gentlemen, we need to discuss a way forward."

Promptly proposing his bank act on her behalf, the Countess cut Lindemann off with a raised hand. "I appreciate your submission, Herr Lindemann, but—" She tarried. "If I take the bank into my full confidence, can you assure me that anything I tell you will reside confidential?"

"Unequivocally, Countess," he substantiated, his mannerism

denoting a binding commitment. "Ze Banque Cantonale Vaudoise has built its reputation on discretion vith clients. If necessary, I am villing to sign a non-disclosure agreement on behalf of ze bank."

"I can sense you are a man of your word, Herr Lindemann, so a non-disclosure agreement will not be necessary."

Going into chapter and verse about how the General Bodrov envelope had been passed down the Kulikovsky generations, the actions taken to evade communist agents and even assassinations, and of late, the threats posed by both Austerberg and Devereux to her retaining the mint, she impressed upon Lindemann the need for lateral thinking to extricate the cache from those seeking it for ulterior motives.

"I must confess, Countess," he responded at the conclusion of her story, "though ve are eminently versed in ze provision of client account secrecy, vhat you are seeking is beyond our intrinsic capabilities."

Dismayed by his response, she sank back into her chair.

"I have some ideas, Countess," Anderson submitted. "But first, can you review what your father is going to do with his inheritance?"

"Fundamentally, he wants to use any acquired assets for the building of a Romanov oriented museum in Darwin to house Russian antiquities."

"Good. How about if the gold is traded on the international stock market for Australian dollars, and you cut a trade-off with Devereux with respect to the eggs?"

"I could have The Firm take care of the gold sale using the Frankfurt office," Fraser volunteered. "Heinrich Metzer could function as the fulcrum point."

"Colby, you're the ace salesman," Anderson continued. "What would you recommend as a bargaining strategy?"

"Well, the objective is to ship the Fabergé eggs to Darwin by some means we are yet to identify. If the Countess removes the eggs from the bank, the moment she steps outside onto Placé Saint-François, Devereux will appropriate them on behalf of the Musée d'Art et d'Histoire as Swiss treasure trove.

"To obviate this happening, the Countess should call for an exploratory meeting with Devereux, followed by a second confab inside the bank, where he can see the eggs, but has no jurisdiction to seize them. She could tender one, perhaps two eggs to Devereux in return for a stamped and authenticated passage of exit from Switzerland with the residual of the eggs. If he is unwilling to comply, then the eggs will remain in the bank vault for eternity. There will be no winners."

"Will you help me with the negotiation, Colby," the Countess implored.

"Sure thing. It will be my pleasure."

"Excuse me, Countess," Lindemann intervened.

"Yes?"

"I hate to bring zhis up, but zhere is ze little matter of bank storage fees to be settled. Examining ze account file, it appears zhat General Bodrov paid for ten years storage up front. Zhat leaves eighty-six years of storage to be resolved."

Shimmering at the affable bank manager, she replied, "That's quite alright, Herr Linderman. What's the bill?"

"Schäfer, can you please oblige us."

Using the computer terminal on Lindemann's desk, he enlightened, "Ze basic cost in 1917 vas a hundred-and-fifty Swiss francs per year for ze three chests. By 1928…let me see…" He banged away on the terminal's keyboard. "…ze cost had risen to a hundred-and-sixty Swiss francs per year.

"Now…applying ze usual cost escalation formula for sixty-eight years, und taking into account currency exchange value fluctuations…mmmm." After performing the calculation, he peered at Linderman. "32,640 Swiss francs."

"Oh, that's a trifling sum compared to the worth of the gold," the Countess indexed. "We'll settle the account after the gold has been sold. However, before we can put any of these proposals into operation, I will need to telephone my father to seek his approval and authorisation. What time is it in Darwin?"

"Twenty-two, thirty," Sorenson supplied.

"Papa will still be up."

Making the call on her mobile phone, she discussed the overtures and options pertaining to the gold and the eggs with Leonid.

After completion, she shared, "My father fully endorses how we intend to dispose of the gold and mediate for the eggs."

"Good," Anderson praised. "Roger, can you contact Heinrich Metzer regarding trading of the gold."

"Okey-dokey. Herr Linderman, may I use your landline?"

"Happy to help."

Making the call to Metzer's smartphone, Fraser probed, "Where are you, Heinrich?"

"I am on Placé Saint-François in my *AMG*, spying on Austerberg and Devereux. Both are outside ze Banque Cantonale Vaudoise, eyeing each other surreptitiously."

"I have some gold trading business for The Firm's Frankfurt office. Can you take care of it?"

"Of course, Roger, but don't you vont your own London office to do the dealing for Ze Firm?"

"There are already too many parties involved in this Romanov venture. If I contact Equities Director Toby Chalcroft, he will want to inform VP Investment Banking Luther Bembridge. That could get very messy. Besides, I'm incognito, and Switzerland is in The Firm's Frankfurt office jurisdiction."

"Oh, I appreciate your position. However, if London Trading Floor Sales Manager Ricky Henshaw gets to know about zhis, he vill have ze kittens."

"Quite, but I'll take care of Ricky, if and when."

"Now, Roger, how much gold are ve talking about?"

"170,028.41 ounces."

"*Wot* did you say?"

"170,028.41 ounces," Fraser echoed.

"*Godt in heaven*, zhat represents a fortune."

"Inarguably," he fortified. "You will realise removal of such a vast amount of gold from the bank only invites an intercept from Austerberg. Hence, the gold will lodge at the Banque Cantonale Vaudoise during the trading period. Buyers of the commodity can either store their purchase at the bank, or withdraw it under the normal high-security conditions.

"I will have Herr Sander Lindemann, Bank Manager at Banque

Cantonale Vaudoise, issue a sell notice to The Firm at Frankfurt for your attention. When trading is complete, the funds minus the zero-point-two percent brokerage fees will be paid into a single client account using electronic funds transfer. I'll give you the account holder name, account number and sort code later."

"Zhis is very generous of you, Roger."

"Well, just make sure my name is not mentioned *vis-à-vis* the gold trading. As far as The Firm is concerned, this is a Frankfurt office initiative headed by yourself."

"Ze next time you come to Frankfurt, Roger, I vill personally treat you to ze best dinner you have ever had."

"Just so long as it's at a French bistro."

"Hah, still not got an appetite for ze German sausage and strudel?"

"I'm afraid not, Heinrich."

"Nevermind. Give me an hour to make some calls to Frankfurt, und I vill telephone you back on ze number you are calling from."

Finishing the conversation, Fraser fixed a collage of apprehensive faces in Lindemann's office. "We're on."

"How long is this effort going to take, Roger?" the Countess enquired.

"If Herr Lindemann can raise a letter of authority to sell the gold and send it by email to The Firm in Frankfurt straightaway, Heinrich will ensure Frankfurt notify the gold buying community. Trading will commence when the Frankfurt stock exchange opens for trading tomorrow at 08:00 local time. New gold sells like hot cakes, so despite the huge quantity, by close of business at 22:00, it should have all been sold." Pausing, he added, "If you so wish, Countess, you can monitor the transactions on Herr Lindemann's terminal, or your own laptop or smartphone."

"So to summarise," Anderson began, "The Firm's Frankfurt office will take care of the gold sale, and with Colby's assistance, the Countess will haggle with Devereux for the Fabergé eggs. The latter can be initiated after we leave the bank."

~ * ~

Restlessly milling around by their cars, on exiting the bank the Countess, her minders and the Cheshire boys instantly drew the attention of the Austerberg union and Devereux's team. Making a big show of opening their jackets indicating they concealed nothing, the opposition displayed disappointed physiognomy.

Stepping over to the *Audi A5* with Richmond, Stephanie solicited, "Monsieur Devereux, could you spare me some time to discuss what we have found in the bank? It might be of interest to you."

"By all means, Countess," he replied. Surprised by the request, he stood bolt upright. "Would you care to meet me in my office at ten tomorrow morning?"

"That will be fine. As well as my minders, I will be bringing Mister Richmond with me."

"For what purpose?"

"Ohh…just to act as my confidante, should the need arise."

"Very well. At ten tomorrow," he reaffirmed, handing her his business card.

"This is the address of the main police station," she stated, slightly perturbed.

"Yes, it is also the address of the local Swiss Federal Office of Culture in Lausanne."

"I see."

"*Au revoir*, Countess."

Reversing to the opposite side of the street, Stephanie said to the Cheshire boys, "Let's have a wash up at the Mövenpick."

As the two parties got into the *Range Rover* and the *M5*, the Austerberg corps followed suit, Devereux and co watching them as the *Grosser* drove by the *Audi* following the Countess and the Englishmen. Always one for baiting authority, Austerberg had the gall to wave to the Swiss officials.

"*Le porc*," Brunner spat out. "One day his jesting and clowning will result in a monumental mistake, and we will have him behind bars."

A third-generation police officer, Marco Brunner had followed in the footsteps of his grandfather and father – both achieving chief inspector rank with the Cantonal Police Corps. Though young Marco had felt the same calling, he had an equal penchant for art. Caught between the two poles, he studied art at the University of Zurich before joining the Swiss Federal Office of Culture. Previous to the Romanov affair, he had gone up against Austerberg and got his fingers burnt. Peeved by the setback, the humiliation stuck, and he fabricated a major grudge against the master criminal. When the Romanov affair came into play, he jumped at the chance to support Patrice Devereux.

"Huh, don't be so sure, Marco," Devereux warned. "The Mincer has the luck of the devil. Besides, the angels are on his side, in the form of the Illuminati."

"He doesn't always work for the Illuminati," Zoe Weber cited. "Sometimes he is solo."

Weber had joined the Swiss Federal Office of Culture after Austerberg embezzled a priceless work from her father's private art gallery by renaissance portrait painter, Hans Besser, whilst masquerading as an antiques dealer. Though reported to the Cantonal Police Corps, they found no conclusive evidence that Austerberg had stolen the portrait. Incensed by the inequity, Weber vowed to bring Austerberg to justice. Underestimating the task, she had tried several times to nail the master criminal through the devolved command of the Swiss Federal Office of Culture. On each occasion, he had managed to slither from her grasp. Amounting to a vast understatement, jailing Austerberg became personal to Weber. She perceived her best chance lay in Austerberg going one step too far, and hoped the Romanov episode would provide that link.

"True," Devereux attested. "But determining that demarcation is near to impossible. From what I can gather, the Illuminati never confirm or deny, if they are involved in criminal activities. Thereby, Austerberg will always put on a front, substantiating he has masters beyond the jurisdiction of international law, meaning the Illuminati."

"Is there really nothing we can do to neutralise the Illuminati, Patrice?" Nicole Steiner questioned.

For Steiner, joining the Swiss Federal Office of Culture became her third choice for employment after she graduated from the University of Bern. Failing to secure the open posts of curator at the Skulpturhalle

Basel and the Centre d'Art Contemporain Genève, she turned to the Swiss Federal Assembly agency as a last resort to launch her career. Not initiative-taking like Brunner and Weber, she performed her duties to the satisfaction of the office but never got emotionally involved in the hunting down of criminal masterminds. She saw the office as a stepping stone to gain a security management post with one of the major Swiss museums or art galleries. When Austerberg appeared on the office radar in connection with the Romanov affair, she imagined if she were part of the team that put him away, that prized entry on her C.V would greatly enhance her ambition.

"That's something I've toyed with for more years than I care to remember," Devereux confided. "Whenever the Illuminati are involved in any undertaking, be it legal or illegal, governments, including our own, turn a blind eye to proceedings. The only way to obviate the Illuminati black angel effect is to catch Austerberg in the act in front of independent witnesses. That is where the Englishmen might come into play."

"How do you mean?"

"Sometimes the shadows are as important as the substance. If we allow Mister Anderson and his cohorts enough latitude to twist Austerberg's tail, maybe The Mincer will make a mistake, and do something rash in front of them."

"But that could lead him to killing them," Brunner interjected.

"Hah! I don't think so. They are civilians, bit players caught up by off-chance in the treasure-hunting arena. Austerberg only disposes of professional competitors. It might be more the case they will vex him to the extent whereby he will put them to sleep for a while. If that should occur, we will be on the spot to record the crime."

*

Whilst taking refreshments in the Mövenpick bar, Stephanie joyously remarked to Anderson, "I can't believe the initiative is now going so well."

"Yes, however, Austerberg will not give up so readily. He'll continue to monitor events before he makes his next move."

"But what can he do?"

"Well, without wishing to appear alarmist, if he gets to know the funds from the gold sale have been transferred to your father's Darwin bank account, he could change his ploy to kidnapping you for ransom."

"That has crossed my mind as well," Sorensen admitted.

"If that's the case," Richmond submitted, "he stands a good chance of being caught in the act by the Cantonal Police Corps, triggering imprisonment. That becomes your buffer, Stephanie. Even so, back in Darwin, it'd be advisable to beef up personal security for all your family."

"My father could use a fraction of the funds realised from the gold sale for that purpose."

"Good," Anderson applauded. "Whether Austerberg is jailed or not, he may decide to cut his losses and go on to the next caper. That appears to be his *raison d'etre*."

"Yes," Fraser supported. "Mustapha Tawfik-Nasseri can bear testament to that."

"Who?" Stephanie enquired.

"Ohh, just someone we came across during our brushes with the Austerberg gang," he categorised, not wishing to put complications in her mind. "You needn't be fretful."

"Now," Richmond began, "turning to the Fabergé eggs, Stephanie, have you ever done any trading negotiations before?"

Hesitating, she then admitted, "In truth, no."

"But you gamble, at the casino?"

"Yes."

"Have you ever played poker?"

"Some, while I was at Turner-Martin Enterprises in Sydney."

"Bartering business deals is a little like playing poker. You do not always need to have the strongest hand to win. It is your opponent who must *think* you have a winning hand, resultant from how you speak, what you say, and your body language."

"You're talking about bluffing?"

"Indeed. In the world of commerce, the seller must be prepared to walk away from a deal if the buyer becomes unreasonable in his aspirations. The very action of the seller packing up the transaction papers gives the buyer time to change his mind, if he truly wants to cut a deal. Be that the case, before the seller reaches the buyer's door to leave, he calls him back."

"And re-opens the parley?"

"Indeed. The seller-buyer interrelation is an age-old procedure conducted for well over two millennia."

"So these are the tricks of your trade used to gain the upper hand with Oxalite buyers," Anderson interposed.

"I knew you would seize on it, Gavin," Richmond cheerily testified. "However, balancing your indignation, be aware that Oxalite salesmen use the same selling model to finalise deals with Oxalite clients."

"Yes, you're right. I was being precious."

"Do you think Devereux could prove to be provocative, Colby?" Stephanie queried.

"Well, the good news is, civil servants worldwide tend not to have the sharpened mentality of buyers from commerce strapped with making a profit. Due to this, Devereux may fire up the motions, or conversely, prove to be a difficult customer. Hard to judge without prior comprehension of the gentlemen. But not to worry. We'll play it by ear and update our tactics according to how he responds to our proposal." Dithering, he offered, "I'll give you some coaching direction after we've had dinner."

Gilding the lily slightly so as to sustain her nerve, nevertheless Richmond's long track record in the seller-buyer forum from Marconi segueing to Brunswick Scorpio was littered with difficult powwows. Often deals were impacted not just by technical compliance and cost. Company internal and external politics including nepotism and personal favours could encroach into the buyer decision making regime. Frequently played when the confab had entered the final vinegar strokes, a demand from left field could furnish a significant ask to the seller. Sometimes it resulted in him walking away under direction from his corporate board, because the requisition lay outside the realms of business protocol or even contravened the law. Richmond had happened on such excesses doing business in South America and the Middle East, zones in which European and North American business etiquette and professional policy could be sidelined in favour of outside factors and third parties.

Whilst consummating an avionics upgrade programme award for Dowty with the Ecuadorian Air Force in Quito, covenant award became contingent on Dowty appointing the nephew of the procurement director at the Ecuadorian Ministry of Defence as Dowty's regional agent for South America. An unprecedented ask, not only did it involve terminating the current incumbent's contract, a man with over twenty-years avionics credentials. It'd also result in commissioning someone with zero avionics clout, his only ace being that he had befriended a lot of military contacts in Ecuador. A knotty dilemma for Richmond to settle, after consideration he acquiesced to a support agency role for the nephew covering Ecuador, Peru, Columbia and Venezuela, under the direction of Dowty's agent for South America.

On another occasion when wrapping up an I.T-based business process management system for the Bahrain National Oil and Gas Authority on behalf of the ACT Group, the chief buyer asked Richmond for not only a kickback, but also a penthouse apartment in London with hot and cold running hookers on call. An integral part of trading in Arab countries, the bung presented no consequential pickle, because it could be catered for as a line item in the contract under the title, 'consultancy fees.' Howbeit, the London pad aspects were totally out of court, the Richmond led team instructed to walk by their employer if the request could not be negated or substituted with a much less costly alternative. In due course, the parties settled on a weekend at the London Mayfair Hotel with access to high-class call girls.

Just two of a myriad of problematical pleas played during the closing stage, Richmond had got used to dealing with the demands in the course of his career.

Also, not immune to client out-on-the-rim requisitions beyond the bounds of the fundamental seller-buyer relationship, Anderson's sense of business ethics had been shaken when Third-World pharmaceutical distribution licensing authorities made it clear they required 'favours' in return for granting the licence. Needless to say, The Firm's London operation engaged Fraser in his troubleshooter role when conventional investment banking methods came up against a brick wall. Many of his escapades involved cutting deals well outside the realms of customary business protocol, the difference being, sometimes it involved facing off with the criminal fraternity with an attendant risk to life and limb.

Based on his impressions of Devereux, Richmond adjudged him to be a straightshooter, untarnished by temptation or personal greed. To prevail at their summit, he tallied that a very frank and open standpoint would be the only way to ensure that Stephanie departed Switzerland with the majority of the fabulous Fabergé eggs. That did not mean laying out all their cards before the Swiss official. Only those pertinent to the eggs. The gold coins could remain on the back burner.

Chapter Seventeen: The Trade-off

Energised by the project, the Countess and her minders plus the Cheshire boys were in Lindemann's office at 07:45 the next morning, crowding around his computer terminal. Already logged on to The Firm's Frankfurt office live gold trading application, they awaited trade opening at 08:00.

A few minutes beforehand, Fraser called Metzer on his mobile phone, the *Obergruppenführer* corroborating that after receiving Lindemann's sell instruction less than twenty-four hours earlier, Frankfurt had alerted the gold market to the sale.

When the market opened, gold was selling at 821 pounds per imperial ounce. At once a flood of buy orders on Frankfurt saw the price drop to 820.50 then 820 pounds per imperial ounce.

Disquieted, the Countess gawped at Fraser.

"Don't be jittery. What we will see during the first half hour of trading is a raft of smaller and speculative buyers as well as the corporate gold boys. Hence because it is a buyer's market the price will decrease. Later, when all of the Romanov gold has been sold, you will begin to see The Firm buying back gold from smaller investors, then selling on to the corporate level. During this part of the task the price per ounce will increase."

"Back to at 823 pounds per imperial ounce?" she enquired.

"Could go higher."

Often akin to a rollercoaster ride, over the course of a day, in value terms commodities trading could hit massive peaks and heart-stopping lows when a fresh batch hit the market. History substantiated speculative buyers only held the stock for a matter of hours, sometimes minutes to make a quick profit before selling on to a corporate buyer, or back to the trading house. Eventually, all the stock became sucked into the coffers of enterprise scale purchasers, its value incrementally increasing until the new batch had been fully absorbed into the primary business layer, where its trading price stabilised.

Richmond and the Countess hung around the computer terminal until gone nine, then departed the bank for the Devereux meeting with her minders in tow.

~ * ~

Entering the police main building, the Countess asked the reception officer for the Swiss Federal Office of Culture. Directed to the second floor, Richmond recalled the last time he had been in a police station, it ended badly.

While at IBM, Joel Kitson, a fellow colleague, had been hauled in after becoming involved in an altercation with anti-capitalist demonstrators, who had invaded a dinner at Grosvenor House given by Parnell-Sargent plc, an international consortium with vast industrial interests. Overcoming meagre security, the activists forced their way into the event shortly after Parnell-Sargent CEO, Warren Gifford, had opened his speech subsequent to over 400 attendees including Richmond and Kitson feasting themselves on a sumptuous dinner. Rampaging around the gathering, they overturned tables, threw eggs at the diners, and attacked anyone opposing their onslaught. Incensed, Kitson laid into two agitators after they had punched him in the face just as London's finest raced into Grosvenor House to quell the fracas. In the free-for-all, Kitson got carted away with others for a night in the cells on charges of disturbing the peace. Twitchy about his workmate's continuing freedom, Richmond had followed the miscreants to Kensington Police Station, saying to the desk sergeant that Kitson had only defended himself under attack. Contentiously, the plea had no effect. Kitson was fined 300 pounds and bound over at a later magistrate's court hearing, the resultant publicity coming to the attention of IBM resulting in his big blue career halting at regional sales director level, Richmond ruminating a huge injustice had taken place.

Despite coaching Stephanie on settlement technique, and assessing Devereux to be a faithful man, he now wondered what unforeseen iniquities might take place within the Swiss officer's jurisdiction.

"*Bonjour*, Countess," Zoe Weber felicitated, drawing the visitor's attention as they trundled into the Swiss Federal Office of Culture, also registering Marco Brunner hovering in the wings. "Monsieur Devereux will be with you shortly." Peering at Richmond, she appended, "I understand you had a close up and personal *tête-è-tête* with Claudette Ducal and Kim Lindberg."

Raising his eyebrows, he retorted, "I didn't realise Swiss Federal Office of Culture intel extended into clandestine consultations, until your boss intercepted us on the same night confessing Nicole Steiner had witnessed my abduction."

"Like Austerberg, we keep our ear to the ground when it comes to recovering treasure trove. All your movements, and those of your English affiliates, have been duly noted."

"Did you know in advance what their intentions were?"

"*Hah*, with complete certainty. Claudette's and Kim's persuasive talents with men are well known in plunder scavenging circles. Based on previous clashes, we calculated at some stage Austerberg would inevitably play that card with one of you Englishmen." She beamed at him. "You seem to have survived intact."

"But for the intervention of a friend, I could have been killed."

"Yes, Herr Metzer — a resourceful redeemer."

"You know about Heinrich?"

"When are you and your chums and acquaintances going to accept nothing escapes us," Brunner pressed. "We know as much about the Romanov affair as Austerberg. The difference being, we are legal, whereas he operates on either side of the law."

Hearing the office door being opened drew Richmond's attention, while Stephanie and her minders were still taking in Weber's last statement.

"Ahh, good morning, Countess," Devereux greeted, as he came into the office. "I must apologise for the lateness of my arrival. Matters of State you understand. I trust that Zoe and Marco have been taking care of you?"

"They've most assuredly been doing that," Stephanie cryptically vouched.

"May I enquire as to why Mister Richmond is chaperoning you?"

"As I said yesterday, he's acting as my confidante, adviser if you will."

"I see."

Sitting down at his desk, he wafted an arm out, beckoning the visitors to take seats on the opposite side of the desk. "Now, what can I do for you?"

"I'd like to discuss a proposition with you," she forwarded.

"I see. And what kind of a proposition are we talking about," he probed, bringing his hands together and interlocking his fingers, as if the action riveted his concentration.

"The kind where both of us benefit from what I have inherited from a safe deposit box at the Banque Cantonale Vaudoise."

"Hhmm, we appear to be talking about Swiss treasure trove."

"No, the heirloom of my father, Count Leonid Nikolaevich Kulikovsky, son of Count Guri Nikolaevich Kulikovsky, and grandson of Colonel Nikolai Kulikovsky and Grand Duchess Olga Alexandrovna, younger sister to Czar Nicholas II of Russia."

"No doubt you produced the necessary documentation to the bank with reference to your ancestry and provenance to the Romanov stash?"

"Indeed."

"Unfortunately, Countess, as explained to your English allies a few days ago, under Swiss law, treasure trove not claimed by the rightful owner after fifty years from deposit in a Swiss bank, belongs to the State."

"So I understand. Albeit, you have no authority to enter the bank and claim the cache. It is only when I withdraw the legacy and step out onto the street that it comes into your domain."

"Correct."

"Well, if I leave without what we have discovered in the bank vault, neither of us will gain anything, will we?"

"True, so what is it you wish to discuss?"

"A reciprocal deal."

"What exactly are you referring to? I won't say your inheritance for obvious reasons, rather what is your find?"

"Eight Fabergé eggs, customised for Czar Nicholas II."

"And what is your proposal?"

"In return for you guaranteeing my safe passage out of Switzerland unhindered by the authorities—" She glanced at Richmond, the Englishman nodding in response. "I will devote one egg to the Swiss Federal Office of Culture to go on public display."

"And you retain the other seven eggs?"

"Yes."

"Hardly an equitable proposition, Countess. It goes against the grain and could raise hackles in ministerial circles. Public administrations expect to come out as foremost winners in all traffic of this nature. At the very least, the Swiss Federal Assembly would want forty percent of the find."

"That is over three eggs," she remonstrated. "I can't justify such an offset."

"Then I cannot guarantee you will leave Switzerland with any of the eggs."

"Then we have an impasse."

"Yes," he validated, raising his eyebrows as if he had the upper hand.

"Looks like the Romanov customised Fabergé eggs will never see the light of day outside the bank." She glinted at her companions. "Monsieur Devereux is playing hard ball. Come, gentlemen," she urged, Richmond smiling narrowly and gesturing his approbation.

As the visitors reached the office door, Devereux hailed, "Wait," Stephanie and co rotating about and staring at the bureaucrat with poker faces. "Let me see if I can persuade my superiors to accept *two* eggs, in return for your unfettered passage out of Switzerland with the remainder. But first, I will need to see them."

"Excellent," Stephanie responded, her entire being doused in gratification. "It will be our pleasure. I intended to make that offer anyway."

~ * ~

Accompanying Stephanie and co to the bank, Devereux and Brunner inspected the eight Fabergé eggs in the vault annex. Anderson stood by should he be needed, while independent arbiter, Sander Lindemann, verified that the Countess's provenance documents were in order authenticating her father's title to the gems. He also certified that the jeweller's mark on each egg was indeed that of Peter Carl Fabergé.

Displaying no emotion, let alone elation at the sight of the unique riches, Devereux accepted the bank manager's judgements.

"So are you satisfied with my claim, Monsieur Devereux?" Stephanie pushed.

"Yes, Countess. Your documentation is perfectly valid."

"Good. Can we go ahead with the pact?"

"Erm," Richmond began, attracting everyone's attention. "Excuse me, Countess." Stepping forward, he said to Devereux, "Could you have a settlement document drawn up by the Swiss Federal Office of Culture apropos the shares of the spoils, and the Countess's warranted, hindrance-free exit from Switzerland?"

"If you really think that is necessary, Mister Richmond."

"Best to be business-like to ensure the arrangement is watertight." Dwelling, he then annexed, "Could you also make sure the document is countersigned by the minister with portfolio for the Swiss Federal Office of Culture, and bears the Swiss Federal Assembly seal?"

"Very well," he agreed, his tone slightly peeved in recognition that Richmond knew his onions. "I'll need a few hours to transact the covenant. Perhaps you could return to my office this afternoon?"

"It'd be our pleasure," the Countess avowed.

After Lindemann had escorted the Swiss officials off the premises, Stephanie and Richmond reviewed the turn of events with Anderson.

"Not as bad as I presumed," she professed. "I imagined beforehand Devereux might give us a hard time, but he seemed to acquiesce to our point of view very quickly."

"Yes, I too foresaw him applying the metaphorical thumbscrews, and the conference lasting hours" Richmond complemented. "I can only conclude he has run this type of arbitration before, and has already worked out the end game. The only bugbear I can envision is the minister not playing ball."

"Is that likely?" Anderson questioned.

"Well, Devereux works in the real world and appears to have some latitude with respect to apportion mediation. If the minister is typical of politicians, he may adopt a different attitude. Procrastination might come into play."

"Why?"

"Associated political factors. Wheels within wheels — is it in line with national policy? Will it leak out into the public domain, causing embarrassment to the government? In the rarified world of national governance, the possible reasons are endless. Most are designed to keep those in power free from accusations of ineptitude and incompetence culminating in resignations."

"So, you're saying," Stephanie interpreted, "if the agreement can be bonded to be kept under wraps, the minister will okay it?"

"Indeed, and here is where Austerberg could play a pernicious card. If he were to find out about the shell out, he could threaten to go to the press with the information."

"And that could be curtailed if both Devereux and I quickly consented to assign a share of the Romanov horde to the Swiss Federal Office of Culture?"

"Indeed. So security is tantamount in all our actions until both the gold is sold, and the egg deal is wrapped up. Austerberg must suspect something is going on, but just what, he is blind to. That's why I was taken. He hoped to learn about our intentions."

"Did Austerberg follow you to the police station?" Anderson examined.

"I'm not sure," Richmond acknowledged. "I kept an eye on the *M5*'s rearview mirror, but didn't see the *Grosser* following us, either going to the cop shop or coming back to the bank."

"Knowing his nature," Stephanie forwarded, "he or one of his gang would've been somewhere in the vicinity."

"Yes," Anderson upheld. "And if that is right, he must be trying to figure out what is going down."

"For sure, but let's not worry about that. It's conjecture anyway." Scintillating, she promoted, "Let's go see what's happening with Roger."

*

Hurrying to Lindemann's office, Stephanie then asked Fraser about the Romanov gold sale.

"The trading price has increased to 825 pounds per imperial ounce," he told her.

"Ohhh, splendid," she crooned. "Things are *really* starting to come together."

"I take it you had a satisfactory session with the Swiss Federal Office of Culture?"

"Yes, Roger. We cut a deal, and after Devereux inspected the gems in the vault, he is parenting the transaction documentation and authorisation."

"Wonderful," Fraser exclaimed. "Howbeit, we'll still have Austerberg to contend with when we leave the bank with your share of the eggs. And he will be in no mood for being a sweetheart when he hears about the gold sale."

"What!"

"Because of its remarkable value and provenance," Fraser vindicated, "the gold trade is already making news in general investment banking circles beyond the gold trading fraternity. Soon the media will catch on, and it will go viral."

"Oh no."

"Of course, since the final trade money will be electronically wired to your father's bank account from The Firm's Frankfurt office," he pledged, "there's nothing Austerberg can do to rob you of the earnings. Certainly not in Switzerland."

"From what I gathered about Austerberg from intel given to my father by Romanov sympathizers and Russian émigrés, his principal objective is the finding and selling of premium jewels and artefacts on the black-market. Coinage does not appear to be of interest to him."

"Coinage is more difficult to dispose of," Anderson labelled.

"And as we are seeing, creates a buzz and thereby possible questions from policing authorities. You can dispose of the gold with the certainty that you have produced the necessary provenance and identification to the Banque Cantonale Vaudoise. Thereby it's legal. Austerberg couldn't do that."

"Absolutely correct," Fraser verified. "Even if he had found the Romanov stockpile at the bottom of Lake Geneva, the logistics of getting it to a buyer undetected, even inside Switzerland, would've been difficult to conceal from the authorities. Particularly so since Devereux has been spying on both Stephanie and Austerberg."

"Yes, I think all along his plan was to let Stephanie discover the horde, then deprive her of it. All that diving at the demarcation spots off Veytaux was merely to bear out Andrey had found nothing."

"So how will he attempt the heist?" Stephanie forwarded.

"Well," Anderson started, "it has to be between the bank and the Mövenpick, at the hotel itself, or during your trek to Geneva-Cointrin Airport. The first and the last options are out on the street, easily witnessed by passers-by with the police quickly called into action. However, the Mövenpick offers a more discrete environment to pilfer your share of the Fabergé eggs."

"How about if I airfreight them to Darwin and use an armed courier service to transport them to the airport."

"Mmmm. With the knowledge that Austerberg is well-connected via the Illuminati, he will probably be able to knobble either the courier service, airport personnel at Geneva and Darwin, or the airfreight service supplier itself." Pausing, he then prescribed, "No, the only sure way of undertaking the eggs will reach the security of your father's bank, is for you to transport them as hand-luggage, with Andrey and Nostro either side of you."

By no means a done deal, to Stephanie and her English confederates many permutations still existed potentially scuppering the caper, the awareness that Austerberg had various alternatives at his disposal to purloin the eggs ensuring the gambol abided in flux. Unlike the opposition, they had no overarching ultra-superpower to call upon to exert dominion over elected administrations, no inside intelligence gleaned from capturing and grilling a foe, and no real capability to counter-monitor the Austerberg gang's goings-on. The only assets in their favour amounted to Austerberg not doing anything contravening Swiss law and thereby being arrested by the Swiss authorities, and a humongous amount of luck coupled with maintaining their nerve.

~ * ~

Returning to the Swiss Federal Office of Culture, Marco Brunner and Nicole Steiner met the Countess and co in Devereux's office. Like Zoe Weber, Nicole took the opportunity to rib the Englishman about his toe-curling wrangle with the Austerberg sirens.

"I've heard that Ducal and Lindberg can be very persuasive with men to the point whereby they are never quite the same again, or worse," she provocatively quipped, her entire being drenched in foxiness.

"Yes," Richmond impishly responded. "I got that message loud and clear from your cohort, Zoe Weber."

She twinkled at Brunner with an air of satisfaction, knowing she'd touched a nerve.

"You must forgive Nicole, Mister Richmond," he begged. "The antics of Ducal and Lindberg have become quite a topic of folklore within treasure trove government enforcement coteries. We regularly exchange intel with our equivalent agencies worldwide. Austerberg's angels of delight are well recorded in the annals of numerous expeditions mounted by Austerberg and intercepted by agencies."

Sorenson whispered something into Stephanie's ear.

"If you have so much incriminating data on Austerberg," she subsequently raised, "why hasn't he been arrested?"

"He's very smart," Brunner conveyed. "Incessantly he is never quite caught in the act."

"But you and other agencies must have chased him."

"Oh we do, but suspicion is one thing, proof is another. He's become a bit of a 'Pink Panther' phantom to enforcement officers, always seeming to be one step ahead in the game."

"But surely he's been seen in the act of fortune searching."

Clive Radford

"Incontestably, Countess. But that act in itself does not break the law. It is only when the hoodlum absconds with the loot that he becomes the quarry of the authorities. To date, as well as a tidy sum of minor thefts or obtaining swag by way of extortion, we know Austerberg has appropriated ten to twelve major assets across the world and disposed of them to private collectors. This includes *Blossoming Chestnut Branches*, a Van Gogh painting stolen from the Foundation E. G. Bührle Gallery in Zurich in 2008. Nonetheless, without proof he remains at large."

"Can't you get him on un-declared earnings?" Richmond tendered.

"Reputedly, he has a residence in Albania, a country without any extradition accords. No doubt he contributes to the Albanian treasury, and they turn a blind eye as to where the funds come from. He has no visible accounts beyond Albania."

"Not even in Switzerland?"

"Ahh, yes, very possibly as a shell company or under a false name. But as you know, the Swiss banking fraternity is not fingered by our Federal Assembly, allowing, shall we call it, unique client banking facilities."

"So, what you're telling us," Stephanie initiated, "is Austerberg will tarry free so long as he plans carefully and is always in advancement of the law."

"Indeed, and he is far from the only criminal mastermind majoring in lucre hunting. We have a further fifteen dossiers on similar alliances with the same M.O. Often they compete for the same bonanza. That's when the fur flies and the corpse rate increases."

"And these other juntas are as equally adept at squirreling out of your clutches?"

"In the main, yes. These are not ordinary criminals, Countess. They are profoundly organised with multiple talents, well-connected, and unfailingly commanded by a gifted orchestrator, like Austerberg. Sometimes the soldier ants – that is the lesser members of the troupe – are caught in the act and brought to justice. But never has an adventurer mastermind been imprisoned. They are always astute enough to stay out of the limelight when the risk of detection becomes heightened."

"We do not hear about such criminal virtuosos in the media," Richmond recounted. "Is that because the chaser and the chased both wish to linger incognito?"

"You could say that Mister Richmond. Neither the perpetrators nor the authorities' thirst for publicity, because the crime falls into such an esoteric bracket."

"Don't you really mean the embarrassing bracket?"

"How so?"

"If my understanding is correct, these adventurer masterminds as you call them must target antiquities linked with governments, or government drives to acquire them. To prevent such duels becoming high profile when things don't work out in the national powers' favour, nothing is ever released to the media."

"You might think that. We couldn't possibly confirm such an accusation."

Just about to delve further into the vagaries of catching felonious wizards, Stephanie and Richmond were distracted when the office door opened, and Devereux joined them.

"I apologise for my lateness," he pleaded. "Gaining clearance for the planned barter became trickier than I had estimated." Sitting at his desk and casting a flustered eye at the visitors, he informed, "The Minister wants all the Fabergé eggs. He says because of their provenance to Czar Nicholas II making them quite unique, they should all be on public display in the Musée d'Art et d'Histoire."

Ashen faced, Stephanie coaxed, "And what did you say?"

"I told him, the eggs would remain at the Banque Cantonale Vaudoise for perpetuity if we did not make a covenant with you."

"And his response?"

"The Minister is a very upright man. He sees no colouration in right and wrong, just candid black and white. As far as Swiss law is concerned regarding treasure trove, he is of the opinion there should be no latitude for negotiation."

"Countess, if I may?" Richmond requested.

She nodded.

"Monsieur Devereux, what kind of man is the minister? I can see he is righteous and honourable, but being a public dignitary, is he also ambitious, keen to see his name attributed to political successes?"

"Huh!" Breaking into a rapacious mien, he designated, "Mister Richmond, I am yet to meet a politician who is *not* ambitious and wants to see his name in lights."

"What's his name?"

"Herr Christoph Ravenstein."

"How about if Count Leonid Nikolaevich Kulikovsky were to agree to a plaque bearing the Minister's name being put on the display casing for the Fabergé eggs in his proposed Romanov Museum in Darwin. It could read something like — Displayed with the kind permission of the Swiss Minister for the Federal Office of Culture, Herr Christoph Ravenstein."

"Mmmm, an interesting proposition."

"He would also take the official credit for unearthing two Fabergé eggs once owned by the Czar, to be displayed in Musée d'Art et d'Histoire," Stephanie reminded Devereux.

"Yes, Countess. Put that together with Mister Richmond's suggestion, and maybe he will change his mind." Cogitating for a moment, he begged, "Please excuse me while I re-contact the Minister."

After the office door had closed, Brunner congratulated, "Very creative once again, Mister Richmond. I wonder what else you have in your box of tricks."

"Yes, show us," Nicole backed, radiating like a vixen, as she sidled over to Richmond. "Colby, isn't it?"

"It is."

"I can see why Claudette and Kim had such fun with you - brains and very handsome. I wonder if I'd have any success if I interrogated you?"

"I'm a happily married man, Miss Steiner, immune to the advances of wrecking sirens like yourself."

"Mmmm, pity."

When Devereux backtracked to his office, he entered exhibiting a broad simper.

"The draw of acclaim and distinction has appealed to the

Minister," he shared, showing them a signed and sealed document outlining the concordance set out by the Countess, and certifying her unrestricted exit from Switzerland with six Fabergé eggs.

Brimming with exultation the triumphant quartet were about to depart when Zoe Weber joined the coterie, closing the door behind her and leaning against it as if wanting to prevent their leaving. Her stony face indicated a twist in the saga.

"You didn't tell us about the gold coins, Countess," she thundered. Glaring at her boss, she specified, "The internet and broadcast media is rife with news about the sale of a vast amount of gold rouble coins on the international market, stored at the Banque Cantonale Vaudoise, and brokered by The Firm's Frankfurt Office. Must be part of the Romanov stash."

Retaining her customary cool, Stephanie replied, "Quite so. But gold coins do not come under the jurisdiction of the Swiss Federal Office of Culture."

"No, but they do by the Swiss Treasury," Devereux insisted. "It would have been courteous to tell us about the gold sale. The Minister is bound to find out."

"But he's already signed and sealed the deal," Richmond reminded him. "Wouldn't look good, if he were to renege on a ratified Federal Assembly bond."

Shaking his napper to convey his vexation, Devereux articulated, "Do not ever come back to Switzerland, Countess. We have long memories, and this episode will not be forgotten."

~ * ~

Throughout the trading day, the price of gold had fluctuated, then risen continuously as Fraser forecast, finalising on 827.50 pounds per imperial ounce at close of business, the Romanov gold realising 140,698,500 pounds. With brokerage fees of 2,813,970 pounds and the outstanding storage fee of 32,640 Swiss francs, equivalent to 23,239 pounds, the residual net came to 137,861,291 pounds.

"Based on today's exchange rate, that's 231,744,830 Australian dollars," Fraser announced, a few hours after Stephanie and co came back to the bank. "The Firm has transferred the balance to your father's Darwin account. Should be enough for him to build a pretty good museum to house the Czar's customised Fabergé eggs and other Romanov artefacts."

"It's much more than he had foreseen," she warranted.

"Now all that remains," Anderson determined, "is for Devereux to collect his two eggs, and us to get you to the airport tomorrow."

"He will be here shortly. Having found out about the gold sale, he's not happy."

"Him making the discovery was inevitable," Fraser notified. "Because of the Romanov connection, news of trading became explosive."

"I just hope the Minister doesn't have second thoughts *vis-à-vis* the agreement," Richmond conveyed. "Governments have been known to tear up contracts."

"That crossed my mind as well," Stephanie volunteered.

"Without meeting Herr Ravenstein, it's impossible to make a judgment pertaining to his nature. Being positive, let's assume he's driven more by the personal kudos he will receive for the two Fabergé eggs being put on display in the Musée d'Art et d'Histoire than standing on ceremony with reference to protocol."

As the hazy veils of dusk drew in, Devereux descended on the bank with his team and a passel of security guards. Escorting them down to the vault, Herr Lindemann made small talk with the ministry envoy, while the Stephanie camp stayed quiet.

"To say this is an unusual occurrence, Herr Lindemann," Devereux stated, "is an understatement."

"Yes, it is unparalleled in my own portfolio," he reciprocated.

"I don't suppose there is any chance you will allow the entire Romanov cache to pass into the hands of the Swiss Federal Assembly?"

"Zhat vould require a change in ze law, Monsieur Devereux. Such a change vould undermine ze Swiss banking industry, bringing about a vast reduction in investments and zhereby taxable bank revenues. It's knock-on effect to our economy vould be devastating. Last year, ze financial sector contributed an estimated eighteen percent of

Switzerland's GDP, und employed approximately 199,000 people representing nearly nine percent of ze total Swiss workforce. 139,000 of whom verk in ze banking sector.

"Long honoured by foreign nations, Swiss neutrality und national sovereignty have fostered a stable environment in vhich ze banking sector is able to develop and thrive. Currently, twenty-nine percent of all funds held outside ze countries of origin, sometimes called offshore funds, are kept in Switzerland. For example, in 2010 Swiss banks managed six-point-two trillion Swiss Francs." Dawdling, his expression became serious. "Can you begin to imagine ze taxable earnings ve contribute to ze Swiss exchequer by managing such a mammoth amount?"

"Yes, but Swiss banks have served as safe havens for the wealth, meaning money laundering, of dictators, despots, mobsters, arms dealers, corrupt bureaucrats and tax cheats."

"You may think zhat, Monsieur Devereux. I couldn't possibly comment."

"It is true that Swiss banks have a legal obligation to record the ultimate beneficial owners of all assets they handle worldwide. But doing so accurately can be tricky in jurisdictions where it's easy for third parties — specifically those further down the fiscal food chain — to mask off who the owners are. Thus, loopholes exist by means of the use of shell companies, trust funds, and proxy directors signing the paperwork without owning the assets."

"Again, I couldn't possibly comment, Monsieur Devereux." Innocently hunching up his shoulders, he set out, "All I can ratify is zhat under ze incumbent rules, banking institutions und cantonal authorities can only report vot is in zheir registers. Inquiring into ze origins of assets, or linkages between individuals, is not permitted."

"A most convenient get-out clause."

"Yes, but von vhich is highly beneficial to ze Swiss economy."

"Mmmm, I pictured you'd say something like that," he coldly remarked, grimacing. "Right, let's get on with it."

After transferring two of the Fabergé eggs into a ruggedised container brought by a Swiss Federal Office of Culture security contingent, Devereux handed over the signed and sealed document permitting Stephanie to leave the country with the remaining six fabulous eggs.

"As I said to you in my office, Countess," Devereux recapped. "Do not ever return to Switzerland."

"You have my word on that, Monsieur Devereux."

"Erm, excuse me, Monsieur Devereux," Anderson began. "Now that the document lays down the Countess's safe exit from Switzerland, can we rely on your office to protect her from a possible interception by Julius Fyodor Austerberg?"

Near to exploding at the further indignation, his face rippled with anger. "We will be in the wings, ready to intervene should the need arise." Hesitating, he appended, "I take it you know the Austerberg clan are lurking on Placé Saint-François?"

"Yes, they are never far from the Countess. Like hungry wolves, they are waiting to feast on the Romanov treasure."

"Quite." His expression relaxed from peeved to flurried. "I would advise a tact of heightened caution."

Chapter Eighteen: Austerberg Play's his Final Hand

After Devereux had departed the bank with his two eggs in tow, a little later Stephanie also made ready to leave, Nostro Kravets entrusted with carrying the original trunk now containing six precious Fabergé eggs.

Surrounded by the Cheshire boys, with Andrey Sorenson at her front, and Kravets by her side, the cortege stood on the steps to the Banque Cantonale Vaudoise main entrance. Behind them Lindemann and Schäfer nervously fidgeted with their ties as they peered left and right along Placé Saint-François. Night had fallen, and with it commerce had ceased for the day, the area near to deserted apart from the odd car careening by at low speed. To the group's right, no more than twenty-metres from the bank, the metallic-lime-green *Mercedes Grosser* lay in wait like a stalking predator.

"Be careful, Countess," the Bank Manager advised.

"We'll be fine, Herr Lindermann."

As the cavalcade took slow steps forward, the doors of the *Grosser* swung open, Austerberg and his cohorts alighting, Zinchenko and Greshnov pointing *Glock 17* guns at their quarry, Lindberg assuming her martial arts fighting position, Ducal glowing with menace, and their boss gleaming as if about to devour his prey.

Perusing in the opposite direction, Stephanie hoped to see Devereux and his team, but no one came into her field of regard.

"Hell's teeth. Trouble-shoot us out of this one, Roger," Anderson quipped to Fraser.

"I think this calls for something way beyond a silver-tongued solution," he responded.

"Come, gentlemen," Stephanie encouraged. "Let us not be intimidated."

As they started to move in the direction of the *Range Rover* and the *M5* parked on the opposite side of Placé Saint-François, the Austerberg led ring barred their way.

"So, we meet again, Countess," Austerberg rehashed, a pinch of bravado mixed with ill omen in his tone. "After our first rendezvous at Port Lausanne-Ouchy, you should have gleaned that my purpose is without latitude or compromise. Huh—" Scanning about his pack, he grinned. "You led us a merry dance when you took off from Lausanne creating the impression you'd found the location of the valuables. It was clever and convincing. Whilst we pursued you, your newly gained confederates sustained the search for the Romanov kitty. I thank you for doing our work for us, but now—" The grin turned sour. "We must relieve you of the Romanov Fabergé eggs. *Viktor, Stanislav.*" He nodded them forward.

"*Shtop*," Austerberg suddenly heard from a source behind them in the shadows, Zinchenko and Greshnov coming to a halt.

Emerging into the moonlight from his hidey-hole, the Cheshire boys right away recognised Heinrich Metzer, holding his *45 Auto Luger* in front of him covering the Austerberg coalition.

"May I know who has me at a disadvantage?" Austerberg nonchalantly summoned.

"Nevermind who I am. Drop your veapons, but do not turn around."

"Judging by your accent, you are German."

Alerting Ducal and Lindberg, the former chirped, "It's that damned kraut again. The one who rescued Richmond from our clutches."

"Less of ze insults, please. I vould hate to have to shoot you for incurring my displeasure," Metzer warned.

Taking a chance, Greshnov whispered something to Austerberg.

"*I repeat*, drop your veapons," he echoed. "Do not test me. As ze frauleins vill confirm, I am an exceptional marksman."

"Very well, mein Herr," Austerberg reacted. "Viktor, Stanislav, put down your shooters."

"And have ze Bruce Lee impersonator relax her posture," Metzer commanded.

"Kim, do as he says."

"Goodt. Now, you vill all climb inside your *Grosser*, and drive avay."

Completing the desired group action, Austerberg slid down the rear nearside window of the *Mercedes* and addressed Metzer. "No doubt, we will meet again, mein Herr." Twisting to face Stephanie and her confederacy, he supplemented, "Pleasure to see you again, Countess. I look forward to our next encounter."

"Give it up now, Herr Austerberg," Stephanie promoted. "The Romanov fortune is mine."

"Spoken without a trace of smugness," he complimented. "Nonetheless, we shall see."

As the lime green saloon took off down Placé Saint-François, Fraser trumpeted, "Heinrich, many thanks for your timely intervention."

"Do you know, Roger," he retorted, sauntering towards the plaintiffs, "I am getting really good at zhis cloak and dagger stuff."

"Herr Metzer," Stephanie called. "I've heard a lot about you from my English friends. Glad that practice lives up to the rhetoric. How can I ever thank you."

"You could start by offering me an extremely expensive dinner, Countess."

~ * ~

After Stephanie had booked flights from Geneva to Darwin for the following day and deposited the Fabergé eggs in the Mövenpick Hotel main safe, she left Sorensen and Kravets on guard duty armed with the *Glock 17* pistols relinquished by Zinchenko and Greshnov. Pumped up after their successful escapade, she and the Englishmen then took the *Obergruppenführer* to two-Michelin stars, haute cuisine restaurant, La Table du Lausanne Palace on Rue de Grand Chêne, less than a kilometre from the Mövenpick.

Once the diners had gorged themselves silly on baked Dover sole with alpine vegetables in a Bretonne sauce, Bresse poultry, foie gras and black diamond truffle pie, washed down with *Jean-Michel Gaunoux Meursault ler Cru*, followed by vanilla soufflé, *brie de meaux dongé*, coffee and liqueurs, they talked about the caper.

"I vas expecting ze Swiss Federal Office of Culture to intervene on your behalf vhen you exited from ze bank," Metzer cited.

"Mmmm, I agree," Anderson supported. "Devereux must have felt exceedingly miffed after finding out about the gold sale, so he left us to swing in the wind."

"Do you really think so?" Stephanie disputed. "Couldn't it be he had to ensure the Swiss share of the spoils were not purloined by Austerberg, and thereby him and his team escorted the security officers to wherever they were going to store them?"

"Maybe, but all the same, knowing Austerberg hovered outside the bank, he could have left say Marco Brunner to keep an eye on proceedings."

"So you assess him to be that vindictive?"

"Admittedly he has no mandate to protect the public. However, he could have let the Cantonal Police Corps in on the act."

"Maybe he discerned that Heinrich would be acting as our guardian angel," Fraser put forward.

"Maybe, but one man against the entire Austerberg mob is a slim shot."

"Ahh, but what a man," Richmond heralded. "Heinrich has exhibited out-and-out cool on two occasions. The first to rescue me, and the second benefitting all of us."

"You are too kind, Colby," Metzer replied. "Any German vorth his salt, vould have done ze same thing."

"Very modest, Heinrich," Fraser commended.

Leaning back in his chair, Anderson voiced, "I wonder what Austerberg is going to do next? I doubt he'll give up. He will try again at the hotel, or during the Countess's journey to Geneva-Cointrin Airport."

"Probably," Stephanie championed. "But let's not allow the spectre to spoil our evening. It's a time for celebration. We have prevailed against all the odds. It was a team effort, Gavin. Without you and your buddies, and our guardian angel, Heinrich, I doubt the Romanov horde would have come to light."

"I suppose the crucial instant arrived when Colby figured out the hyphen sign on that yellowing piece of paper was in fact a negative operator, meaning an inverse logic sign. That led us to the true concealment point on the lakebed, two kilometres east of Gland."

"Well before we go sucking each other's dicks — if you'll forgive the indelicacy, Stephanie," Richmond began, "the game is not over yet."

"Yes, he's right," Fraser endorsed. "The final whistle will only be blown when Stephanie and her minders are safely aboard the Darwin flight at Geneva-Cointrin Airport, along with the Romanov Fabergé eggs."

*

As Anderson had predicted, when the partygoers returned to the Mövenpick, they saw the lime green *Grosser* parked no more than twenty-five metres from the hotel entrance, the audacious Austerberg waving to them from his back seat position.

"Huh, I must say, he's got some nerve," Anderson applauded.

"All psychopaths have nerve," Fraser qualified. "It goes with the territory."

"My father's agents think he might have killed, or had third parties kill a myriad of adversaries," Stephanie recalled. "Howbeit, like his other lawbreaking activities, nothing has ever been proved. He seems to be eminently adept at covering his tracks."

"Right, here is vhere I leave you," Metzer tattled, catching their attention. "I vill be slinking back into ze shadows. Vhen you depart ze hotel for ze airport. I vill be in ze vicinity."

"Stephanie and her minders will travel in the *Range Rover*," Anderson detailed. "We will follow in the *M5*."

"Zhen I vill follow you in my *C63 AMG*."

Divining their adversary to take measures when they entered the hotel, instead Austerberg lingered in the *Grosser*. As to why he had allowed them free entry remained unsolved. Did he have something up his sleeve that he intended to play in the morning? Stephanie assumed he'd found out about the flight tickets she'd booked to Darwin, so he'd reckon she was going nowhere until the following day.

Congregating around the bar, they tried to fathom if he might try something during the night to abscond with the trunk containing the six Fabergé eggs. That appeared to be remote because it'd involve overpowering Sorensen and Kravets, and holding up hotel staff. A definite case of provable robbery, they concluded Austerberg could not risk such an action. No, the morning would provide the next interdictor zone for him.

~ * ~

Anderson got little sleep that night. Though he had slept normally amidst the operation since meeting Stephanie, the following morning represented the high noon point of the operation. Anything could happen.

Sometimes he had endured the same insomnia when Oxalite projects reached criticality – a point at which business success or failure occurred. Primarily consummate with new drug development, like Project Unicorn, after years of research consuming perhaps the equivalent gross national product of a small developing country, it came to the milestone of breakthrough after clinical testing, whereby country drug administration authorities had to give their blessing to market the new miracle. Not always a given, regulatory bodies could deny the issuing of a license for both political and business reasons, Anderson the guy commissioned by Oxalite to sort out the impasse in double-quick time. Consequently, nights before meeting with drug administration authorities tended to attract sleep disorder.

After several hours of restlessness, he turned on his bedside light and read from Huxley's *Point Counter Point*, a favourite satire novel he'd brought with him from home, hoping it'd induce drowsiness bringing about sleep. There had been a time when he couldn't contemplate leaving home on business or vacation without a portable cassette player to indulge his predilection for his Rolling Stones albums committed to tape. But that obsession had waned by his late thirties, his consumption of the world's greatest rock and roll band restricted to home listening. By the time the Cheshire boys had set off for Switzerland, his absorption in the Stones and other majestic luminaries from his nascent years had dwindled further, the pressures of the pharmaceutical industry coupled with domesticity leaving little spare time to indulge in his musical cravings.

As he ploughed through the Huxley, he heard the strains of *Stray Cat Blues* - a Stones song from their masterpiece *Beggar's Banquet* album - filter into his open bedroom window from a passing open-top car, probably filled with jubilant nighthawks returning home from the Barriére Casino at Montreux. The mesmerising jangle of electric guitars and a syncopating rhythm section had him harking back to when he played the album more or less continuously. Momentarily he stopped reading, his mind focused on the first time he played *Beggar's Banquet* in his eighth year. His elder brother, Donnell, had told him, if he continued to be bewitched by rock music, he'd never pass his eleven-plus examinations. Smiling at the remembrance, he reengaged the novel, the soporific effect of reading soon having him nodding off.

Like Anderson, on occasion Richmond had problems sleeping when business matters troubled him. Never one to come home and bleat about his dilemmas to Carolyn, habitually he said nothing, preferring to work out the conundrum in his mind. After the intellectual rigours of university, he'd entered into an uncomplicated period during his first few years in the workplace, but as his responsibilities grew, the challenges multiplied. Assuredly home life relaxations balanced his work issues, bringing a sense of equilibrium to his life. But nonetheless, ever-increasing revenue-bearing requirements from his employers tested the upper limits of his fortitude and endurance.

Soon after graduating, he'd worked out that for success in sales management, team selection and training were key to accomplishing company-set objectives. Get that process right, and the burden on the sales manager lessens. Albeit, with his professional attitude, he took nothing for granted, *force majeure* often the unpredictable sideswipe cutting deep into carefully conceived plans, necessitating the implementation of fallback plan-B strategies. Though the scheme had served him well to date, he never counted his chickens, and abided vigilant to the unforeseen.

Since the Cheshire boys first showdown with Austerberg, the Romanov affair had ignited disquiet as well as excitement, causing him sleeping difficulties. And without doubt being kidnapped shook him.

Albeit, knowing tomorrow represented the final facedown, that night he slept without interruption.

A completely different kettle of fish when it came to work pressures, Fraser took everything in his stride, whether it be analyst or trouble-shooter tasks. A talented analyst from the off with an inborn capacity to handle both clients and co-workers, such as rapacious stock traders, nothing had given him major heartache in the often slippery and volatile world of investment banking. He put it down to a rational mindset coupled with good intuition to read market trends and thereby steer clients into profitable investments. Anticipating he could apply his talents to sorting out onerous and delicate situations arising in the business beyond the realms of line managers, The Firm's London operation had made him their trouble-shooter.

Using this combined foundation as a launch platform, his contribution to assisting the Countess realise her assets came so naturally that he never flip-flopped, or conjured up misgivings. Just like the labour he actioned every day of his working life, here was a commodity requiring translation into currency. All it took was a connection to the ever-dependable Heinrich Metzer, and 'your Uncle Robert is your mother's brother,' as he had said to many an investor. Outside of that turning of the wheel, his trouble-shooting experience had endowed him with mettle, enabling him not to become bothered by devious felons and chancers bearing artillery. To Fraser, the Stephanie Nightingale intrigue had become yet another trouble-shooting exercise.

~ * ~

Awakening to the peep-peep of his alarm clock at seven-thirty, the Huxley still lay open in Anderson's lap. Quickly showering and dressing, he then took the elevator down to the ground floor and strolled to the restaurant, Fraser and Richmond waving to him to join them for breakfast. Soon Stephanie and her minders consolidated the assembly, the combined group discussing their final arrangements for the drive to the airport. Not quite on tenterhooks but mindful that the passage could be eventful; after finishing the preparation they kept the conversation to light-hearted subjects and the continuing glorious weather.

Later in the morning, Stephanie retrieved the trunk containing the Romanov jewels from the hotel main safe, Sorensen and Kravets having taken turns to stand guard over the depository throughout the night. After checking out, Sorensen brought the *Range Rover* to the hotel entrance, Richmond pulling up in the *BMW M5* behind him. With Anderson and Fraser flanking Stephanie, and Kravets carrying the trunk to their front, the group browsed left and right from the hotel entrance, the *Grosser* coming into their view, parked very nearby. Though people milled in and out of the Mövenpick, and passersby inhabited the area to the front of the hotel, it didn't mean Austerberg and co wouldn't try a heist.

Sure enough, as soon as the Countess and her escort moved towards the *Range Rover*, Austerberg and his deputies alighted from the *Mercedes*. Quickly surrounding them, Zinchenko prodded a replacement *Glock 17* into her back, Greshnov similarly covering Kravets with his substitute revolver. Completing the stop and seizure, Ducal and Lindberg stood next to Anderson and Fraser pushing discreet *Ruger LCP* firearms into their sides. Absorbed by their own goals, bystanders tarried oblivious to the holdup.

"Good morning, Countess," Austerberg felicitated in his customary flippant manner, a broad gleam magnifying his aristocratic features, but as usual, his glass eye stayed lifeless. "So glad you have brought the prize for me."

"In your dreams, Austerberg. The Romanov legacy belongs to my father, Count Leonid Nikolaevich Kulikovsky."

"Come, come, there is no need to be hostile. You are a worthy opponent and have presented a creditable challenge to us. But now is the time to concede that you have lost, and I have won." His phiz transformed into a serious countenance. "Now, have your man hand over the trunk to Stanislav."

"No."

"Countess, I admire your courage, but you are in no position to bargain."

"You won't try anything in public."

Scanning about, he raised his eyebrows. "But we are. People are too consumed with their own affairs to notice what we're doing. See for yourself."

She flashed her optics left and right, judging Austerberg's admission to be correct.

"The treasure, Countess," he demanded. Nodding to his accomplices, they pushed their heaters further into their targets.

"That's enough, Herr Austerberg," the opposing camarillas heard, as Devereux and his aides appeared from inside the hotel.

Taken aback by the Swiss official's appearance out of nowhere, Austerberg blathered, "Monsieur Devereux, we meet yet again. I supposed you had no further interest in the conclusion to this matter."

"An incorrect assumption," he replied, stepping forward to stand opposite the main protagonist, while Brunner, Steiner and Weber positioned themselves around the tight-knit group.

"You have your share of the loot," the master racketeer complained. "Why intervene in my business?"

"Let's not be coy, Julius. What you are attempting to do is daylight robbery."

"But you have no delegated authority to stop us."

"No, but the Cantonal Police Corps has." Nodding at Weber, she raised a smartphone for all to see. "The Lausanne Police number is already keyed into the phone. Zoe only has to press send, and they will be here within minutes."

"So, it's a *fait accompli*," Austerberg categorised.

"Indeed. You are barely operating on the right side of the law. Cut your losses, maintain your freedom, and withdraw. Anything less, and I will have you charged under the Swiss Law and Order Act."

Considering his position for a moment, Austerberg cultivated a sly, sinister comportment, then chuckled before gesturing to his team to withdraw and return to the *Grosser*.

As the car sped off, Anderson congratulated, "Your timing was immaculate, Monsieur Devereux."

"The Department felt obliged to fully honour our joint settlement with the Countess. We've been concealed at the hotel for the last few hours, monitoring both you and the Austerberg gang. I don't think they'll give you any more trouble."

"You didn't afford us the same protection when we exited the Banque Cantonale Vaudoise last night," Stephanie reminded him.

"My first duty amounted to ensuring the two Fabergé eggs you bestowed were safely enshrined in the Musée d'Art et d'Histoire. Besides, I distinguished your guardian angel protector, Herr Metzer, resided in the vicinity of the bank, ready to come to your assistance."

"Mmmm, fine margins for error, Monsieur Devereux," Anderson classified.

"This entire campaign you and the Countess have waged has fine margins for error, Mister Anderson," he rebuked, his facial muscles twitching with disdain. "You have been decidedly fortunate to survive a confrontation normally culminating in body bags. The illegal treasure trove hawker domain is littered with the corpses of those foolhardy enough to go up against professional cartels."

~ * ~

With the *M5* leading and the *Range Rover* behind, the cavalcade set off for Geneva-Cointrin Airport. Above, a deep yellow, Van Gogh sun glowed in another cerulean-blue sky dotted with the odd fair-weather cumulus cloud, the idyllic backdrop making Anderson appreciate the difference between normality and the ultimate episode of the Romanov affair.

As they passed along the road parallel to Lake Geneva, he gazed south-west to a point opposite Gland on the west shoreline and reflected on the dive he'd made to discover the stainless-steel box containing the paper with the Romanov kitty bank name and account number. Aware from previous scuba-diving sorties, a deep dive should only be attempted after a series of shallower immersions, he accepted he'd been impetuous, even reckless. His underwater pilgrimages in the Bahamas had taken place in his early thirties, soon after he married Francine, and when he could claim to be mega-fit. Now in his early fifties, during the intervening decades, apart from tennis in the summer months, exercise had been sparse, and his fitness had waned. Deep diving puts all kinds of strains on the human body, particularly the lungs and the heart. He could have emerged from the underwater trawl feeling queasy or even worse. How could he ever explain his actions to Francine, if something severe had happened? Why did he say he could do it without a second thought? It came down to the adrenalin rush created by Stephanie's crusade.

As his management responsibilities multiplied at Oxalite, Anderson spent more time at their Welwyn Garden City plant, rather than in the field transacting pharmaceutical license deals with overseas business partners and drug administration authorities. The former, he found to be relatively dull and mundane, the latter, a haven for exhilarating adventure. After graduating from Edinburgh, he'd been comfortable in risky environments such as on North Sea oil rigs and in the sweltering deserts of the Middle East with his first employer, petrochemicals giant, Scale. Since those intoxicating days, opportunities for pulse-raising business forays had been few and far between. That coupled with family holidays while Michelle and Wyatt were growing up, restricted Gavin to placid undertakings, his sense of risk-taking reeled in. By the time the Cheshire boys came together, he had assumed he'd never engage in a hazardous gamble ever again. The Romanov affair changed that. With his appetite for risk reignited, prudence became sidelined.

Despite being abducted, involvement in the treasure-seeking odyssey disturbed Richmond a lot less than his biggest fear — demise by way of flying. Sure, he had some hairy moments during his sales and marketing career, principally in South America and in the Middle East interacting with near-to psychotic military officers and unscrupulous buyers with underworld affiliations. But statistically, though flying lasted as the safest means of travel, statistics also disclosed that the more he flew, the incidence of a flight disaster increased. The prospect of Carolyn losing her husband, and Amanda and Suzi their father, gave him the flutters. But what could he do? From the outset of his international sales and marketing career, he knew it called for extensive flight travel. With his low threshold of boredom, eight-thirty to five office-based duties crushed him. He constantly yearned for the irregularity of working hours and environment variations offered by meeting new people in different countries. Taking an office-based job definitely evaporated flight statistics concerns, but he discerned it'd turn him grouchy with both work colleagues and his family. Something to be avoided.

Before the Switzerland trip, he had broached the two million air miles mark without a major incident. The only out-of-the-ordinary events occurring were due to severe weather conditions, meaning fog and snow, sometimes causing aircraft to make multiple attempts at landing. Occasionally flights he'd been on were grounded due to a flight deck annunciator logging an aircraft equipment failure during taxiing, but he'd never been on a flight when the aircraft suffered a critical failure resulting in the stewardess instructing passengers to fasten their seat buckles, and reinforcing life jackets were beneath their seats. Maybe his luck would hold firm until he retired, but that watershed moment lay a long way into the future, way past the conventional sixty-five retirement age. Besides, even when he did hang up his sales and marketing spurs, he'd still be jet-setting privately with Carolyn and maybe his daughters to far flung holiday destinations.

Fraser had gotten so used to precarious missions via his trouble-shooting role at The Firm that the Romanov affair barely cut into his anxiety and distress register. Major wrongdoing by chancers in the financial services sector, typically complex, money-laundering operations attracted the most severe means by the culprits to nurture the gamble and their continuing freedom. A rare event, Fraser achieved a positive state of mind to potentially violent miscreants, because when cornered they were more motivated to lessen their jail sentence by surrendering, rather than loosing off artillery, the stance enabling him to conduct his delegations with cold reassurance.

For him, the Romanov affair constituted nothing more than one of his mildly dangerous trouble-shooting campaigns. Though independent assessors might view his unruffled detachment as unwise, even naive, in Fraser's mind, he had to adopt the daredevil in his makeup, or he'd never have agreed to enact the trouble-shooter role. Certainly, he'd taken onboard how ruthless Austerberg and co could become to accomplish their goals, but still he figured if he executed proven methods to manage the wrangle, no harm would come to him.

As the column neared the airport, Richmond briefed, "I'll park the M5 in the short-stay car park, then we can join Stephanie outside the departures terminal as arranged."

When the Cheshire boys hiked it to the meeting point, they found the *Range Rover* awaiting them. While the Englishman escorted Stephanie and Kravets into the terminal with the traveller's luggage including the jewels trunk, Sorensen returned the *Range Rover* to Hertz Car Rental, then rejoined the party.

About to thank her confederates for their invaluable help, before Stephanie could speak, the Austerberg gang descended on them again, guns angled into midriffs.

"I think the phrase you are looking for rhymes with clucking bell," Richmond enlightened Anderson, noticing he displayed aggravated lineaments.

"You don't give up, do you," Anderson bleated, as the raiders corralled their prey into a quiet part of the terminal.

"Rarely, Mister Anderson," Austerberg flatly avowed. "And this caper is starting to annoy me. There are far too many players and subsidiaries for my liking. Usually when this occurs, there is work for the undertaker." Revolving to face Stephanie and beaming, he directed, "And now, it is finally time for you to hand over your Romanov patrimony."

"No."

"Countess, Monsieur Devereux and his band of acolytes will not be coming to your rescue on this occasion." Becoming stern, he warned, "Please do not force me to instruct Viktor to drag the trunk from your aide's grasp after shooting him. You will notice we have added silencers to our pistols, so no one will hear."

"*Shtop*," the two groups heard, before Metzer appeared behind the assailants.

"I recognise that voice," Austerberg proclaimed. "It is the German gentleman with a pronounced Bavarian accent."

"Indeed, it is. You vill put down your veapons."

"And if we don't?"

"My *45 Auto Luger* is also fitted vith a silencer. I can shoot you vithout drawing any attention from ze public."

Dolefully shaking his noodle, he mumbled, "God-damned kraut," then instructed, "Viktor, Stanislav, gentlewomen, do it." Seeing Ducal and Lindberg refraining from obeying the command, he reiterated, "Ladies, if you please."

All four antagonists dropped their weapons.

Swiveling about to address Metzer, Austerberg complimented, "You are a clever and resourceful man. Why don't you join my team? You could make a lot of money."

"I don't think so, Herr Austerberg. I already have a lot of money, und a predilection for safeguarding my freedom. Zhat means staying on ze right side of ze law."

"You anticipated our final move, didn't you?"

"I vas concealed in a position outside ze hotel, ready to come to my friend's rescue, should you set upon zhem. Monsieur Devereux intervened, so I speculated you vould make one last try at ze airport. So I drove here ahead of you in my ultra-fast *C63 AMG*."

"Are you sure I can't tempt you?"

"No," he pressed. "Roger, pick up zheir firearms."

Fraser did his bidding.

"Now give von to Gavin und Colby, and ve vill keep Herr Austerberg and his troops entertained while ze Countess and her minders check in at ze Qantas desk."

Close to overcome with emotion, Stephanie threw her arms around each of the Englishmen and thanked them for their beyond price support, Metzer also the recipient of her affection.

Before making off, she committed, "When my father's museum is built, all your names will be inscribed on a plaque at its entrance, thanking you for your invaluable contribution to ensuring the Fabergé eggs safe return to their rightful owner." Radiating at them, she parted with, "Goodbye, gentlemen."

After Stephanie and her minders disappeared into a throng of people milling around the departure terminal, Metzer and the Cheshire boys continued to keep Austerberg and his cohorts at bay to ensure no last minute intervention.

"You are lucky that I can see the funny side of this escapade," Austerberg informed his captors. "Under different circumstances, I could have all of you tracked down and liquidated. However, I have enjoyed our set-to's, so rest assured, no one will be coming after you." Desisting and assuming mournful qualities inviting condolence, he then requested, "Now, may we have our weapons back?"

"I don't think so, Herr Austerberg," Anderson replied. "No slight intended, but having seen your, shall we call them - dubious methods at first hand - I'm inclined to say it's best that you and your faction leave without them."

"It's a classic ploy," Metzer complemented. "First gain your adversaries confidence, zhen renege on ze deal. If ve gave ze artillery back, you vould turn zhem on us."

"Mmmm. Very wise," Austerberg conceded. "I must say, it would be a temptation to let Viktor and Stanislav play football with your craniums." Becoming grave, he affixed, "Take great care never to cross my path ever again. If there should be a second coming together, none of you will survive. Now—" The undaunted radiance returned. "On a lighter note, we must be away. First reported by sources close to me and substantiated in German newspapers, last night I received confirmation of a priceless Inca gold statue encrusted in diamonds and rubies to be found on the Peruvian Altiplano Plateau, requiring my attention. Goodbye, gentlemen."

Without reciprocating, the Cheshire boys and Metzer watched as the Austerberg coterie left the departures terminal.

"So that's why Greshnov acquired *Die Welt* and *Junge Freiheit,*" Anderson settled.

"Yes," Richmond supported. "While we were rummaging around that townhouse basement on Chem. de Beau Rivage, he must have been putting in place the instruments for the Peruvian jaunt."

"What are we going to do with these shooters?" Fraser voiced.

"Keep them until we are sure he has really gone," Anderson advocated. Turning to the *Obergruppenführer,* he said, "Well, Heinrich, you've saved us yet again. As a thank you, we're going to take you for a humongous slap-up lunch at the Brasserie La Riviera."

"Thank you. I vould very much like zhat. It vill afford ze opportunity to see if zhat bolshie corporal vaiter has learnt to respect his betters. If not, I vill introduce him to more persuasive means in ze dungeon of my schloss. I have already ordered von of those Tucker Telephones to be used by ze Austerberg frauleins to torture Colby."

Not sure if he was serious or not, Anderson merely replied, "Quite."

Chapter Nineteen: Normal Service Resumed

For the balance of their vacation, the Englishmen resumed sailing the Argonaut on Lake Geneva and losing money in the Casino Barriére at Montreux, the twin pastimes refreshing their beings and purging the unexpected stress accumulated during the Romanov affair. Meanwhile, Metzer returned to his schloss to renew torturing delinquent traders and stroppy waiters who had incurred his displeasure.

"I'm reminded of the novel *Journey* by James A. Michener," Fraser expressed as they stared out on the view over the lake from a Port Lausanne-Ouchy quayside café, after returning from a sail.

"Yes, you're right," Anderson supported. "I've read *Journey* and there is a similarity, though Lake Geneva is far larger compared to the Yukon Lake Michener describes in his novel."

"I've read *The Bridges at Toko-Ri* by the same author," Richmond threw into the pot. "What is *Journey* about?"

"*Journey* is a riveting account of the obstacles four English aristocrats, and their Irish servant, have to overcome as they journey from England to Canada in 1897 to 1899, and haul across the cruel Canadian terrain to the Klondike gold fields at Dawson Yukon. Vivid and sweeping, it features Michener's probing insights into the follies and grandeur of the human spirit, and the depiction of a mystical lake, becoming a symbol of tranquillity and dream for the fortune seekers."

"Sounds similar to *Campbell's Kingdom* by Hammond Innes, except the prize is oil found in a small valley in the Canadian Rocky Mountains."

"Do you know," Fraser began, "it's only at moments like this when you can hit pause for long enough to really absorb your surroundings, that true appreciation of the setting can occur."

"It's a product of taking time out from the hustle and bustle of work and home life," Anderson propounded. "Immersion in a backcloth like this fully opens the psychic valve and suddenly the natural world becomes apparent in all its raging beauty."

About to delve further into bucolic rhetoric, they heard a female voice behind them say, "Roger, is that you?"

Twisting about, Fraser logged curvy and captivating man-eater, Alice Vaughan, from The Firm's London operation human resources department.

"Alice—" he blurted, staggered to see her. "What brings you to this heaven on Earth?"

"I'm on holiday with Sarah Williams from accounts."

"If I recollect correctly, Sarah has a big, bad boyfriend, who beats anyone he remotely suspects of even talking to her."

"She dumped him. We're on a girl's only frolic."

After Fraser made all-round introductions, he enquired, "So where is Sarah?"

"She's getting togged-out for a night at the casino. We're going to lasso a couple of high rollers and have a tremendous time at their expense."

"The usual vixens on the mercenary prowl approach then," he categorised, then annexed, "actually, I'm surprised that you've left your man-hunting ground at The Firm."

"Well—" She came over all hurt. "They're treating me like a piranha."

"You mean, a pariah?"

She recoiled, a quizzical expression flowering. "Do I?"

"Actually, you've got it right. You are a piranha when it comes to eating men."

"Oh, Roger, don't be such a fuddy-duddy. It's just fun." She dallied before issuing him a flirtatious simper. "Now before I go, what can I do for you, handsome? Promise you the last dance at the Lausanne Palace ballroom, a twosome in a jacuzzi, or perhaps a blowjob?"

"*What*!" His jaw dropped. "I never know if you are serious or just kidding, Alice."

"Well, I'll let you be the judge of that." she purred, poking her tongue into her cheek.

Grinning wickedly, she then sashayed off, her hips swinging from side to side, attracting young male attention like salmon to a lure, then turned, broke into a radiant twinkle and called back, "See you later."

"She's hot," Richmond saluted.

"Yes. Alice is The Firm's prize-winning prick teaser. She and other bewitching nymphets get exceedingly frisky at our Christmas parties and social events. Personally, they have subjected me to some very embarrassing moments, some in front of executive board members, and even Charlotte. I can neutralise the former by making light but convincing remarks, but if it's the latter, ceaselessly I end up in the doghouse licking my wounds."

"Oh, Roger, Charlotte is a gorgeous honey," Anderson insisted. "Difficult to believe she turns into a harridan if some office floozy makes inappropriate or false comments about you in her presence."

"Quite right. The punishment is 'more honoured in the breach than the observance' to quote from *Hamlet*. Suspicion as opposed to fact is all that is needed for my doghouse penance."

"And what form does this punishment take?"

"Tied to the kitchen sink or the lawn mower for the entire weekend. Denial of pass outs to attend a Kappa Corinthians soiree, or a meeting of the Hazelwood & District Gentlemen's Club. They vary in line with the unproven misdemeanour."

"Does it include denial of conjugal rights?"

"Oh no, independent of doghouse blues – that is always on offer. Charlotte is very assertive in the bedroom. She always has been, and she still has the looks and body of a debutante."

"Peals as fascinating," Richmond applauded. "Are you going to serialise your diaries in the Sunday Times?"

"Hah, I'm not sure they'd have any uniqueness, attracting publication. They merely reflect the status quo norm."

Consulting the day indicator in his *Montblanc* watch, Anderson exclaimed, "We're nearing exit time, gentlemen. In just a few days, we'll be back in our hot seats. For me, that means tackling the latest pains thrown up by Project Unicorn."

"Well that scheme effects all of us," Fraser identified. "You for the in-house development, Colby for the I.T support system, and me for the finance."

"We're coming to a stage," Anderson outlined, "when I'll have to seek approval to proceed further from the Oxalite corporate board." Biting his lower lip, he declared, "There are a couple of board members who always oppose any drug development on risk grounds. Even though I produce a risk-reward document spelling out how catastrophe is minimised to less than half of one percent, they still put me through the mill."

"Yes, the Firm's London operation contains similar merchants of doom," Fraser admitted. "I remember Trading Floor Sales Manager, Ricky Henshaw, having the thumbscrews applied to him, and coming out of the board room white as a ghost. I told him, *illegitimi non carborundum*."

"Don't let the bastards grind you down," Anderson interpreted.

"Precisely."

"Middle management is always susceptible to the most severe caning when the business goes pear-shaped or a revolutionary technique is put forward to either solve a business pain or increase market share," Richmond interjected. "In my time in the I.T arena, I've been the recipient of cold water and derision by corporate boards when I've put forward a business plan to say expand company operations into new spheres to lessen dependency on volatile core markets. Even when authorised and proved to yield profit, those against the plan invariably give faint praise when it bears fruit."

"Yep, there's a fine line," Anderson stated, "between being seen as a threat to shall we call them - board members with obsolete intellectual equipment accompanied by suspect business nous - and fulfilling your designated role with inventive business strategies sanctioned by the board as a whole."

"So it is, and so it will always be. Who's to say if we ever reach the exalted height of board membership, we wouldn't chop away the legs of up-and-coming middle management virtuosos to preserve our positions."

"Mmmm," Anderson and Fraser both murmured.

"Maybe it's better just to be satisfied with the money we earn at present, rather than spoiling our scruples by participating at board level," Anderson proposed.

"Yes," Fraser supported. "Just before we left for this holiday, a trader came into my office proclaiming, 'I'm going to earn a shedload of money,' after a commodities stock went ballistic. 'Yep,' I replied, 'you'll become rich as Jeff Tracy, maybe even Ant and Dec or Keith Lemon.' 'Who's Jeff Tracy? A successful trader, I've never heard of,' he inquired. 'No,' I stipulated. 'He runs Thunderbirds.'

"The point is, he was as happy as Larry just to be in a job that can provide astronomical amounts of commission. At the end of the day, money is money, independent of how it was earnt. We work for money much more than the reflected glow of job title kudos."

"Exactly," Richmond advocated. "We're all comfortably well off and very happy for most of the time. Why jeopardise that for more power and a few more k?" Stopping abruptly, he then babbled, "Good god. You see that boy wearing the lederhosen and pork pie hat over by the ice cream parlour, Gavin?"

"What about him?"

"If my eyes don't deceive me, he's a near replica of Jasper Wainwright, our classmate from Christleton Junior School."

Scanning in the given direction, Anderson replied, "Yes, there is a passing resemblance, and Jasper did have a penchant for pork pie hats. I'm astonished that you memorised him."

"*Hah*, Jasper was unforgettable." A perky cast sprung up on Richmond's boatrace. "Nice lad, but he had a tendency to act the goat in front of teachers. Got him into a lot of hot water. Didn't he come from the Eaton Hall Farm estate at Waverton?"

"Yeah. His father was a worker at the farm. Sometime after you left, he told one teacher his ambition was to focus on rural studies and become a master ploughboy. Didn't go down well. The teacher thought Jasper was being cheeky. I lost contact with him after Christleton Junior School, but I understand his japes continued into his secondary education, and he got a reputation for appearing simple."

"What happened to him?"

"Jasper. He became a fully qualified village idiot, but my mother told me he went on to manage Eaton Hall Farm."

"So, all that tomfoolery was just a cosmetic front?"

"I wouldn't go as far as that. By all accounts he prolonged the village idiot motif even when he took over the farm!"

With the Cheshire boys thoroughly spaced out, the conversation freewheeled into other domains, further family socials explored, vexing thorns in the side crunched, the world put to right, until Fraser reviewed, "Do you know, I don't think Nostro Kravets said a single word in open forum throughout the entire Romanov caper."

"For sure," Anderson backed. "Prompts the pump, was he truly alive — a sentient being? Having said that, Sorensen turned out to be a man of few words as well."

"Maybe that can be emblematised in legacy terms," Richmond suggested. "Both inherited pro-czarist leanings from past generations, and clearly, they venerate Count Leonid Nikolaevich Kulikovsky. Tasked with protecting his daughter, they were deferential and assumed traditional Russian guardian guises."

"Does explain the lack of dialogue," Anderson accepted. "It was the same for Austerberg's and Devereux's underlings in his company. I suppose it just goes to show that in the presence of a boss, his supernumeraries tend to be tight-lipped, allowing him to lead two-way debate with other party chiefs."

Their confab cascaded back into the Romanov affair, the Cheshire boys wondering how the Countess, a.k.a., Stephanie Nightingale would fare down under. Appreciating her skills and virtues, they deduced she'd continue to conduct an exciting and productive life.

~ * ~

Feeling nostalgic, the last day of their sojourn saw the Englishmen journey to Geneva-Cointrin Airport, say farewell to the M5, then wheel their cases into the departures terminal making for the BA London Gatwick Airport check-in.

"Watch out, the sisters grimm are closing in on us," Richmond warned, seeing the familiar twosome trundling up behind them.

"Mister Anderson, Mister Fraser, Mister Richmond," Gertrude acknowledged. "How was your holiday?"

"Oh, er…" Gawping at his companions and winking, Anderson replied, "…very relaxing—"

Before he could go any further, she cut him off. "Evelyn had some luck at the casino," she enthused. "She came away with over 3,000 Swiss francs to the good, and we had a wonderful time exploring Lausanne. Such a clean and tidy city. And—" She glittered with pride. "We got to meet the Mayor of Lausanne at a showing of *La Traviata* in the Théâtre de Lausanne. What about that!"

"I think I left my parasol in that taxi," Evelyn spouted, after fiddling about with her belongings.

"Ohh, really, Evelyn," her sister admonished. "You'd forget your noggin if it weren't affixed to your neck. How many times have I told you to check for everything before alighting from a taxi."

"Can we go back for it?"

"Don't be ridiculous," she chastised, clearly irked at the prospect. "I'm not charging all over Switzerland in pursuit of a parasol that can be replaced for less than twenty pounds at Harrods. Besides, we'll miss our flight." She scintillated at the Englishmen. "I'm sorry, Mister Anderson. What were you saying about your holiday?"

"Oh er…it turned out to be quiet," he defended, glancing at his companions for support.

Adding credence to the claim, Richmond and Fraser nodded positively.

"Quite so," Richmond endorsed.

"Yes, it approximated a church fete," Fraser appended. "Nothing as thrilling as winning 3,000 Swiss francs or meeting the Mayor of Lausanne."

"Funny," she retorted, displaying a dubious visage. "I thought I saw the three of you outside the Mövenpick Hotel with a stunning blonde, and some most peculiar-looking people who seemed to be crowding around her."

"Us?" Anderson contested. "I don't think so. We spent most of our time sailing on Lake Geneva."

"Huh, I must have been mistaken."

"Gertrude, I'd really like to find that parasol," Evelyn begged. "It was a particular favourite."

"*Ohhh.*" She threw her head back. "The most I'm prepared to do is request the airport authorities to send the blessed thing on to you, should it be handed in." Spying behind her, she saw a lost baggage counter. "Come on. Let's report your tragic loss."

With that they lumbered away from the Cheshire boys, Gertrude still admonishing her sister.

After glimpsing at each other, Anderson pigeonholed, "We all seem hesitant to talk about the Romanov affair."

"It's like after Stephanie returned to Darwin for the family's provenance," Richmond recounted. "I said, if someone had told me we'd become embroiled in the hunt for a priceless heirloom whilst in Lausanne, I'd never have believed them."

"And I remarked, it does bear all the hallmarks of the implausible," Fraser recalled.

"So are we going to keep the escapade to ourselves?" Anderson queried. "Not even telling our families."

"I'd be inclined to that tact," Richmond upheld.

"Yes," Fraser promoted. "Opening up will only foster a barrage of knock-on questions."

"Looks like we'll be drawing a line under the Romanov affair forever," Anderson summarised.

~ * ~

Back in Blighty, the Cheshire boys sustained their taciturn stance, only conveying to family, friends and work colleagues how they had enjoyed the pleasures of sailing the Argonaut on Lake Geneva and losing their stakes at the Casino Barriére at Montreux.

Albeit, when they congregated as a threesome at a posh London restaurant or some other social haunt, the Romanov affair became reviewed and regaled. Knowing such a quicksilver adventure was unlikely to cross their paths again, they amplified the light-hearted and amusing moments at the expense of reenacting the more onerous aspects and came to position the escapade as a welcome distraction from convention.

Some years later, Anderson received a communication from the Countess, saying her father's inheritance had been used to build a Romanov Museum in Darwin. Further, and as promised, the names of those involved in helping her expedite the treasure find, including Richmond, Fraser and himself, had been built into a plaque, positioned at the entrance to the museum, for all the world to see.

Subsequently when the museum opened, it attracted universal media attention. The families and employers of the three Cheshire boys made aware of their involvement, when their names on the plaque were beamed into sitting rooms from television transmissions. Forced to admit there had been more to their Lausanne trip than sailing and gambling, the Englishmen gave a censored version of events to their wives and children, their kith and kin fussing over them like mewling grannies.

For Anderson it seemed prophetic that a distant intrigue had unlocked such unexpected sentimentality. In quieter moments, he mentally revisited the Romanov episode under the influence of *Chivas Regal* or other liberating intoxicants, gauging it to be manna from heaven.

Also by the Author
at
Rogue Phoenix Press

Incident at Lahore Basin

Whilst on business in Pakistan, ex-RAF officer and businessman Dale Latham comes close to death when his helicopter is downed by a ground to air missile. Hospitalised, he meets Chanda Govinda, a persecuted Christian Indian and helps her escape across the Pakistan-India border. Although there is no evidence linking Latham's involvement with Chanda, Muslim zealot police chief Aman aims to imprison him. With his top-secret knowledge, HMG fear Latham will end up in the hands of Pakistani intelligence. MI6 agent Ross Hunter is dispatched to appraise the situation, and if necessary, liquidate Latham. When Latham is abducted by terrorists, Hunter rescues him, saying that Aman set him up for the ultimate fall. Without evidence, Aman is forced to allow Latham to leave Pakistan, avoiding a bullet from Hunter.

Chapter 1: Tempest

Flameout! Pilot Wing Commander Dale Latham's Tornado zoomed groundward. As the aircraft stalled, rolled and flipped over into a spiral dive, its altimeter decremented at an astonishing rate.

He had to act fast. Initiating the engines start-up procedure, he managed to engage one RB199. Singing into life the turbofan generated thrust, allowing Latham to push the stick forward making the aircraft nose down, then increase throttle setting to full power. Miraculously, the Tornado settled, enabling him to apply back pressure to the stick levelling the wings, the aeroplane regaining steady-state flight, Latham recovering altitude as he tried to ignite the second RB199.

Approaching RAF Lossiemouth, backtracking from a combined RAF-Luftwaffe sortie over the Rhineland, navigator-weapons officer, Flight Lieutenant Harry Beaumont, warned of severe hailstorm conditions ahead. As the Tornado slowed from supersonic speed and descended from 30,000 feet over the Moray Firth channel, she hit the inclement weather. Far worse than expected, a freak set of climatic conditions had conspired to generate the mother of all storm clouds, cumulonimbus building a trail blazer of epic proportions.

As the Tornado passed beneath 15,000 feet, she encountered heavy rain and tennis-ball- sized hailstones, the contaminants ingested into the engine's inlet ducts leading to dual-turbofan flameout.

Whilst Latham struggled to re-start the second RB199, Beaumont contacted Lossiemouth Air Traffic Control, advising their predicament. Asked if the Tornado wanted to register a Mayday call, Beaumont answered in the negative. Confident of Latham's flying skills, he knew the pilot would be reluctant to pull the ejector seat handle, releasing the canopy and sending both aircrew into space, abandoning the Tornado to crash into the Moray Firth.

Latham had never lost an aircraft. He certainly did not intend to let the £14m fighter-bomber end up in the drink. Albeit the second engine refused to spark into life, further ingestion of the life-threatening hale defeating his attempts. Though capable of flight on a single engine, prudence dictated under the tempest onslaught, having both turbofans operational equated with minimising further danger. Gaining height, the Tornado rose above the cumulonimbus wrecker, permitting the second engine inlet duct to clear of ice debris. Sustaining the re-start protocol, at last the stagnant RB199 burst into life, the gained extra thrust making the aeroplane nose-up. Deciding not to risk landing at Lossiemouth through the storm, Latham called RAF Leuchars, requesting permission for an emergency landing.

South of Lossiemouth by 90 miles, Leuchars allowed the Tornado to land without any further troubles, her aircrew reporting the flameout incident, and staying until clement weather prevailed over the Moray Firth locale, allowing then to return to Lossiemouth.

Beaumont's assessment of Latham had been spot-on. Wholly aware that the UK taxpayer owned the platforms he carried out missions on, spanning his RAF flight career, Latham had made it his business to ensure any aircraft allocated to his charge remained in one piece from take-off to landing. A trait inherited from his father; a sense of responsibility in all matters came to dominate his life from an early age.

Sometimes the quality resulted in gladness and fulfilment, whereas on other occasions, it got him into hot water, his innate sentiment to duty subduing imperilment factors.

About the Author

Clive Radford began writing at school, then university but mainly through subsequent life experience.

His poetry has been published in numerous poetry magazines such as The Journal, The Cannon's Mouth, Poetry Monthly, Poetry Now, Storming Heaven, Poetry Nottingham, Scripsi and Modern Review, plus in many compilations by United Press.

A series of his short stories and poems have been published by Ether Books. The Arts Council has sponsored publication of his novels 'One Night in Tunisia' and 'The Sounds of Silence'. His contemporary satire 'Doghouse Blues' was number one in Harper Collins Authonomy chart and has been awarded gold medal status. It has been published by Black Rose. His spy thriller 'Zavrazin' has been published by Triplicity Publishing. It's companion sequel 'Nexus Bullet' is published by Ex-L-Ence Publishing. His three-book series 'Disclosures of a Femme Fatale Addict' has been published by Wild Dreams Publishing and Miraclaire Publishing. His science fiction novel 'Maggie's Farm', suspense-thriller, 'Incident at Lahore Basin', contemporary thriller, 'Alpha Centauri, satires 'Doghouse Blues 2', 'Doghouse Blues 3' and 'Doghouse Blues Revised and Remastered' plus his action-adventure/rite of passage 'Desolation Argonauts'are published by Rogue Phoenix Press. Melange Books has published his mystery thriller, 'Monsoon in the Making' and 'The Spiral Staircase and other Novellas', a mix of psychological, modern satire and rite of passage sagas. Miraclaire Publishing has published his poetry collection, 'Poems of Life.'

'One Night in Tunisia', 'Zavrazin' and 'Nexus Bullet' have all been converted into three-act screenplays.

Currently, he is crafting a number of works including 'University Disclosures', a rite of passage saga, 'Mozart meets McCartney', a mystery, 'Wokeland', a dystopian social science fiction, and 'The Speed House in James Street', a coming-of-age saga.

His work has a distinctive voice setting it apart and appealing to those fascinated by intrigue, and who question status quo accepted views.

www.ingramcontent.com/pod-product-compliance
Lightning Source LLC
Chambersburg PA
CBHW071906220626
47052CB00002B/224